W9-BZV-667

PLAYING WITH FIRE

PLAYING WITH FIRE

Patricia Hall

This first world edition published 2018
in Great Britain and the USA by
SEVERN HOUSE PUBLISHERS LTD of
Eardley House, 4 Uxbridge Street, London W8 7SY
Trade paperback edition first published
in Great Britain and the USA 2018 by
SEVERN HOUSE PUBLISHERS LTD

British Library Cataloguing in Publication Data
A CIP catalogue record for this title is available from the British Library.

ISBN-13: 978-0-7278-8826-6 (cased)
ISBN-13: 978-1-84751-949-8 (trade paper)
ISBN-13: 978-1-4483-0159-1 (e-book)

All Severn House titles are printed on acid-free paper.

Severn House Publishers support the Forest Stewardship Council™ [FSC™],
the leading international forest certification organisation.
All our titles that are printed on FSC certified paper carry the FSC logo.

MIX
Paper from
responsible sources
FSC
www.fsc.org   FSC® C013056

Typeset by Palimpsest Book Production Ltd.,
Falkirk, Stirlingshire, Scotland.
Printed and bound in Great Britain by
TJ International, Padstow, Cornwall.

ONE

Detective Sergeant Harry Barnard stood thoughtfully on one side of Greek Street in Soho gazing up at one of the narrow Georgian buildings on the opposite side of the road. Thrown up as a speculative town house for an eighteenth-century family, it had fallen inexorably on hard times until very recently. Barnard was not taken in by the discreet bookshop on the ground floor which advertised very little in its window behind smeared glass and peeling paint, and then only the most innocuous titles. He knew all about the more lurid stock it specialized in, which was kept well-hidden for favoured customers. But tonight his attention at three o'clock on a chilly autumn morning was on the upper stories which had been recently renovated. Three floors had been gutted, which the sergeant had been aware of as an army of builders had been working there to turn it into a smart dining and drinking club. It had remained below Barnard's professional radar since it had opened, until the weekend just ended. Then it had exploded into a scene of intense interest to the police when a young girl had plummeted from one of the windows on the top floor and died instantly, he had been told, on the narrow pavement below less than an hour earlier.

Harry Barnard had been called from his bed to help, torn reluctantly from his girlfriend's warm embrace and instructed to go straight to Greek Street to back-up uniformed officers. What concerned him when he had arrived at the Late Supper Club was to find that the dead body, if that was what it was, had already been removed by ambulance, although the site was still cordoned off and the bloodstains all too visible and sticky on the pavement. Only a solitary uniformed copper remained outside the door to secure the premises and explain what had happened, although all the windows on the upper floors were still ablaze with light.

'Was she alive, then, when they took her away?' Barnard asked angrily of the uniformed constable who was standing with his back to the wall looking distinctly anxious.

'Not so you'd notice, Sarge,' the officer mumbled. 'But they insisted she should go to Casualty so I couldn't make them leave her on the pavement, could I? The manager of the club insisted and the ambulance men seemed to think they could save her. I couldn't argue with that, could I?'

'OK, but I'm told she's dead now even if she wasn't then, so I'll track her down at the hospital,' Barnard said with ill grace before he turned to the club door which was ajar and went up the narrow stairs, thickly carpeted, to discover that most of the clients must have left the scene hurriedly, abandoning drinks and food on tables which had obviously been well populated before what the manager was insisting was a tragic accident had happened. Barnard did not necessarily disbelieve the officer on duty, but he was uneasy about the fact that the body had been removed so fast and the crowd which must have filled the club well into the small hours had been able and evidently eager to vanish so quickly. He suspected that their reasons might not be entirely innocent but, after a quick look round, Barnard concluded that there was not a lot he could do on his own in the small hours of the morning with staff and clients long gone and not even a body to examine. If anything illegal had been happening there had been more than enough time to hide it.

'I'll be back first thing,' he told Hugh Mercer, who had identified himself as the manager, and who was hovering close to the top of the narrow stairs with keys in his hand and ill-concealed impatience in his eyes. He was a heavyweight, with the broad shoulders of a rugby forward, all muscle not fat, wearing a well-cut suit Barnard knew came from a tailor who was well out of his own league, and with a supercilious expression and an accent, or more like a drawl, Barnard did not normally hear in Soho and which he did not warm to. Mercer's clean-cut profile and well-barbered hair only emphasized the fact that this was a man as confident in his abilities as the sergeant was in his own and, he assumed, with a social status and a range of contacts that might well extend as far as the commissioner at Scotland Yard itself. The chilly blue eyes which Mercer shifted around the untidy debris left behind by his departed clients clanged warning bells in Barnard's head: Mercer's priority was obviously to please the living, leaving no room at all for sympathy for the anonymous young girl who had died and whom so far no one had apparently identified at the scene or laid claim to in the morgue. She must, he thought, have come into the club with somebody older, but whoever that was had made themselves as scarce as everybody else.

'I'll want a list of the clients who were here last night and the staff who were on duty,' Barnard said, leaving no room for debate. 'I assume you know who brought her in?'

'That should be easy enough to check,' Mercer said. 'But the door staff have all gone home. I can get them back first thing for you if you like.'

'I do like,' Barnard said flatly. 'The nick was told it was a non-fatal accident but it seems to be worse than that. I'll check with the hospital to see whether this poor kid is actually alive or dead as you don't seem to have made that call. Have you no idea who she is, or who brought her here?'

Mercer scowled and made as if to argue, but he thought better of it quickly as Barnard grabbed his arm and squeezed hard.

'No idea, Officer,' he said. 'I don't personally monitor everyone who comes through the doors. I have staff to do that and, as I told you, they are long gone. There was no request from your station to keep them here racking up unnecessary overtime.'

'So I'll see you in the morning, eight o'clock, and don't be late,' Barnard said. 'And I will want to know exactly who was here last night, every T crossed and I dotted,' he added before spinning on his heel and taking the stairs two at a time to the street door below. As he slammed the door and revved the engine of his car, his mood lightened slightly. With a bit of luck Kate would be awake and welcome him back into bed, which would be a bonus that would maybe make his early hours' trip worthwhile for him at least.

As he manoeuvred the car off the pavement the constable still standing uncertainly outside the club stepped forward and tapped on the driver's window.

'I forgot to mention,' he said when Barnard wound the window down. 'Some bloke went in there just before you turned up. I didn't see him come out.'

'You didn't ask him who he was?' Barnard snapped. 'I didn't see any sign of anyone else up there. The manager was waiting to lock up so I doubt there was anyone still inside.'

'There were still quite a few people coming and going while the ambulance was here. I didn't think to take their names, Sarge.'

'OK, I'll check it out with the manager in the morning. But I don't rate your chances of making it into CID very highly.'

Back in Greek Street outside the Late Supper Club the next morning to meet the manager for the second time, Barnard parked half on the pavement again, leaving just about enough space for a passing cab to squeeze past. He crossed the road to the main door of the club, which he found was still locked, and rang the bell impatiently, almost sure that Mercer had ignored their appointment. He waited and the door was eventually opened by the man he had spoken to the previous night, looking even more in control and unruffled by events than he had before.

'Right, Mr Mercer,' Barnard said as the manager waved him into a seat in his tidy office, feeling justifiably irritated by the club manager's relaxed attitude. 'The bad news is that your young victim was found to be dead when she arrived at hospital.'

Mercer took a sharp breath and sat down at his desk. 'She's not my bloody victim, is she? What's that supposed to mean exactly, Sergeant?'

'I would say that it means you are responsible for the safety of people while they're on these licensed premises and failed pretty miserably last night,' Barnard said, not bothering to hide his irritation. 'This may simply be a tragic accident. There's no way of telling yet so there will be a post-mortem. But I saw this girl briefly in the morgue. She was only a kid, not old enough to drink, probably not even old enough to be in here at all. So let's talk about your club and exactly what happened in the early hours, shall we? From the moment you opened the doors to the moment this girl made her unusual exit. She fell face first and will be hard to identify unless one or more of your people tell us who she is. If we have to wait for her to be reported missing we may be waiting a long time. I think you said last night that you were a members' club. What exactly am I supposed to understand by that, from your perspective?'

'You know what I mean, Sergeant,' Mercer said, his voice unsympathetic. 'There's a membership fee, isn't there? A very serious membership fee, more than enough to keep the riff-raff out. And only members are allowed in. Members and their guests. We are very strict about that. We don't have any old hoi polloi walking in off the street. We have some quite well-known people coming in – musicians, artists, mainly the creative types as it's always been in Soho. But they like their privacy. And a lot of them have incomes these days which would make you blink. They can afford to pay for their privacy.'

'That should make our inquiries much easier, shouldn't it?' Barnard snapped. 'I assume you have a register of members and they sign in so you know exactly who's here and who's not. So you'll be able to identify this poor kid, I expect, and link her to the member who signed her in. She was only a teenager, not much more than a child, about fifteen or sixteen, one of the hospital doctors who examined her was saying.'

Mercer's eyes swivelled away for a moment and Barnard thought for a second that he detected a panic which was quickly veiled. 'Obviously she wasn't a member,' Mercer said. 'She must have been signed in by someone.'

'And your door staff didn't notice she was underage?'

'The place was buzzing,' Mercer said. 'We were packed out by midnight. And you know the way they dress these days – skirts up to their knickers, all that heavy make-up round the eyes. She might have been sixteen but she was going on twenty-three.'

'But you'll have a record of who brought her in,' Barnard said. 'And her name in your visitors' book. That must be routine, easy to check? If she wasn't carrying any ID, and she doesn't seem to have been, she might be hard to place otherwise.'

Mercer shrugged, his eyes blank and his half-smile bland. 'We won't necessarily have a written record,' he said. 'As I say, it was very busy last night. Sometimes the door staff don't get the details of all the guests members bring in, do they? Not written down anyway. I'll check.'

'You should have done that already, Mr Mercer,' Barnard said. 'Surely the door staff know who's come in alone and who hasn't. You may be a members' club but the licensing laws still apply. And from what the uniformed officer who was first on the scene told me last night, this girl didn't look to him as if she was old enough to be here under any circumstances, signed in or not.

Somewhere, I expect, a mother and father are wondering why their daughter didn't come home last night and are beginning to fear the worst.'

Mercer's expression hardened and he dashed a bead of sweat from his forehead impatiently. 'It's these damn kids running round after the damn bands,' he said, his voice harsh. 'We don't talk about our clients or we'd be completely overrun with them, shouting and screaming and making a nuisance of themselves. You've seen them chasing the Beatles around outside the Palladium, screaming from the roof at Heathrow when they go to America. You must know what they're like. Our members here are looking for a relaxed night out, away from their camp followers. We try to guarantee that. Complete discretion at all times. But we know some of the kids still try to get in—'

'But she didn't just get in, did she?' Barnard snapped. 'The bobby on duty said she'd been drinking at the very least. He could smell the booze on her. There'll be a post-mortem in the circumstances, and the pathologist will certainly be asking for blood tests to see if there was anything worse going on. I can smell the cannabis in here even this morning. Did she smoke anything, d'you know? Or take anything stronger? The toxicology will tell us so you might as well say now if you know what she got up to. Are drugs available in your exclusive club, Mr Mercer? And if so, who uses them and who might have given them to an underage girl who shouldn't have been here in the first place?'

'You know what Soho's like, Sergeant,' Mercer said with the slightest of shrugs, his face rigidly bland. 'It's nothing new. It's been the same for years, since before the war. It used to be booze in the old days – lots of booze and jazz and the odd bit of dope, and a pretty relaxed attitude to sex, and you lot didn't take a lot of notice. It was live and let live. Now the poets and jazz singers and artists are moving on and it's the rock stars moving in so it's suddenly top of your blacklist. Why's that, Sergeant? What's the difference? Why is a paralytic drummer in a band so much worse than Dylan Thomas the poet drinking himself stupid every night?'

'The difference is that I don't think Dylan Thomas had many kids chasing after him while a young girl must have thought it was a good idea to come here to see the singer or the drummer

– or whoever it was drew who her in, or maybe signed her in – and now she's dead. In any case, we know for a fact that there are more drugs on the streets now and more dangerous drugs around,' Barnard said. 'Scotland Yard is worried and you probably know there's a new law going through to crack down on it all. So let's have a close look at your membership lists and the people who signed in here last night. I want to know who this girl is, where she came from and how she got in, who bought her drinks or gave her drugs and what she took that sent her through that window head first. And if I don't get some answers we'll be going to the magistrates to get this place closed down.'

Mercer smiled faintly and Barnard knew that was a threat this man did not believe was real. To have set this pricey-looking enterprise up in such a prominent location, Mercer must have had some rock-solid support from somewhere, and Barnard was beginning to wonder how much he had paid for it and who to.

'The bobby outside said someone came into the club about the time the ambulance left. Does that ring any bells, Mr Mercer?' Barnard persisted.

The manager shrugged. 'Not that I recall,' he said. 'I'd cleared the place out by the time you rolled up. And you saw me lock up. I think your bobby's mistaken.'

'Maybe,' Barnard said, knowing that for the officer to mention it to CID at all he would have to be pretty sure of his facts. Every young bobby's ambition was to join CID. 'We'll talk about it later when you've done the paperwork I need. We really don't want anyone left out of this investigation who ought to be in it, do we?'

'Of course not, Sergeant,' Mercer said.

'Well, I'll leave you to press on with what you need to do while I go to talk to my boss. At the moment we've got this down as an unexplained death, quite possibly an accident. But one way or another it has to be explained and it could get a whole lot worse than that.'

Barnard was back at the nick by mid-morning, leaving Hugh Mercer to trawl through his books and membership lists in no doubt that he would be hearing from the police again within a few hours. The sergeant had found no satisfactory lead into his inquiries yet but he was aware that the tragedy at the Late Supper Club was somehow meshing into a web of worries which had been bothering him for months. He knew as well as Mercer did that there had been drugs fairly freely available for years in the strip clubs and pubs and dubious entertainment venues and cafes of Soho. It had been the seedy bohemian centre of London since before the war with a cosmopolitan population which attracted outsiders looking for excitement and an element of risk and the chance to see the famous – or notorious – at play. It was one of the reasons why he enjoyed working there and he reckoned he knew how to take its temperature and keep its illegality within bounds without driving away the clients the bars and pubs and clubs and restaurants relied on and the relatively harmless entertainment they indulged in. What was new was the fact that the new celebrities patronizing the up-and-coming venues like the Late Supper Club were attracting followers much younger and more unpredictable than of old.

And recently he had picked up another undercurrent which was not normal. It was not just that Soho was pulling in new clients from further afield looking for excitement they could not get in the suburbs and with money in their pockets to pay for it. There was also, he reckoned, a new reticence among the contacts he had relied on for as long as he had worked in the crowded narrow streets to tell him what was going on under the glittering, frenetic surface of the place. There were faces he did not know and who walked away quickly when he appeared, transactions which were concealed round corners when a uniformed officer walked at the regulation pace down Greek Street or round Soho Square on patrol, and an increasing number, not just of drunks later at night, staggering and falling down as they always had done for years, but of much younger punters who walked unsteadily in circles with glazed eyes looking for something they did not seem to be able to find.

It was not just Barnard who was uneasy. The nick had been put on alert by Scotland Yard, who told them that the inflow of banned substances through the docks was increasing. And some of it, Barnard guessed, or even a lot of it, was reaching his manor. If the girl who had plunged out of the club window in Greek Street had been using drugs, then a simple accident was not necessarily the way to describe what had ended her life. She needed to be identified urgently and her route to the Late Supper Club checked out. In the end the suppliers needed to be found before any more victims ended up dead on the pavement. And for that to happen he had to persuade Mercer and the clients who were in his club last night to help him, and that might not be easy as a significant proportion of them might be involved themselves and more likely to try to pull strings at the Yard to keep their names out of the papers rather than cooperate with queries from the local nick.

Time was, Barnard thought, that such a response was confined to a strata of society which regarded itself as a distinct cut above most coppers. But there were new and different aristocrats now with just as much money in their pockets as the traditional kind, who were often crippled by the debts and mortgages which hung around their family mansions. And the new young stars too might well expect, with a sense of entitlement that used to take generations to breed, that they would be able to remain above the law where ordinary mortals might expect to fall foul of it. It was time, Barnard thought, to consult the boss.

He hung his coat and hat up as carefully as usual when he got back to his desk in the CID squad room, straightened his new Liberty print tie and smoothed his hair, which was widely regarded as too long by his senior officers, before reporting to the DCI along the corridor. Barnard and DCI Keith Jackson had never had the easiest of relationships. The precise, puritanical Scot, his person and his desk always immaculate and his manner unbending, did not hide his dislike of Barnard's enthusiasm for swinging London's fashion, music and lifestyle, something which Jackson evidently could not even begin to comprehend on aesthetic or moral grounds. He was like the ultimate parent watching a whole generation of wild teenagers and young adults chuck their lives away.

'So what exactly have you asked the manager to do?' Jackson asked sharply. 'I don't care how much his members value their privacy. A girl is dead, perhaps not as accidentally as we are being led to believe. I want the names and addresses of everyone who was in that club last night, not just when she fell but before that as well. I want to know who took her there and what she had to drink or smoke or inject or whatever else they get up to these days. You know the Yard want some progress on drugs in Soho. They're so worried that they are halfway to setting up a special squad to concentrate on the trade. They know stuff is coming in but so far they don't have a clue who's distributing it or where. But from what I hear this is not just marijuana. There are all sorts of dangerous substances floating about that even the doctors don't know the effect of yet.'

'I'll ask the pathologist to make sure we know exactly what she had taken,' Barnard said. 'I've got the manager going through all the paperwork and I'll check it out later. I've told him I want details of everyone who was in that club last night. Someone who was in there must know who she was. Someone older must have taken her in.'

'Right. Someone who should have known better,' Jackson snapped. 'You have to ask what the parents were thinking, letting a young girl out in Soho at that time of night.'

'Sir,' Barnard agreed.

'And on another matter,' Jackson ploughed on, and Barnard had a good idea what that matter might be simply from the expression of impatience on his face. 'You haven't heard anything about where your friend Ray Robertson has vanished to, have you? Anything on the bush telegraph, even after all this time? Anything from the Soho contacts you think so highly of? Now his brother is safely locked up he might be tempted back into the mainstream, don't you think?'

'To my knowledge, Ray Robertson never dealt in drugs,' Barnard said carefully. He had hoped that Robertson's disappearance would be the end of a long-standing connection which went back to the East End school from which they both had been evacuated during the war. But he was well aware that his bosses were still linking his own name to his old schoolfriend with depressing regularity as if the relationship had never changed.

'I haven't seen or heard from him since I last picked up his trail out in Essex. I thought he must have gone abroad after Georgie was sent down, but he wouldn't have contacted me anyway. He must know I was furious with him for putting my girlfriend's life at risk, leaving her there at that farmhouse without telling anyone.'

'Well, that's what you keep telling me,' Jackson said, not hiding his scepticism. He glanced at his watch. 'You'd better get over to the morgue. The post-mortem is due to start at eleven. We haven't indicated yet that it might be more than an accident, so they won't be treating it as urgent. If you're convinced there's more to it, make sure they prioritize the blood tests. And then chase the manager at the club again for all the information he's got. I don't care how well known some of his members are. Notorious might be a better word. Either way they're not above the law and they won't get any favours here. Get on with it, Sergeant. You've a lot of lost ground to make up after your last little adventure. You can be sure that the Yard are watching your every move, and probably the other lot as well. The spooks'll be keeping a close eye. Once you've come to their attention they don't forget about you. I don't think they ever let go.'

'Guv,' Barnard muttered as he turned away, not bothering to hide his anger but too wary to make any comment.

'Don't forget to see if you can track Robertson down either,' Jackson added as Barnard opened his office door, and he knew it was not just an afterthought. Someone somewhere had the missing Ray Robertson, once his boyhood protector, in his sights, and he did not fancy becoming collateral damage.

TWO

Kate O'Donnell was having what passed for a quiet day at the office. She had slept late, only vaguely aware of Harry Barnard's second early departure after which, she realized, she must have fallen deeply asleep again. That was hardly surprising, she thought with a satisfied smile as she had rolled out from among the tangled sheets. She had washed and dressed quickly, not bothered with more than a cup of coffee and had almost run down the hill from Barnard's flat to Archway Road and the Underground station. Clutching a paper bag containing a couple of iced buns in lieu of breakfast, she had been relieved to find that the photographers' room at Ken Fellows' agency, where she remained the only female photographer on the staff, was still crowded with her colleagues while Ken's office, behind its glass screen, remained unlit and empty.

'Where is he?' she now asked the half-dozen men who seemed to be milling about aimlessly.

'Held up on the Central line apparently,' one of the more approachable older men deigned to inform her. 'He should be here soon.'

'Right,' Kate said, taking a bite of a sticky bun, settling at her desk and opening her file of recent pictures which she guessed she might as well make a start on filing. But she had hardly begun to make an impression on her chosen task when she was waved over to the phone at the end of the room and heard a voice on a crackly line which she barely recognized, although it had once been very familiar.

'Kate?' it asked urgently. 'I got your number from Tess. I didn't know who else to ring.'

'Who's that?' Kate asked, not because she was not entirely sure, but more because she was not sure this would be a conversation she wanted to have. 'It's a terrible line.'

'It's Dave, Dave Donovan, la. I need some help, Katie.'

'Where are you?' she asked, trying to hide her surprise at hearing from a boyfriend she had finished with, to his intense discontent, soon after she had met Harry Barnard. 'Are you in London again?' she asked, her voice cautiously neutral.

'No, no, I'm ringing you from my mam's phone in Aintree. I'm ringing about my girlfriend, Marie Collins. Do you remember her, la?'

'I don't think so,' Kate mumbled.

'You must remember her,' Dave said querulously, as if Kate's memory lapse, if that was what it was, was some sort of moral lapse as well. 'Well, anyway, she's in London and I can't get hold of her. She gave me a phone number but no one ever answers. She went a couple of weeks ago and I've been trying for days to get hold of her.'

'What's she doing down here?' Kate asked, relieved that Dave at least had a girlfriend, even if she was missing, and that he was not on some misguided mission to restart their own relationship.

'I told her not to go – begged her, like – but she thinks she's another Cilla Black and is sure she can make it down there. Singing with my band round Merseyside wasn't good enough for her, so she took off to look for a manager who'll get her a recording contract. Solo, you know? She tried Brian Epstein up here – the Beatles' manager? – but he turned her down. I think Cilla's the only girl he handles. And Marie was full of herself, full of plans, but I've not heard from her for weeks now. I'm getting really worried.'

'Is she another Cilla?' Kate asked. 'Really that good? There must be hundreds of girls in Liverpool who think that.'

'She's pretty good,' Dave said, but Kate could hear the faint reluctance in his voice. She could imagine how he would resent it if this Marie really did do well in London where he had failed.

'But not that good?'

'No, I don't think so. But if she's been turned down again she'll be heartbroken. I really need to find her.'

'London's a big place, Dave. You know that,' Kate said, feeling slightly panicked at the magnitude of what Dave was suggesting and remembering how the city had so thoroughly chewed him up and spat him out when he had brought his whole group south to try to make a name for themselves. 'Have you no idea where she's been staying? Or who with?'

'I told you, no one's answering the phone number she gave me.'

'Do you have an address, and a photograph maybe? I could go round there and see if I can find out if she's moved, and if so where to,' Kate said doubtfully. 'People move around all the time – you know that. It's difficult to find decent places to live. The landlords rip you off.'

'Yeah, yeah, that's why I called you. I sent you a picture – one of the publicity shots she had taken to show Brian Epstein. And the address, though I don't know where it is exactly. It doesn't seem very detailed to me. A number and a road, that's all. Anyway, I posted it to what I thought was still your place with Tess and when you didn't get back to me I rang there and she said you weren't living there any more. What's going on, Katie?'

'Never mind, it's complicated,' Kate said. 'But Tess will have kept the post for me.' There was no reason at all why she should account to Dave Donovan for anything after all this time. 'I can go round to the flat after work and pick the photo up.' She sighed. 'I'll see what I can do,' she said. 'But I don't hold out high hopes. And if that doesn't work I can't think of anything else you can do apart from reporting it to the police.'

'So you're still with that smartie-pants London bizzie who fancied you when your brother Tom was in trouble?' Dave asked aggressively, and in spite of the background noise on the long-distance line, Kate could tell that he still resented the fact that Barnard had taken his place in her affections. 'Tess said that you weren't really sharing the flat with her any more. Just paying the rent.'

'I told you. It's complicated. You don't need to know. I'll pick up your stuff and see what I can do with it,' Kate said without, she hoped, much sign of enthusiasm and dodging the still slightly fraught issue of where she was living. She didn't want anything more about that getting back to the sharp eyes of her zealous mother in Liverpool. But Dave did not seem to appreciate that maybe Marie was another girlfriend like she had been, with ambitions that had overtaken her affections and, like her, had run into Dave's deep suspicion of women who wanted careers of their own. Reluctantly she gave him Barnard's home phone number at the flat.

'Better to catch me there than here at work,' she said. 'I'll talk to Harry Barnard anyway when I see him later and see what he thinks.'

'Do you have to?' Dave asked, and she wondered how that touch of jealousy had survived so long if this Marie was such a serious girlfriend that she had slotted into Kate's vacant place.

'I told you. I don't think the police will do anything unless someone reports her missing,' she said. She wondered whether Donovan would actually use the number anyway if it meant involving Harry, who was much more likely to answer the phone than she was.

'I'll pick up the details from Tess and see what we can do,' she said, although she knew that there was probably no way she could track down a missing girl who might have her own good reasons for leaving Dave Donovan high and dry on Merseyside. After all, he had just reminded her of those very good reasons she had had herself.

Harry Barnard took his time on the way to the hospital for the post-mortem. He had just enough time, he thought, to call on a few of his contacts and try to uncover just why so many of the legitimate and less legitimate businesses which lined the relatively quiet morning streets were suddenly less willing to talk to him. But he got nowhere until he passed an Italian bar much like the one where he and Kate often shared lunch and found the proprietor sweeping broken glass from his doorway.

'What happened?' he asked the owner who he knew simply as Mario.

Mario shrugged massively and raised his hands in the air. 'A car,' he said. 'Nearly came through the window. Didn't stop. I didn't even look for a number – it gave me such a shock. An accident, I suppose. These things happen.'

'Did you call the police when it happened?' Barnard asked, but he knew from the way Mario's eyes slid past him to scan the street in both directions warily that he hadn't and probably wouldn't the next time either. And he was sure that there would be a next time if someone had really taken up where Ray Robertson had left off.

'No point is there, Sergeant? You won't catch him.'

'And you really don't know who "him" is?'

Mario shrugged again, scooped up a shovel full of broken glass and pitched it into a bucket.

'Didn't you see the driver or get the car number?'

'Just a passing car,' he said. 'An accident. Bad driving. Young men don't concentrate. They watch the girls.'

'But usually they stop when they hit something,' Barnard said. 'Do you have insurance?' he asked, knowing the answer before Mario shook his head emphatically.

'Nothing like that,' Mario insisted, although they both knew he was lying. There had been a time not so long ago when the only 'insurance' around on some of the narrow, crowded streets of Soho was the criminal kind, and it was not only Mario's situation which convinced him that maybe those days had returned. He just hoped that DCI Jackson's suspicion that Ray Robertson might be relaunching at least one of his former enterprises was a nightmare too far to become a reality. For him personally, the implications would be seriously unwelcome. He sighed and glanced at his watch.

'I have to be somewhere,' he said. 'A young girl died in Greek Street last night after a fall. But I'll be back, I promise.'

'*Que sera, sera*,' Mario said, although he did not look as though he meant it any more than Barnard went along with the sentiment. What the sergeant wanted to know as he set off again towards the hospital was who was really behind the resurgence of a protection racket on these streets if it wasn't Robertson? He did not believe this was just a few petty criminals riding their luck. Someone would be organizing it and whoever that was would be trouble. He knew his manor well enough to feel anxiety in the air as eyes slid away from him as he hurried away from the damaged bar. He was aware that since the Robertson brothers had been absent from Soho's streets – one incarcerated and the other evidently keeping a very low profile for reasons of his own – the atmosphere had lightened. But this morning the fear was undoubtedly back and seemed to linger in every narrow lane and back alley and behind the unusual number of doors which were closed tight and, he guessed, locked and bolted by locals confused by what was going on.

The post-mortem, on the other hand, turned out to be predictable and straightforward. Barnard watched from a decent distance as the cause of death for the young girl on the slab was only too evident from the shattered state of her body and particularly her head and face.

'It was a high floor window, a serious height,' he said to the pathologist. 'They're tall, those old houses. And she looks as though she went out with some force.'

'Depends what she was doing when she fell, or jumped maybe, though I think that's less likely,' the doctor said. 'Or if she was pushed. There's no definitive way of telling. But the head and facial injuries are very severe, as you can see.'

'But you think that's possible, looking at the injuries? I mean, could she have been pushed?' Barnard asked.

'I've no idea, Sergeant. Talking to witnesses is your job. All I can tell you is that apart from other injuries, mainly broken bones, she suffered a blow across the face and forehead which undoubtedly killed her. When the test results come back I can tell you whether she was drunk or, what do they call it? Stoned? Or if she had taken anything even stronger. Heroin, perhaps, though it must have been inhaled. I can't see any obvious signs of injection. And to be honest I don't know much about this LSD some of the youngsters are experimenting with, but I believe it can have a very powerful effect on some susceptible people. Nightmares, hallucinations, you name it. I heard from a colleague who had dealt with a young man who had tried to jump off a bridge – reckoned he could fly. Dangerous stuff apparently. It seems it's difficult to detect but the effects can last a long time. It works its way out of the body quickly, though, so it doesn't often show up in tests. Anyway, I'll let you know as soon as I have results.'

'I'm going back to the club now to pin the manager down,' Barnard said. 'But whether we'll ever identify everyone who was there last night, I'm not sure. People are supposed to sign in but there doesn't seem to be any guarantee that guests' names are taken. And this kid can hardly be a member. Did you find anything to identify her when she was brought in? Anything in her pockets?'

'A purse with a couple of pound notes in it. That's all. Nothing convenient with a name and address on. It's over there in that dish.'

'It's not much to fund a night in a club like that. She must have been with someone. I'll take it anyway and see if the manager has found anything else she might have left behind – coat or a bag maybe. It's very odd if that's all she had on her. And if no one has come forward because they were with her it may be quite hard to find out who she is.' He put the relics into an evidence bag and put it in his pocket. It was not much to show for a life so prematurely snuffed out, he thought.

He glanced at the pale face from which the blood had been partly cleaned, the lips with a gash across them, the front teeth smashed, the nose crushed as much as broken, the eyes blackened and closed and the untidy blonde hair matted with blood and dirt, and he tried to take in just how young she must have been. Somewhere, he thought, a family would very likely be wondering where their daughter was and he knew he would have to go through the missing persons reports that had come in either late last night or this morning to see if he could identify her that way. The family might not even have realized yet that she had not come home last night and reported her missing. He hoped that the unlucky female PC sent to break the news of her death did not arrive before her parents had even realized she had gone. And if she was not identifiable from those overnight reports then they would have to work backwards, knowing that it was possible that she had been missing for weeks or months, adrift in a city where young girls were often regarded simply as prey. It was never easy and the longer news was delayed the more those waiting would be distraught as hope was slowly snuffed out by the lack of official answers and the passage of time.

'Do you have any colleagues who could help us reconstruct her face?' he asked.

The doctor looked at him across the table. 'I'll ask around,' he said. 'I know there have been some experiments in that sort of area. I read something somewhere about a Russian who reckoned he had recreated the face of Ivan the Terrible. But it's all experimental. I don't think anyone's taking it very seriously and I guess Scotland Yard would just laugh at you. I'll look in the literature, though. Keep me in touch.'

THREE

On his way back to the Late Supper Club, Barnard put his head round the door of Ken Fellows' photographic agency, but Kate O'Donnell's desk was empty.

'Is she out on a job?' he asked a photographer who was busy loading his camera.

'I'm not sure where she's gone,' he said with not much sign of interest. 'She asked Ken for a couple of hours off and just went. It's all right for those with a pretty face, isn't it?'

Barnard closed the door behind him with rather more force than necessary and made his way back into the street, looping round to Greek Street where he caught his quarry, Hugh Mercer, striding up the stairs of his club holding a bacon sandwich in a greasy paper bag held well away from his suit in one hand and a cup of coffee in the other. He did not look pleased to see DS Barnard.

'There's no catering staff on till later,' he said, swallowing hard and panting slightly. 'A man's got to eat.'

'You've got an appetite, have you?' Barnard said. 'A kid out of the window's all in a night's work?'

'I told you last night. I've no idea who she is – or was. Or who brought her in. Is she really dead?'

'Dead on arrival,' Barnard said. 'And pretty much unrecognizable. So now you and me are going to sit down and go through your paperwork to see exactly who she might be. And who brought her here. You're not telling me that a kid of that age made it to a private Soho club all on her own.'

'If you say so,' Mercer agreed with ill grace.

For a moment, Barnard saw red and pushed the man, who with a rugby player's physique must have weighed twice as much as he did himself, against the bannister and held him there with his spine pressed hard against the wood.

'Have you made any progress since I saw you earlier?' he asked.

'Yes, yes, Sergeant,' Mercer said, flushing slightly and obviously fighting the instinct to hit out, his hands balling ominously.

Just give me a reason to arrest you, Barnard thought, recognizing a man who was not used to being treated with anything less than respect by police officers.

'I've sorted out some stuff for you,' Mercer said. 'But I've still no idea who this kid is. Not a clue. People who came in as members may not have signed everyone in properly. I told you, it was very busy last night. The door staff may not have done a very good job. You know how it is.'

'No, I don't know how it is,' Barnard snapped, easing away from him slightly. 'I've never been a manager of a club, but I do know the rules. This girl was very young, most likely underage, and she died. I want to know who she is, who she came with, whether she drank anything she shouldn't have, or smoked something, and how and why she went out of that window. And if you can't provide some answers, I promise you I'll have this place closed down.'

'A few of your colleagues wouldn't be very pleased about that,' Mercer snapped back unexpectedly. 'We pay enough insurance and not just to friends of yours.'

'What's that supposed to mean?' Barnard replied quickly, although he was not as surprised as he pretended to be.

'Never mind,' Mercer said, and Barnard guessed that he had already said more than he had intended. The manager led the way into his office and pointed to a number of papers and ledgers on his desk.

'Membership lists, registers people sign in with, going back six months, staff names and addresses – what more will you want?'

'This will do to be going on with,' the sergeant said, taking Mercer's chair at the desk and waving him away. 'Don't go anywhere until I've finished – I may need to check details with you. This girl obviously didn't get in here all on her own. I need to find out who brought her here and left her dead on the pavement without a word of explanation as to how that happened. I need to talk to that man – and I guess it's a man – very much indeed. And anyone who might have been a witness. It may all take some considerable time.'

'I'll get on with my breakfast then,' Mercer said, but he caught the hostility in Barnard's eyes clearly enough. 'If there's anything I can do to help . . .' he added quickly. 'Anything at all.'

'I'll let you know if I need you,' Barnard said dismissively, but by the time he had gone through the books thoroughly he had found no trace of the girl who had died or any indication who might have brought her to the club. Frustrated, he closed up the manager's records, left his desk and went into the main club room, where he found Mercer sitting in the bar area with a large Scotch in front of him. He sat down across the table from him.

'She wasn't signed in, as far as I can see from what you've given me,' he said. 'And you say there's no sign of a bag or a coat which might belong to her. Isn't that very odd?'

'I don't know,' Mercer said. 'I don't know much about what these hysterical kids who chase pop stars get up to. She may have left her stuff outside and followed someone she recognized through the doors.'

'Possible, I suppose,' Barnard said sceptically. 'That's the other thing I wondered about. You said you were pulling in some big names, but I don't see any serious stars on your list for that night. Did they not turn up? Or are you trying to keep them out of the limelight, because I should warn you that if that's what you are doing my boss will not be best pleased. I'm going to be talking to as many people as I can track down that I know were here that night and I guess that if they saw the likes of a Beatle or a Rolling Stone or one of this new group – what are they called? The Rainmen? – they are going to be full of it. It's a secret they won't keep to themselves.'

Mercer took a swig of his drink, then a deep breath, and Barnard could see the fury behind his bland facade.

'I'll check it out,' he said. 'I'll get back to you. Sometimes some of the stars ask to be kept off the register to avoid fans like this stupid girl who fell out of the window . . .'

'You'll do that and you'll do it quickly,' Barnard said. 'Or I'll have you – and whoever you think you can keep out of the limelight – for perverting the course of justice. And you won't like that.' But he did not think that Mercer seemed to be as bothered by his threat as he had expected, and he thought that that in itself was worrying.

After spending most of the day between the Late Supper Club and the nick without feeling as if he had made anything like progress,

Barnard decided to see if he could check one of those niggling loose ends which had been bothering him since long before the anonymous young girl had plunged from the Soho club window. More than one of his contacts had suggested obliquely that someone – no one was ever very specific, eyes swivelled away when Barnard tried to pin down details – had recently seen Ray Robertson around his old haunts. And there had been a time a couple of weeks ago that he had himself seen someone he thought was Ray but the figure had vanished among the Oxford Street crowds before he could catch up with him. Not that he imagined that Ray would greet his old schoolfriend with anything like enthusiasm. They had parted on bad terms, with Barnard blaming Robertson for endangering Kate's life in the pursuit of his financial advantage and Robertson furious that Barnard had later admitted that if he had to choose between his job and his former friend he would not hesitate to arrest him.

There had been a time when they were sent away from their East End school as evacuees to a farm in the country when they'd been close. As the oldest of the three boys, Ray had protected Harry from his younger brother Georgie, who had been a bully even before he had left primary school and who could indulge in vicious violence if provoked. Years later, when Ray had set up as a boxing promoter and he was confident that Barnard could make it in the ring, he had done his best to make sure he did. But the relationship did not survive Barnard's decision to join the police, which the Robertson boys, as members of one of the most notorious criminal families in the East End, regarded as a betrayal too far.

Before setting off for home, the sergeant parked his car close to the rear doors of the Delilah Club with a sigh and decided that tonight, as the timing would probably see at least some of the management on the premises, might be the time to try to pin the rumours about Ray down. If nothing else, Barnard thought, a definite answer to the question whether or not Robertson was back in Soho might keep the powers that be at the Yard at bay for a while and DCI Jackson off his back at the nick.

He had already checked out that the Delilah still belonged to Robertson, which did not surprise him. It had been the scene of some of his greatest publicity triumphs in the days when he and his brother Georgie were minor celebrities who entertained the great and the good at boxing galas which, it was claimed, raised substantial amounts of money for sporting charities, although Barnard had often wondered how much the brothers creamed off for themselves. But once they had been exposed as more on the wrong side of the law than the right, their influence quickly evaporated like morning mist and Ray had effectively disappeared after his last encounter with the sergeant, as much to keep out of Harry's way after putting his girlfriend at risk as to avoid the crooks whose ill-gotten gains he had apparently appropriated that night. But somehow he still appeared to be in charge of the Delilah, which had once been his pride and joy, and when Barnard raised the subject of his boss with Derek Baker, the harassed-looking stand-in manager of the club, he shrugged with obvious anxiety.

'Dunno, mate,' he said with a hunted look. 'I get instructions from some lawyer down Holborn way. I never see anything of Mr Robertson. In fact, I've never set eyes on him as it goes.'

'Can you give me the name of this contact, the lawyer?' Barnard asked but Baker looked dubious and sucked in his cheeks like a plumber facing an untraceable leak.

'Don't think so, mate,' he said. 'You'd need some paperwork for something like that, something legal, wouldn't you? Really couldn't do anything like that off my own bat. I'd be out of a job, wouldn't I? Not a very patient man, is he, Mr Robertson, by the sound of it? Likes loyalty.'

'Fair enough,' Barnard said equably, not wanting warning signals to go out too firmly on what was only a hunch that if there were upheavals going on in Soho's underworld it was a fair guess that Ray was in some way likely to be involved, even at a distance, even possibly from abroad. 'Don't worry your head about it. It wasn't anything important.'

'Right,' Baker said. 'I'll get on with my job then.'

'I did hear, though, that some of the businesses around here are being pestered by some new protection racket. A bit of serious harassing, maybe? Broken windows at least, threats and intimidation on top. Have you come across anything like that at all?'

Derek Baker shrugged. 'Can't say that's a problem I've had,' he said. 'I can't imagine Mr Robertson would put up with anything like that, can you?'

'Maybe not,' Barnard conceded. 'But if you have any trouble, let us know, won't you? It's something that easily gets out of hand and we've been free of it for a while. So keep in touch.'

Baker nodded without enthusiasm as Barnard decided to leave him to make what he would of this renewed interest from the law. Baker knew very well that his absent boss knew all there was to know about protection in the tightly knit square mile of Soho and that Ray would in all likelihood also find out very quickly about the sergeant's long-delayed visit to the club. To be on the safe side, Baker went into the office, picked up the phone and dialled the solicitor's number. Better to keep the boss up to date, he thought, as let him find out from less friendly sources.

For his part, Barnard also knew very well that Robertson would want to know exactly what Harry was up to if it involved the club and that Baker would inevitably tell him. Robertson had, unlike his younger brother Georgie, stayed out of jail for so long by keeping at least one step ahead of the opposition on both sides of the law.

A chance encounter outside the still-closed doors of the club only confirmed Barnard's suspicions. Vincent Beaufort was never hard to spot. At a time when the Metropolitan Police blew hot and cold on Soho's homosexual men as they waited with ill grace for the new, more liberal law to be enacted, Beaufort never disguised for a moment his still illegal tastes and specialized in the sort of flamboyant outfits which would seriously challenge any passing bobby to stop him if they felt in the mood. This evening he was evidently intent on an evening out on the town in a purple check suit, a mustard cravat and his signature floppy broad-brimmed felt hat. Barnard put an arm across the pavement to stop him in his tracks, though not with any great force.

'Vincent,' he said, surveying the outfit with mock outrage. 'Where the hell do you think you are going dressed like that? I should stay well away from the nick if I was you, or you'll be hauled in for gross provocation.'

'Flash Harry,' Beaufort said weakly. 'Nice to see you too.'

'A moment of your time,' Barnard demanded. 'I get the distinct feeling that something's going down on my manor that I don't know about. Protection from a new source, maybe – a cafe trashed this very morning by a passing car? Ring any bells for you?'

Beaufort attempted a smile, but it did not seem to Barnard that his heart was in it and he shrugged instead. 'You know I don't get involved in anything like that,' Vincent said, aiming for a look of injured innocence which did not quite convince.

'I know all that,' Barnard said. 'But I also know you keep your eyes and ears open. So what have you heard?'

Beaufort scanned the busy corner outside the Delilah and dropped his voice until Barnard had to struggle to hear him. 'A lot of people thought it was Ray Robertson making a comeback, but I'm not sure that's right,' Beaufort said in little more than a whisper. 'There are new faces. And new tactics. Violent tactics, like a car going through a cafe window and not stopping, just reversing away in a cloud of dust. And there seems to be more drugs on the street too, and new varieties we haven't seen before. But that's all I know. And all I want to know. Asking questions seems to be a very bad idea according to anyone who's tried it.'

'Anyone I should look out for in particular?' Barnard asked. 'I need a bit of help here.'

'There's a tall, dark bloke around who seems to be taking an unusual interest in some of the businesses who are complaining. The people who make the threats are the usual riff-raff – sounds as if they're parroting someone else, though. And someone told me they had seen this dark bloke talking to some of them, as if they were in charge.'

'A description would be good,' Barnard suggested. 'Or even a name. D'you mean dark as in West Indian, someone up from Notting Hill?'

'No, no, not black,' Vincent said. 'Dark hair, dark eyes, pale skin, could be Italian maybe. Smart suit and hat. Quite dishy, a friend of mine said. But I've not heard a name.'

'Let me know if you do,' Barnard said.

'Sure, but now I have to go. I'm going to be late for my date.'

'You live dangerously,' Barnard said, making a half-hearted attempt to stop him, but he knew he was wasting his time. If Beaufort felt like helping with his inquiries he would usually do it willingly, if discreetly, enough. But today he was clearly not in a very helpful mood, and Barnard felt it was more and more urgent to find out who was spreading this level of anxiety among the locals and why.

Watching Beaufort dodge the traffic around Piccadilly Circus, DS Barnard made a decision which he did not intend to pass on to DCI Jackson at this stage in the game. His first call tomorrow would not be in Soho but further east. That was where, if he could not track down Ray Robertson in person, he could at least chat to his mother, who was the one person who might know where her older son was hiding. Whether he would be able to prise the information out of the old lady he somewhat doubted, but it had to be worth a try.

When he finally got home to his flat in Highgate that evening, Harry Barnard was almost as frustrated by the lack of information he had gained from the Late Supper Club's documentation as he had been at the start of the day. The DCI had not been impressed but had contented himself with urging the sergeant to try harder tomorrow. Barnard found Kate in the kitchen beginning to cook supper. He put his arms round her and kissed the back of her neck.

'I thought you'd be hungry,' she said. 'I certainly am.'

'I looked for you earlier but no one at your office seemed to know where you were.'

'Right,' Kate said. 'You'd better sit down. I need to talk to you.'

'That sounds ominous,' Barnard said, selecting a bottle of wine and pouring her a glass. But he listened with growing disbelief as she described how she had spent part of her day since she had spoken to Dave Donovan that morning.

'He must be joking,' Barnard said, not bothering to hide his anger. 'How the hell does he think you can track down one girl somewhere in London? It's not possible.'

Kate shrugged and passed him the envelope with Marie's photograph, the usual glossy black and white publicity picture, a bit tattered round the margins. She wondered how long Brian Epstein had kept the picture around his office before handing it back with the desperate disappointment that would have gone with his decision not to take Marie on.

'You said you were dealing with a case, a girl who was killed,' Kate said. 'That isn't her, is it?'

Barnard shook his head. 'No, that's not her. The girl who died was a bottle blonde, straight hair, not curls, a short cut – you know, Vidal Sassoon style. Much younger than this one, too, though it's difficult to tell very much about what she looked like. She had terrible injuries to her face. And anyway, Dave's girlfriend looks like a redhead. Is that right?'

'Yes, I think so,' Kate said. Marie was a new addition to Dave's line-up around the Merseyside clubs and Kate only vaguely remembered her from the days when Dave Donovan had played at the Cavern once or twice and tried out various singers, though not many of them were women. But as soon as Cilla Black had made her breakthrough she imagined that there would be any number of young women and girls in Liverpool attempting to ride on her coat-tails once it was plain that a girl could make it just as well as the boys. And perhaps dying your hair red was part of every female singer's strategy now Cilla had hit the big time. Marie was unlikely to be the only one.

'So what else did Dave give you?' Barnard asked, knowing that he would be wasting his time trying to talk Kate out of trying to help. He had known her long enough now to realize that Scouse loyalties were strong and long-lasting.

Kate pulled a sheet of lined paper from a notebook out of her handbag and passed it to Barnard.

'A phone number and what he said he remembered of the address she had given him. But I looked in the A to Z. There are dozens of Western Roads in London. There's no district code so it could be any of them. And that's the name of the manager she was supposed to be coming down to audition for. Jack Mansfield. I haven't tried him yet but Dave said he made some sort of promise to Marie.'

Barnard ran an eye over the list. 'It would take you weeks to work your way round these roads,' he said. 'Is that what you were doing when you asked the boss for time off at lunchtime?'

Kate shrugged slightly. 'Just a couple of the central ones,' she said. 'But I didn't get anywhere. No one had heard of her. I'll have to go to see this manager. He may know where she is. If she's really been to see him he must have an address in London for her.'

'Till you do, the phone number is the best bet,' Barnard said, unwilling to pour too much cold water on Kate's plans. 'Keep trying that. If you can't get a reply I can probably get it traced. What's the district code?'

'LAK,' Kate said. 'I've no idea where that is. Have you?'

'Not offhand, but it's easy enough to find out,' Barnard said, reaching for the telephone directory. They looked in the index of exchanges. 'Lakeside is Wimbledon. That's an odd place for an ambitious rock and roll singer to hang out, isn't it? Maybe she knows someone who lives down there and she's staying with them. Are you sure this isn't just a lovers' tiff? She's disappeared because she wanted to disappear and leave Dave behind?'

'I don't know, Harry,' Kate said. 'I really don't know.'

'Well, I reckon it'll be easier to try the manager first to see if she turned up for her audition, and if so what he told her afterwards. Didn't Dave think of that?'

'He's not got a phone at home,' Kate said. 'Not many people have up Scotland Road, even now a lot of the slum houses have been pulled down. And trunk calls are expensive anyway. And he may not have the manager's number. But I'm sure this Mansfield man won't be too difficult to track down from this end. It's Friday tomorrow. I'll try then, before the weekend. And he gave me the number of a bass player down from Liverpool, who's been playing with the Rainmen. He might have heard of another Scouser looking to make it big.'

Barnard looked at Kate for a long moment.

'Are you sure you want to do this?' he asked. 'It's not as if you owe Donovan anything.'

'Are you jealous, Harry?' she asked him with a grin. 'I don't believe it.'

'Of that Scouse freeloader? Never in a million years,' he said, refilling their wine glasses and raising his in an ironic toast. 'He had his chance and you blew him out of the water. That should be more than enough.'

Kate spent her lunch hour the next day tracking down Jack Mansfield, who turned out to have an office in Denmark Street, London's so-called Tin Pan Alley, which was an easy walk from her own office in Frith Street. Although she reckoned that she knew Soho pretty well by now, she had not been to Denmark Street before and was surprised to find it a bustling haunt of musicians – mainly young men in jeans and leather jackets hurrying between the surviving tall houses on both sides of the road which she reckoned must date back a couple of centuries at least. The beat of music thudded out of premises which offered everything from sheet music to recordings, even seeping out of steep entrances here and there leading to staircases evidently going down below ground into basement studios. For a moment, she stopped dead in her tracks as she came face-to-face with a familiar figure she knew she should recognize, but it was not until he had turned quickly into a studio entrance and disappeared that she realized it was Mick Jagger of the Rolling Stones.

She worked her way down the rows of houses looking for the number where the phone book had indicated that Mansfield's management agency was based, but she had to search the list of occupants outside the door more than once before she spotted his name. She had no idea how Marie Collins had heard of the man but his small, slightly tarnished nameplate did not indicate a flourishing business of any kind, least of all one which aimed to secure publicity and contracts for singers and musicians. She pushed open the street door streaked with flaking paint and followed the signs pointing up the bare and rubbish-strewn wooden staircase. The place looked as though it would go up in flames in minutes if you dropped a lighted match. At the top of the stairs she found another door with Mansfield's name on it and pushed it open to find herself face-to-face with a girl who looked as if she was still in her early teens. She was the sole occupant of a tiny, cluttered office, sitting behind a typewriter, totally absorbed in painting her nails.

'I'm looking for Mr Mansfield, Jack Mansfield,' Kate said sharply. 'Is he in?'

'Who's asking?' the girl questioned, glancing up without enthusiasm.

'My name's Kate O'Donnell but I'm really here because I'm trying to track down someone I think is one of his clients. A singer called Marie Collins from Liverpool. Do you know if she's made contact yet? She had an appointment but I'm not sure when it was.'

'Another one from Liverpool,' the girl said sulkily. 'Strikes me the whole bleeding town's heading south. You too by the sound of it.'

'Has Mr Mansfield seen Marie then?' Kate asked with a sense of relief, ignoring the not very veiled insults to her accent and her home city. 'People back home are worried about her . . .'

'I'll ask him,' the girl said. 'I'm only a temp. I don't know much about what he does. I just do the typing and answer the phone. I've only been here a week.' She got to her feet, pulling her miniskirt down below her knickers as she straightened up before she knocked on the inner door behind her and put her head round it.

'There's someone here asking about one of your clients, Mr Mansfield,' she said. 'Do you want to see her?'

Kate could only hear a muffled answer which did not sound at all enthusiastic but, as the girl pushed the door open further and waved her inside, she assumed the reply was affirmative and went in. She smiled with as much confidence as she could muster but could tell from the even denser clutter in the rather small main office that Mansfield was not in the same league as Brian Epstein who, even outside the music business, had become something of a legend who could, many ambitious musicians believed, turn base metal into gold on the strength of what he had achieved for the Beatles. Here, files and posters and tapes were piled on every surface and, as Mansfield turned the record which was playing down a notch, he looked distinctly the worse for wear. He was in shirtsleeves and looked as if he had not slept for a week, with purple bags under his eyes and deep creases around his mouth. He lit a cigarette from the butt of the previous one with hands which shook, threatening to thicken the already dense air to a serious fog. Kate found herself watching carefully where he put the dead match and wondered how singers coped with the atmosphere, which was already catching at her throat.

'Who is it you're looking for, darling?' he asked, closing one of his desk drawers with a clunk, leaving Kate unsurprised to recognize the distinct whiff of alcohol hanging in the air beneath the cigarette smoke and the heaps of shaking sheet music.

'Marie Collins,' Kate said. 'She came down from Merseyside a couple of weeks ago but she hasn't been in touch with her boyfriend since and he's worried about her. Did she come to see you? She told him she was going to.'

'Don't remember the name,' Mansfield said, digging into the paperwork piled on his desk and pulling out a dog-eared desk diary. He turned over the scrawled pages slowly. 'She can't have made much of an impression even if she did turn up. You've got to be a bit special to make it as a girl in this game. There's not many that succeed. There's not many Cilla Blacks out there.'

'She's doing OK,' Kate said sharply. 'And Sandy Shaw.'

'With the bare feet?' Mansfield asked dismissively. 'She won't last. You need something a bit more sexy than bare feet.'

'So did Marie turn up here?' Kate persisted. 'If so, I thought you might know where she was staying. Her boyfriend really wants to know where she is. He's not getting an answer to the phone number she gave him.'

'I don't remember her and I can't find her in my book. And believe me, everything goes into this book.'

Kate could imagine that it was genuinely his lifeline, given the state of chaos which surrounded him. 'If she wrote to you wouldn't you have kept the letter?' she asked. 'Won't your secretary have a file?'

'She's only a temp,' Mansfield said dismissively. 'I don't think she's got around to filing. The girl who was here left me in the lurch a couple of weeks back. They never seem to stay long.'

Kate could easily understand why that might be the case.

'So how would you listen to her voice if she did come in? Would she bring a tape herself or would you take her to a studio to record a reel? I saw there were some studios downstairs.'

'I'd listen to a tape of her own first off. I haven't got time or money to nursemaid them myself. And if she sounded any good I'd help her make a showreel, professional quality. But she'd have to be bloody good. Girls can't get away with the grunting and shouting and a few stock chords some of the boys can get by with. It's a different ball game. They don't usually play guitar and they have to sing in tune. And after that, if it was OK, we'd play it to the record companies. But as I say, it's mainly lads in groups who come looking for a break. I had the Kinks in here once but they moved on.' Mansfield stared into the distance for a while and Kate wondered how many chances like that he had missed. The Kinks were riding high now.

'So you haven't done any of that for Marie?'

'Nope, I don't think so,' Mansfield said. 'I told you, I don't get many girls coming through here and I'd certainly remember anyone with an accent like yours. Sorry.' His hand hovered over the telephone and it was obvious that he was anxious to get rid of her.

'Can I leave you my number in case she turns up?' she asked.

'Give it to the typist girl,' Mansfield said dismissively.

Looking at the heaps of paper on his desk, Kate decided that was probably a good idea. Anything left with Mansfield looked as if it would sink without trace. Kate went back into the secretary's office and gave her a sheet from her notebook with her name and details on it.

'Did he see her?' the girl asked.

'He doesn't seem to remember whether he did or not,' Kate said. 'Is he always like that?'

'Pretty much,' she said. 'He's better earlier in the day. He generally starts drinking at lunchtime. We usually close the office up by about four o'clock.'

To Kate's surprise, the connecting door was suddenly flung open and Mansfield stuck his head out.

'Did she have red hair, your Liverpool friend?' he asked. 'A mop of red hair?'

'Yes, that's right. She was a blonde but we think she dyed it,' Kate said. 'So you did see her?'

'Ellie Fox, that's who she is. Not Marie at all. Not any more. We decided on a new name so she's down in my book as Ellie Fox. I did a reel for her and she was supposed to be coming in to see me again yesterday. But she didn't turn up, did she? I've not seen her again. They're none of them reliable these kids. Pain in the bloody neck, most of them. No wonder they don't get anywhere.'

'She gave her boyfriend a phone number, a Lakeside number?' Kate asked.

'Where is bloody Lakeside?' Mansfield said.

'Wimbledon,' Kate said. 'Sounds as if I'll have to track her down there. If I find her I'll tell her to get in touch.'

'I shouldn't bother,' Mansfield said. 'She seemed to be more interested in her ruddy social life, to be honest. Said she'd met someone from a major group. Didn't say which so I don't know who she considers major. And the record company wasn't interested in her stuff anyway. I told her to come back so it's down to her, isn't it? If she can't be bothered why should I be?'

FOUR

Sergeant Harry Barnard sat in his parked car just off the Whitechapel Road feeling unusually and unexpectedly emotional. He must be getting old, he thought irritably as he surveyed what was left of the gym Ray Robertson had set up before Barnard himself was more than a skinny East End teenager, hovering on the edge of a criminality which was where he knew Ray was already well entrenched. In his case it was obvious Robertson was essentially joining the family business and Harry had no doubt that if he had asked he would have been recruited too by Ray's mother, who took over after his father had sailed with the troops to Normandy and failed to come home. But for reasons which he had never fathomed, Ray seemed to have different plans for Barnard. Far from encouraging him to join the gang, he went out of his way to tell him repeatedly that he showed promise with his fists in the ring rather than on the street and had put a lot of time and a lot of effort into his training at his newly launched gym down the road in Whitechapel.

The gym was still standing, though only just. It had never been anything other than a barn of a place with little spent on maintenance apart from the boxing rings and equipment, but now it was almost derelict, clearly abandoned and bearing official notices that it was to be demolished along with the rest of the street in a redevelopment scheme, one of many being completed by the local council to, as they saw it, complete the modernization of East London after the war. Ray Robertson might have hung on to the Delilah Club even after his apparent disappearance, but had evidently not been able to hang on here. The fight posters still hung outside, torn and tattered and fluttering in the wind. They were all that was left not only of Barnard's unfulfilled teenager's dreams, but those of dozens of other East End lads who had hoped to fight their way out of the slums by skill rather than crime. Ray Robertson had evidently abandoned this long-cherished project and did not look like coming back any time soon, if at all.

The sergeant eased the car back into the busy Whitechapel Road and headed further east, parking close to Bethnal Green station where, the last time he had visited Ma Robertson, a couple of streets of pre-war terraced houses had still been standing, looking determined to ignore the natural dilapidation of pre-First World War homes thrown up for the dockers and then the additional sideswipes of the Blitz, which had left gaps like rotten teeth on both sides of the street. He crossed the main road and made his way down Alma Street, immediately aware that the place was seriously more ruined than the last time he had been there. Most of the houses were plastered with the same sort of notices that had been attached to Ray Robertson's gym and some were already vacant with their windows and doors securely boarded up. The green paint on the door of Ma Robertson's home was faded and streaked and there were signs that the ubiquitous demolition notice had been ripped away. Barnard smiled faintly. Ma Robertson had promised to fight for her house to the bitter end the last time he had spoken to her and it looked as if that was exactly what she was going to do. But at the very least a light showed through the front window, obscured by net curtains, and when he knocked the door was quickly opened. The old woman looked a little greyer, a little more bent, but still with the implacable expression and the unforgiving cold eyes he remembered, still in control and obviously still as determined as ever to remain in her home.

'Oh, it's you,' she said without even the faintest of smiles. 'You'd best come in, duck, although unless you can get the council off my back I've not much use for you or anyone else right now.' She led the way into the living room, which looked to Barnard much the same as it had fifteen or twenty years ago. Ma Robertson must have pocketed substantial sums of money over the years she had been active as a guiding hand in East End crime, but she had always refused to move house. How she had avoided prosecution herself Barnard had never understood, but he supposed it was largely because there had never been anyone among her friends and relations who would give evidence against her. She had been well protected and no doubt still was.

'The houses are finally coming down then?' Barnard asked.

'So they say,' Ma Robertson said. 'I've told them it'll be over my dead body.'

'Haven't they offered you a new place? They can't put you on the street, surely?'

'A place in an old folks' home,' Ma Robertson almost spat. 'Not even a flat in one of the new blocks. A bloody home to wait to die in. My old man would be spitting tacks. Those two sons of mine have as much idea about family as a bag of rotten fish from Billingsgate.'

'Surely Ray can do something better than an old folks' home for you,' Barnard said, surprised. 'He built that massive house out in Epping for his missus. Hasn't he still got that?'

'How should I know?' Ray's mother said.

'Really,' Barnard said, genuinely surprised, 'I thought he would have kept in touch. Actually, it was Ray I was looking for. You don't know where he is, do you? I need to talk to him.'

Ma Robertson shrugged. Her older son, never her favourite, was obviously seriously out of favour, and Barnard guessed he would not get much help here.

'He doesn't tell me anything these days,' she said. 'I haven't seen him for months. I might as well not have sons the way Georgie and Ray have turned out, one in jail and the other vanished off the face of the earth.'

'You may not have seen Ray but have you heard from him?' Barnard came back quickly. 'There's still some official interest in his whereabouts and I don't think it's going to go away.'

'I reckon he's gone abroad,' Ma Robertson said just a bit too quickly. 'He always said he wanted to travel.'

Barnard tried to hide his scepticism at that. He had never once heard Ray Robertson exhibit the slightest interest in 'abroad' and as far as he knew none of the family had ever had a holiday any further away than Margate or the well-appointed house in Epping Forest that Ray had built for himself and his former wife when his empire was flourishing. He was quite sure that whoever at the Yard wanted to interview Robertson would be keeping a close eye on whether that comfortable mansion was being used or not, although he also knew that if Ray needed to leave the country he would not trouble the passport office to help him.

'Georgie's lodged an appeal,' Ma Robertson said suddenly, switching back to the incarceration of her favourite son.

'Yes, I knew that,' Barnard said, his face closing suddenly.

Georgie Robertson's violent criminal career had ended far too close to himself and Kate O'Donnell for him to wish for anything other than an abject failure for that thankfully slow legal exercise.

'I suppose you'd throw away the key?' she snapped.

'Something like that,' Barnard said flatly. 'It's all over, Ma,' he added. 'Georgie, Ray, the family firm, even your street, by the sound of it. The East End the way you knew it is finished. But if Ray does pop up one day, tell him I want to talk to him. It'd be in his interest.' And with that he left the house, slamming the door behind him, feeling he had probably left it loose on its hinges and that when push came to shove that was exactly what it deserved.

Kate got back to Barnard's flat before him that evening and began to prepare a meal. It might look a bit like bribery, but she wanted a favour and was not entirely sure that he would be keen on offering it. When they had finished eating she cleared the table and then sat beside him on the sofa.

'I need a bit of help,' she said. 'I want to go to this road in Wimbledon where I think Marie Collins is staying. I looked at the Tube map but I thought it would be much quicker to go by car. Would you take me over there? Please?'

Barnard looked at her without much enthusiasm.

'You're keeping this up then?' he asked. 'I'm sure you're wasting your time. If this man Mansfield has never seen her again the chances are that she came to London for something else entirely and she wants nothing more to do with Dave Donovan. She's probably met a new bloke in Wimbledon. Donovan will just have to get his head round that.'

'You may be right,' Kate said. 'Mansfield did say he thought she'd met someone from one of the more successful groups, but I won't be able to convince Dave that she's moved on unless I've actually talked to Marie. Anything less and he'll be on the next train down, and I really can't be doing with that.' And nor can you, she thought, although she didn't want to spell that out. 'Come on,' she said. 'It's not that far in a car and I thought Wimbledon was an attractive place. Doesn't it have a common, or something? And tennis?'

'All of that,' Barnard admitted reluctantly. 'Though the tennis is a one-off thing in the summer. It's long over for this year. I suppose we could go to one of the pubs on the common after we've tracked this girl down.'

'That would be good,' Kate said. 'It sounds quite like country. Let's do it and then we can get Dave off our backs.'

Barnard sighed. 'Come on then,' he said. 'A quick knock on her door and then we'll explore the pubs on Wimbledon Common. It's a good evening for a bit of fresh air. The clocks will change soon and then it'll be dark before we finish work. But if she's not there that's the end of it, Katie. Donovan can't expect you to organize search parties for this girl all over London. It's an impossible task, believe me. The Met itself would find it hard to track her down with the information you've got. We're finding it impossible to identify this kid who fell out of the window at the club in Greek Street and she's young enough to have a family somewhere.'

The road Marie Collins was supposedly living in was not at the smart end of Wimbledon at the top of the hill close to the common. They drove over the river at Putney, across the wide expanse of green space and down the hill past the railway station and the shopping centre before turning left and following the District Line and mainline railway towards Wandsworth and Tooting. The houses became smaller and terraced with tatty strips of front garden more often no more than a foot or so from the pavement. This was not the Wimbledon of the All England Tennis Club and substantial houses worth tens of thousands close to the wide-open spaces at the top of the hill. It was a south London suburb of working-class families reliant on low-paid jobs, squeezed into small houses where children slept packed two or three to a room. There was less dilapidation here than in the Liverpool inner city which Kate knew so well, but not much more space, she thought. She watched the house numbers carefully.

'That's the house,' she said as Barnard cruised slowly close to the kerb. He pulled up.

'You go,' he said. 'I don't want my fingerprints anywhere near this. I'm well out of my comfort zone.'

Kate got out of the car and knocked on the front door. It was some time before a man in shirtsleeves opened it and looked anxiously behind him to where she could hear the Z Cars theme tune playing on television. She pulled Marie's photograph out of her bag and thrust it towards him quickly before he had time to close the door in her face.

'I wonder if you can help me,' she said with what she hoped was her most appealing smile. 'I'm trying to track down this girl from Liverpool. It's for her boyfriend, actually. He's not been able to contact her and he thought she was staying here a few weeks ago. Do you know her, by any chance?'

The man glanced at the picture and shrugged. 'Not a clue, duck,' he said. 'Me and my missus have lived here for years and we've got three kids. There's no room for lodgers, sorry.'

Kate put out a hand to stop him closing the door on her. 'Is this your phone number?' she asked hastily.

'We don't have a bloody phone,' he said angrily and closed the door firmly in her face, keen to get back to the telly. It was, she thought, an awful long way to come for nothing. She got back into the car and slumped back in her seat with a sigh.

'That was a waste of time,' she said. 'They've lived there for years and don't know who she is. I think it's time to go and find something more interesting to do. I'll ring Dave again tomorrow and break it to him gently. I think she's been telling him porky pies. She's never been down here at all. She's made it all up, including the phone number. I guess you were right. She's dumped him and doesn't want him to find her.'

'Well, you know the man better than I do,' Barnard said. 'From what you told me about him it must be a possibility. Especially if she's as ambitious as he says she is. If she wants to be the next Cilla Black she's not going to want a loser like Dave Donovan hanging round her neck, is she?'

'I asked about the number too, but he said he didn't even have a phone,' Kate said. 'You said you could try to trace it for me. I wouldn't make a very good detective, would I?'

'Oh, I wouldn't be too sure about that,' Barnard said, slipping the car back into gear and out into the traffic stream again. 'You don't do too badly whenever I've seen you poking your nose in where it's not wanted. You bring DCI Jackson out in a rash.' He threw her a smile to take the sting out of his words, although she knew he was not entirely joking.

'Will you see if you can trace the number so I've got something to tell Dave when I call him again? Please?'

'After the weekend,' he said. 'Though it's always possible she just invented it to keep him quiet.'

'Oh dear,' Kate said.

'Now let's go and have a drink in Wimbledon Village. It's supposed to be a smart suburb, though I can't say I've seen much sign of it yet. They always say if you're a Londoner you're either a north of the river person or a south of the river person. It doesn't look like much of a contest so far to me.'

FIVE

D S Harry Barnard had not even got his coat off and his new tie aligned to his satisfaction in the CID room on Monday morning before he got a summons from DCI Jackson.

'There's been some trouble at the queer pub,' Jackson said. 'Someone's been taken to Casualty at death's door apparently. You'd better get over there. Fred Watson's gone down with some uniforms in case we need a murder team but you know those poofs better than anyone. Go and lend a hand and check with the hospital. First report was that the victim was male and unconscious but see what you can find out. And if he's not unconscious, get a word with him if you can. It's probably no more than a lovers' falling out. They tell me these people can be a bit temperamental.'

'Sir,' Barnard said, his stomach tightening. He had been sure that the tensions which had built up over the last few weeks would eventually bubble to the surface and he hoped that whoever had been hurt was not anyone he knew. He had not been entirely joking when he had told Vincent Beaufort to keep a low profile. Prejudices always seemed to ebb and flow unpredictably and there was violence swirling in the Soho air just now, quite possibly made worse by the approaching change in the law.

'And, Sergeant,' Jackson said as Barnard turned to go.

'Sir?'

'Have you made any progress on the girl who fell from the window?'

'Not really,' Barnard said. 'I was going to follow-up today on some of the people who were in the club that night. Someone must have taken her in . . .'

'Well, I think we should prioritize the attack on the pub for the moment. It'll make a bigger impact than an accident and a girl whose name we don't even know yet. The Yard keep telling me that they are setting up some sort of specialist unit to deal with drugs so I'll see if I can push them into action on the Late Supper

Club business themselves if you think drugs were involved. A raid on the place could sort them out, I should think. We know drugs are a growing problem but a turf war over protection will be much worse and frighten the locals and the punters far more. Are you quite sure Ray Robertson isn't trying to stage a comeback?'

'As sure as I can be, sir,' Barnard said, his hand still on the door handle.

'Right, carry on then, Sergeant. See if this man is still alive. If he's not we'll have to pay him some attention even if his morals leave something to be desired.'

The pub was no more than a ten-minute walk away and Barnard could see uniformed officers outside and a gaggle of bystanders watching what was going on in a sullen silence. Some of the bystanders he recognized; others were strangers and he wondered whether some had been attracted to the scene because this was the queer pub and there were some people around who objected to its very existence. He elbowed his way through the throng, pushed the closed door open and shut it behind him. DI Watson flashed a look in his direction but said nothing. Watson was coming up to retirement and was one of the officers who looked most critically in Barnard's direction when their paths crossed. From his flamboyant clothes to his flash car, the sergeant offended his sense of what a detective should look like and how he should conduct himself. Barnard guessed that when they got back to the nick he would do his best to persuade the DCI that he could cope very well without the sergeant's help.

'Guv,' he said by way of greeting. 'Do we know who the victim is?'

'The barman, apparently,' Watson said, with a significant look. 'Friend of yours, was he?'

'I know him,' Barnard said. 'Goes by the name of Len Stevenson. He's worked here for a while. Couple of years maybe.'

'Poofter, is he?'

'Almost certainly,' the sergeant said, thinking that he could end his career very fast if the DI sneered at the victim and he lost his own temper. He took a deep breath, glanced around the bar with close attention for a moment and realized even in the relatively dim light that it had been comprehensively trashed, bottles smashed, glass scattered across overturned chairs and tables and a strong smell of spilt liquor permeating everything.

'Looks as if he might have been lying here all night,' Watson said. 'Judging by the state he was in I don't think he was beaten up this morning – more likely after closing time. He wasn't bleeding, more congealed. Could be a lovers' tiff maybe. You can check out the regulars later. I'm sure you know them all. Is there any regular antagonism to the existence of this place? They're not very discreet, are they?'

'We get occasional complaints, the odd punch thrown at closing time as people come out of other pubs,' Barnard said before he took a deep breath and changed the subject.

'I've been following up some incidents that look like somebody's trying to get a protection racket going again,' he said. 'Could be part of the same thing and Stevenson made the mistake of resisting. He fancies himself as a bit of a peacemaker if there's trouble in here. There are a few people who reckon they can have a bit of fun at the customer's expense occasionally. Stevenson's a big lad and knows how to handle himself. Intruders don't generally hang around long. But he could have picked the wrong people this time. Whoever's behind the protection racket drove a car into an Italian cafe yesterday morning because the owner didn't want to pay "insurance". And nobody's talking about it. In fact, nobody's talking about anything much, as it goes. Everybody's very edgy.'

DI Watson looked at Barnard for a long moment and then nodded reluctantly. 'Maybe you can make yourself useful then,' he said. 'Get out among your contacts, your poofs and your toms, and find out exactly what's going on. If whoever half killed the barman is involved in anything else I want statements, descriptions of anyone who's been making threats, every last detail. Don't take no for an answer from anybody, male, female or any other beggar – or bugger – in between. I'll see you back at the nick about four and we'll see what you've got. It looks as if these shirt-lifters are going to be made legal before we know where we are, so we'd better show willing at least.'

'Guv,' Barnard said and spun away from him on his heel to conceal the anger in his eyes. His younger brother had killed himself as a teenager long before any change in the law had been dreamed of and he had regretted almost every day since then that he had never guessed what his secret was and never helped him. It was not something he had ever talked about at work and never would, but Kate knew and, to his surprise, she understood.

He did not have far to go to start his inquiries. As he pushed his way through the watching bystanders outside the pub – officially the Grenadier but generally known simply as the queer pub or quite often by much less acceptable names – his arm was seized and he found himself pulled into an alleyway on the other side of the road.

'I thought you might not be far away, Vincent,' he said to Vince Beaufort, who did not look as though he had been to bed the previous night. His eyes were sunken, his make-up smeared and his clothes rumpled. 'Late night, was it?'

'None of your business,' Beaufort said. 'So what happened here? Your bobbies won't tell me anything.'

'I don't suppose they will,' Barnard said. 'DI Watson's in charge. The only place he wants to see you is behind bars, along with all your friends and acquaintances, so watch out. So far, he has this down as a lovers' tiff that went too far. Does that make any sort of sense to you?'

Beaufort shook his head. 'If it's Len you're talking about, the barman? No, he's got a long-term partner,' he said. 'I know all you straight men think we sleep with someone new every night, but that's not always true. Not everyone plays the field and he didn't.'

'So someone has to help me follow up the other possibility,' Barnard said.

'Which is?' Beaufort said.

'It's down to whoever is behind the thugs who are trying to get a protection racket going again.'

Vincent shuddered histrionically and said nothing.

'Someone must know,' Barnard said. 'My boss thinks it must be Ray Robertson, which is not that unlikely, I suppose. Before he got into his flamboyant phase with the boxing charities he wasn't averse to milking the local pubs and clubs.'

'Most people think Mr Robertson's abroad somewhere. You hardly ever hear his name mentioned these days. There are new people around now, more violent people, and no one seems to know who they are or where they came from.'

'Cockneys, are they? Or Italians from round Clerkenwell branching out? They're a vicious lot if they're not running your local shop. Or the Maltese trying to expand into Ray Robertson's old territory?'

Beaufort shrugged again. 'Any one of those,' he said. 'Could be. But rougher and tougher than when the Maltese and Mr Robertson's lot carved it up between them. This lot look like they enjoy the violence. They do it for fun. People are scared, Flash, really scared.'

'Keep your eyes open for me, Vince,' Barnard said quietly.

Beaufort glanced around the still-watching crowd before turning his back on them and dropping his voice to a whisper. 'I told you, there's one bloke who hangs about, dark fellow, quite a dish to look at, a bit Spanish looking. I've no idea who he is but he's definitely on the scene quite often, not doing a lot, just watching. I could fancy him but he has a chilly look in his eyes and he definitely isn't one of us.'

'You haven't got any idea of a name?'

''Fraid not, and I'm not going to try to find out either,' Beaufort said. 'This feller's not one you'd want to cross. There's something bad going on, you can be sure of that, and I'd put money on him being at the heart of it.'

'OK,' Barnard said. 'Keep in touch, yes?'

'All right,' Vince said, and he tried to sidle unobtrusively away down the alley behind them, breaking into a trot before he had gone more than a couple of hundred yards and disappearing round a corner as if he had never been there at all.

Kate O'Donnell ordered a sandwich and a cappuccino at the Blue Lagoon, which was where she often met Harry Barnard for lunch, but today the sergeant had cried off, claiming he was too busy to take a lunch break. She was trying to work out the best time to phone Dave Donovan in Liverpool to pass on what had happened to Marie Collins with her agent, although she knew that what she had learned would not please Dave much or help him track her down. The fact that Jack Mansfield claimed to have passed her songs to a record company might encourage her boyfriend slightly but the fact that they had not wanted to produce them would be a blow, and the fact that Marie had not come back to talk to Mansfield at all would only pile the pressure on. She pulled the list of possible addresses she had checked against the A–Z from her bag and decided that she was thrown back on that as the only strand of information she could follow up and that Harry was undoubtedly right when he said it would be like looking for the proverbial needle. Even knowing Marie's new stage name, which she might be using, it was likely to be a thankless task. And if she was really trying to dump Dave she might have simply made the address up.

She sighed, took another bite of her chicken sandwich and was aware that someone was hovering above her with a loaded plate in one hand and a cup of coffee in the other and an inquiring expression on his face.

'D'you mind if I sit here?' a man asked with an uncertain smile. 'It's a bit full now.'

'Feel free,' she said, glancing around the cafe's bustling lunchtime crowds. 'I'll be going in a minute.'

'Can I get you another coffee?' he asked. 'If you've got time, that is?'

Kate focused on the man hesitating above her and decided that the tall, dark stranger with hair a few inches longer than many bosses would find acceptable might be a welcome distraction from her slightly desiccated lunch and the absence of Harry, who had seemed unusually worried that morning, answering an early phone call and gulping down no more than a strong coffee for breakfast.

'A quick one,' she said. 'Cappuccino. Why not?' Leaving his own lunch on her table, the man went back to the counter to join the queue again.

'You look a bit glum,' he said as he put the coffee in front of her and slid into the chair opposite. 'Do you always have lunch by yourself?'

'Not often,' Kate said. 'My boyfriend's busy today.' She thought it was worth putting down a marker in case he thought she was available for more than a casual chat.

'Ah,' the man said. 'That's a shame. I'm Bob by the way.'

'Kate,' she said, feeling exposed and trying hard to sound neutral.

'And with that accent you're not from these parts, are you? So where's home?'

'Liverpool,' she said defensively.

'Ah,' he said again, not hiding his scepticism. 'Of course. I thought it might be Glasgow. But I suppose you lived next door to John Lennon, did you, when you were a little girl?'

'I went to the same college as he did, actually,' Kate said firmly. 'It's my one claim to fame.'

'You're kidding?' Bob came back, looking slightly stunned.

'No, I'm not. He wasn't my best mate or anything, but I knew him and Cynthia, his wife, when we were all students.'

'So are you a musician too?' Bob asked, still looking sceptical.

Kate shook her head. 'No, it was the college of art and I was doing photography. I can't remember what he was supposed to be doing: you could say he wasn't a very studious student but he could draw. Funny pictures too. He was well known for it. But after that the band went off to Germany and played in clubs in Hamburg. I didn't see him again for years, until he came back in a group to play in the Cavern Club and make their name.'

'Well, well, that's amazing. They certainly put Liverpool on the map, didn't they? No one in London had a clue what was going on up there until they burst on the scene and the girls went crazy.'

'It had been going on in Liverpool for years,' she said.

'No way?'

Kate finished her sandwich and the coffee he had bought her and pulled her jacket over her shoulders. 'I must get back to work,' she said.

'So did you get a job as a photographer?' Bob asked quickly, and it was clear that he wanted to prolong the conversation. 'That's quite unusual for a girl, isn't it?'

'Not unheard of these days,' she said sharply. 'This is the sixties, not the thirties.'

'Oops, sorry,' he said. 'I suppose you specialize, do you? Lots of babies and small children maybe, little dogs and cats for birthday cards? That sort of thing.'

'Not exactly,' she said, not hiding her irritation. 'I work for an agency for magazines and newspapers.'

'Saving the babies and small children for when you get married then, are you? When you give up work?'

Kate looked at him stonily, wondering if he was deliberately trying to provoke. She stood up and pushed her chair hard underneath the table, destabilizing his coffee so that it filled its saucer.

'There was some sort of happening going on in a pub round the corner this morning, lots of police around,' he said quickly. 'Is that the sort of thing you take pictures of then?'

'I don't know what was going on there,' Kate said. 'I didn't notice anything unusual and I don't usually do news pictures. But why do you think I'd want to give up work anyway? I enjoy what I do. I worked hard to qualify for it.'

'Sorry, sorry, I'm sure you did,' he said. 'I can see why Liverpool's got the reputation it's got, what with you and Cilla Black both. A bit spiky. I just hope your boyfriend can handle it. What does he do?'

On the point of answering as casually as the question had been asked, she suddenly felt very cold and shivered slightly. 'This and that, you know what Soho's like,' she said and pushed through the tables, heading for the door as quickly as she could. What had seemed like a chance encounter suddenly did not seem quite like that any more. She made her way slowly back towards the Ken Fellows Agency and was not too surprised to see Harry Barnard himself waiting for her by the door, leaning against the doorpost with his hat pushed back and a cigarette in hand. She was surprised at how pleased she was to see him and offered her cheek for a quick kiss.

'Sorry I couldn't make it for lunch,' he said. 'There's been an attack on the barman at the queer pub and this one is definitely not an accident – it's attempted murder by the look of it and the pub's been trashed. It's all getting very heavy, so there's a major panic on. I'm just heading to Casualty to see if he's come round yet. He was unconscious when he was taken in. I'll probably be late back tonight. DI Fred Watson's in charge and he doesn't like me much. He'll pick my brains, keep me pinned down as long as he can and take the credit, I expect.'

Kate hesitated for a moment and then told herself that Harry would not thank her for presenting him with more anxiety just now. 'I may go and check one or two more of those addresses for Dave tonight and then see if I can get him by phone, tell him what's going on,' she said. 'And see if I can track down the bass player he thought might help. Kevin Dunne, he's called. Dave and his girlfriend both knew him before he came down here to join the Rainmen.'

'Jason Destry's group?'

'That's right. They're doing very well at the moment,' Kate said. 'Not quite the Beatles but I'm sure that's where they'd like to go. I don't think I ever met Kevin Dunne back home, though, but he might have some idea where Dave's Marie is. It's a small world, the music business, especially around Liverpool. Everyone knows everyone else up there and a lot of them stick together when they come to London.'

'There's so much going on at the moment. What I need is just a hint that it wasn't an accident. You can ask your bass player if he was at the club too, but it would be a bit of a long shot. I still reckon you're wasting your time trying to find Marie,' he said. 'Anyway, good luck. I'll see you later, Katie. Take care.'

She watched him push through the lunchtime crowds towards Oxford Street and the Middlesex Hospital and wondered if she had been imagining an unusual interest in Harry Barnard from Bob, the casual customer looking for an empty seat who had chatted her up in the Blue Lagoon. Wasn't it much more likely that the good-looking, dark-haired man had sat at her table because he fancied her, not from any more ulterior motive? Perhaps she shouldn't underestimate her own charms, she thought wryly. But she was sure that she was not being completely paranoid to think that once she and Barnard had crossed the path of the secret state they might try to forget but they would probably never be forgotten. She shivered again before pushing open the office door and climbing the narrow wooden stairs to the photographers' room on the first floor and dropping into her chair, still feeling a worm of anxiety in her own stomach. She thought she had made a new life well away from Liverpool, but more and more the waters of the Mersey seemed to be seeping back to lap around her ankles in unpredictable and slightly threatening ways.

SIX

Realizing by now that groups had managers and even if musicians were not always available at the end of a phone line their manager almost certainly would be, Kate called Jack Mansfield that afternoon and asked him if he knew who the Rainbirds' manager was.

'What do you want to know that for?' he asked aggressively.

'Someone I knew in Liverpool has just gone to work with them,' she said, stretching the truth only a little.

'I heard they'd taken on another Scouser,' Mansfield said, sounding as if he was describing some particularly unpleasant infectious disease. 'A bass player. You haven't tracked down Ellie Fox, have you? I got a flicker of interest in her reel in the end.'

'No, her boyfriend's coming to London, though. You might find him on your doorstep in the next couple of days. He seems to think you're to blame for the girl dumping him.'

'I can do without that sort of hassle,' Mansfield said. 'I tell all my boys and girls I'm not in charge of their love lives or their other tastes in leisure activities.'

'So where can I contact the Rainbirds?' Kate asked. 'They're not shacked up in some country mansion miles from anywhere, are they? Are they that successful already?'

'They've certainly shot up the charts lately,' Mansfield said, a fact which clearly irritated him. 'I did read somewhere that Jason was looking for a house out of town. That's what all the lads who've done well seem to be doing.' He riffled through the address file which was almost buried on his desk and repeated the details of their manager down the phone to her.

His offices seemed to be located on the north side of Oxford Street in an area devoted more to restaurants than the music business, although Kate was not sure whether that was a sign of higher status than Denmark Street or lower. When she walked through the shopping crowds into Charlotte Street the building did not look much different from the one where Mansfield had his agency, although when she presented herself at the reception desk it struck her as a more efficient operation, cleaner, tidier and better cared for.

'Well, I can't go handing out band members' addresses and phone numbers to just anyone who walks in off the street,' the girl behind the desk said officiously. 'Their last single did really well and they're hoping the new one will do even better. If that happens we'll soon be getting hysterical young girls chasing round after Jason with their knickers in a twist. Maybe not for Kevin, though, as he's not been in the band long. I don't think many of the fans have cottoned on to him yet, though he's quite dishy, isn't he?'

'I knew him in Liverpool,' Kate said quickly. 'I've known him for years . . .' she said, pushing the truth to its outer limits.

'Yes, I can tell that from your accent,' the receptionist said, unimpressed. 'I thought you must be foreign or something.'

Kate had to take a deep breath before she could speak again. 'Do you think you could pass a message to Kevin for me? If I give you a phone number? Then it's up to him if he wants to contact me.'

'I suppose that would be all right,' she said without any enthusiasm. 'Give me the details and I'll pass them on next time I see the band. Though I don't know when that will be. They've been working all hours on the new recordings. And Jason's bought himself a new house somewhere in the country so I guess they'll be going down there for the weekend. It's got a swimming pool . . .' She stopped, realizing that she had perhaps gone over the top. 'Well, I don't know if it's heated. It's getting a bit chilly for it now if not.'

By the middle of the afternoon, Sergeant Barnard felt as if he had worn the leather off the soles of his shoes without much result. He had trawled the shops and bars, cafes and restaurants, bookshops from legitimate – very few, to very dodgy – very many, trying to measure the extent of the harassment which, eyes turning away and lips pursed told him clearly enough what was going on but about which no one would utter a word. Neither cajoling nor bullying nor even modest bribery opened mouths today, as they usually did, though apart from the trashing of the Grenadier and the assault on the barman, there was no sign of overt violence on anyone else's premises today or on the street. But the mood was sullen, as if the whole of Soho was holding its breath waiting for something else to happen. DI Fred Watson was not impressed by the lack of progress, and when Barnard reported back to the nick he sent him straight back out on to the streets again to keep on asking questions they both knew by now he was not likely to get answers to.

'I thought I should follow up the death at the Late Supper Club,' he suggested, but it was obvious that Watson was not interested.

'There's no evidence that was anything more than an accident,' he said. 'Until we get an ID there's nothing much we can do. Concentrate on whoever is trying to take over the rackets on the streets again. If they're as ruthless as they seem to be we'll have a war on our hands before the week's out. The Maltese had a deal with the Robertsons and that kept the peace for a long while, according to DCI Jackson. I've no doubt you knew even more about that than he does. But with Ray Robertson apparently retired now, or at least lying very low, anything could happen. Someone will try to fill the gap. They probably already are.'

But by the middle of the afternoon Barnard was tired and frustrated and, finding himself passing his old friend Evie's front door, which was still firmly closed this early in the working day, he banged sharply on it. She opened the door a crack, wearing jeans and a loose sweater, her make-up not yet completed.

'Flash,' she said with a genuine smile. 'Long time no see.'

'How's it going, honey?' he asked, aware that undressed, as it were, she looked more unwell than she should have done. The circles under her eyes were darker than he remembered them and her face thinner, and the cigarette she held trembled between her fingers.

'A cup of tea?' she asked, holding the door open for him. 'Or something stronger?'

'Tea will do fine,' he said. 'Are you OK? You don't really look it.'

'Not too bad,' she said, but her words carried little conviction.

He followed her up the stairs to her room and threw himself into the armchair by the window.

She picked up a bottle of Scotch and waved it in his direction. 'You sure you won't?'

Barnard shook his head but Evie poured herself a generous slug, which worried him even more, although he knew questions were obviously not going to be very welcome. He would have to tread almost as carefully here as he was having to do on the street, and quite likely for the same reason.

'Do you remember DI Fred Watson?' he asked. 'Went to the south coast for a while but he's back and I'm on a case with him. And I'm not his favourite person anyway, without breathing alcohol on him in the middle of the day.'

'I do remember him,' Evie said. 'Made a speciality of rounding up as many toms as you could fit in the cells and keeping us there all night. Lovely man. So what are you doing with him?'

'The barman from the queer pub got beaten up along with his bar and he's not regained consciousness yet. Len Stevenson. You know him?'

Evie nodded and turned away with a shudder to brew tea and pour him a mug which he sipped slowly as he watched her dress, appreciative but without any sense of temptation. He was, to his own surprise, a changed man, in some respects at least.

'What's going on, Evie?' he asked quietly. 'Everyone's clammed up. No one's saying a word. I've never known anything like this.'

She sat down at her mirror and began to paint her face carefully. 'I know what you mean but I don't know what's causing it – or who. People have stopped talking to each other. People are scared but I'm not sure who of. I'm surprised someone hasn't passed something on to you. That's unusual, isn't it? I always thought you had your finger on the pulse one way or another. There wasn't much that escaped your notice.'

Barnard drained his tea and sighed. 'I must be losing my touch,' he said. 'Or . . .' He hesitated. 'There are a lot of new faces around, new businesses starting up, new traders on the streets.'

'I heard about the kid who fell out of the window at that posh new club – what's it called?'

'The Late Supper Club,' Barnard said. He glanced at his watch. 'I must follow that up as well as the attack on the barman.'

'That sounded awful,' Evie said. 'Was she really just a teenager?'

''Fraid so,' he said. 'And we haven't even managed to identify her yet.'

Evie shuddered. 'She must have parents somewhere worried

sick if she's not come home. If my kid got into that sort of trouble . . .'

'She's OK, isn't she?' Barnard asked quickly. 'I thought you said she was being well looked after.' Perhaps problems with the child, who must be almost a teenager herself by now, was why Evie looked less radiant than she used to. The make-up helped but when he had first known her she barely needed it.

'She is, she is,' Evie said quickly. 'She's still with my mother and doing well at school. She'll be fine.'

'How old is she now?'

'Nearly eleven.'

'Not taking herself off to nightclubs then,' Barnard said. 'But a hostage to fortune?'

'Maybe,' Evie said quietly.

'I'll find out who took that kid to the Late Supper Club,' Barnard said. 'I promise.'

But it was almost the end of the day before the sergeant could find time to try to fulfil that promise. The club's door was locked when he tried it and he had to knock repeatedly before he heard someone thumping heavily down the stairs and opening several bolts and a key before pulling the door slightly open and squinting through the narrow aperture he was holding firm.

'We don't open until nine,' a voice said.

'Detective Sergeant Barnard, and you open when I tell you to,' Barnard said in a tone which did not leave any room for argument. The door eventually inched open but so slowly that Barnard lost patience and pushed so hard that the skinny young man in slightly grubby chef's whites stumbled backwards and almost fell.

'Bloody hell,' he said. 'Keep your hair on.'

'Has Mr Mercer put you here to keep the police out?' Barnard snapped. 'That's a dangerous thing for a licensee to do, isn't it? Is he here?'

'He's gone out,' the boy muttered. 'Told me not to let anyone in. I'm supposed to be prepping stuff in the kitchen. One of us does an early shift every night.'

'Well, I'll wait for him and in the meantime you and I can have a bit of a chat, all right? I'm sure you can catch up with your prepping later.'

'He won't like that,' the boy said, looking even more anxious than when he had opened the door.

'Well, he'll have to put up with it,' Barnard said. 'A young girl died here two nights ago and I've yet to hear a satisfactory explanation as to how that happened. So we can have a chat here or you can come down to the police station with me and we'll have it there, but one way or another it will happen, and so will a lot more questions and answers with a lot more of your colleagues and your boss and as many of your clients as I can track down. I want to know who that kid was and how she died. So what's it to be?'

'Stay here,' he said, looking sulky.

'Right, we'll go upstairs where it's a bit more comfortable, shall we? Lock the front door again if that's how the boss likes it.'

When the front entrance was securely locked Barnard followed the youth upstairs and they sat opposite each other at one of the round tables close to the bar, Barnard with his notebook out and the youth with his hands buried underneath his apron. He twisted his fingers together as he seemed to take on board what he had committed himself to.

'Right, let's start with your name and address and job.'

'Stephen Bright, and I live at home with my mother in Croydon – though quite often I stay over here if we're running very late, sleep in the kitchen . . .'

Barnard raised a mental eyebrow at that but didn't pursue it. It could stay in the closet for now for use later if it was needed, he thought. Stephen Bright was obviously not the sharpest knife in the drawer.

'And how long have you worked here?' he asked.

'Since it opened, but I worked for Mr Mercer before, when he was a manager at Newbury Racecourse. He asked me to come with him.'

'Quite a compliment, wasn't it? You don't look old enough.'

'I met him when I did my National Service, back a bit now. I was in the Army Catering Corps, in a squad which looked after the officers' mess at Lincoln. Mr Mercer was an officer there. He was a good bloke and I heard he'd gone to Newbury and I looked him up when I got out. I knew he had a lot of horsey friends. I saw him going off hunting once. Anyway, I've worked for him ever since.'

'Right, but I suppose you spend most of your time in the kitchen, so how much do you know about what goes on up here?' He glanced around the bar and the tables already set for dinner. 'Do you know who comes and goes? How people carry on? Mr Mercer says he has built up quite an exclusive clientele in quite a short time. Do you get to see any of them?'

'Hear about them, at least,' Stephen said with a look of animation in his eyes. 'The waiters are in and out of here all night. They're busy but we get the best bits relayed – the amount of champagne they've drunk, the night a drummer knocked back a whole bottle of Scotch, or the ones who are on drugs. Sometimes I'm up here myself if they're very busy. I might have to push the pudding trolley round and get an eyeful more than I should if I'm lucky.'

'And are many of them on drugs?' Barnard asked.

The young man twisted his hands together even more frantically under the apron, knowing he had said too much. 'Well, I wouldn't really know but the word in the kitchen is that some are.'

'Any names?'

'No, no, I couldn't tell you. It's just gossip,'

'And any gossip about who brings the stuff in?'

'No, no, I've no idea,' Stephen said, looking several shades paler than he had when Barnard had started his questioning.

The sergeant guessed he had hit the wall between what the kitchen worker regarded as innocuous 'gossip' and what he knew was deadly dangerous in all sorts of ways. Rather more slowly than Barnard had expected, Bright seemed to understand now that he had perhaps said more than his employer would approve of.

'So going back to the night the girl fell,' Barnard resumed. 'Mr Mercer had been telling me about his famous clients but when it came to the lists of people who he said were here that night there didn't seem to be anyone very well known on them at all. I'd expected at least John Lennon and Mick Jagger and Marianne Faithfull but it all looked very tame.'

'Yes, well, it's not always like that, not every night. I think he likes to advertise his celebrities but they're not here all the time,' he said. 'Not every night.'

'You mean your boss tells a few tall tales, or people like that don't come here at all? He makes it up?'

'Some come, sometimes,' Bright muttered.

'And the night before last? Was anyone interesting here that night?'

'Someone told me Jason Destry of the Rainmen was here but I didn't see him,' Bright said.

'And he's not on any of Mr Mercer's lists,' Barnard said thoughtfully. 'Don't you think that's a bit odd?'

'I expect they have to sign in just like anyone else, even if they come in the back way. But if they do that they can stay pretty much out of sight round the back or even go upstairs.'

'Upstairs?'

'There's a private room upstairs,' Bright said reluctantly.

'And that's where the young girl fell from, the top window?'

'I think so, yes.'

'Well, I'll check up on that with your boss,' Barnard said. 'So let's get on to what you know about people using drugs in here.'

'Who said that?' Bright asked, obviously annoyed and deciding rather late in the day to be more cautious. 'I don't know anything about that.'

'It was pretty obvious when I came here the other night that a fair number of people had been using marijuana,' Barnard said. 'You could still smell it long after people had gone home. And I'm told the girl who died had taken something, though the laboratories haven't sorted out exactly what yet. Some things they don't even have tests for. You said the waiters told you people were using drugs, but did they tell you who was using, and what they were using?'

'Not names, no,' Bright said quickly, obviously very clear now that he had got himself in far deeper than he intended.

'Did you use them?'

'Course not. I'd lose my job.'

'But you knew they were around, on the premises?'

Bright nodded reluctantly.

'And did you know who was supplying them?'

'Course not,' Bright said again. 'Look, I've got stuff to get on with in the kitchen. I'll be in trouble if everything's not prepped when the chef comes in. You need to be asking Mr Mercer these things, not me. None of it's anything to do with me.'

'You're right,' Barnard said. 'I'll hang on here for Mr Mercer if you're expecting him soon.'

'You won't tell him I've been talking to you, will you?' Bright asked, wringing his hands again in his apron. The full implications of what he had told Barnard seemed to have penetrated at last.

'Course not,' Harry Barnard said blandly. 'Why would I?'

SEVEN

Kate caught up with Dave Donovan when she got back to Barnard's flat that evening. She guessed he was sitting very close to the phone – it was picked up so quickly – and she could hear the tension in his voice even over a crackly long-distance line.

'Have you found her?' he asked.

'I'm afraid not,' Kate said. 'Though I have talked to Jack Mansfield, her manager. He says Marie turned up there and made a tape for him and decided on a stage name. Ellie Fox.'

'Sounds awful,' Dave said angrily. 'What's wrong with her own name?'

'I'm not sure,' Kate said. 'I think people often use different names for singing and acting. Look at Ringo Starr. Anyway, that's not all he said. He said he would offer the reel to some record labels and she should come back to see him. But she didn't turn up, and the record labels didn't want to take her on anyway, so he's more or less washed his hands of her. So we don't know where she is or what she's doing. I'm sorry, Dave, but London's a big place and there are an awful lot of Western Roads.'

'She can't just vanish,' Dave said.

'Don't panic,' Kate said quickly. 'The other thing I've done is leave a message with the Rainbirds' manager's agency for Kevin Dunne but I've no idea if he'll get back to me. He won't recognize my name so he may not phone me back.' There was silence at the other end of the line, a faint, empty crackle was all that could be detected across the miles which separated them, and Kate was not surprised when Dave's choked response came back.

'I'll come down there,' he said. 'I need to be doing something myself. I can't leave it all to you.'

'I don't know how that will help,' Kate said doubtfully. 'The best bet is if Kevin Dunne contacts me. Let's see if he knows where the Scousers get together. You can bet your life there'll be a pub somewhere that's a little Liverpool Pier Head. And I've asked my boyfriend to try to identify the phone number as people at the address in Wimbledon had never heard of her, and they had lived there for years. It wasn't their number. We went round to check it out. They didn't even have a phone.'

'We?' Donovan asked, his voice full of suspicion again. 'That's you and your bizzy?'

'Mmm,' Kate murmured. She could hear that there was still bitterness in Dave's voice even though the water which had flowed under that bridge would have kept the Mersey in spate for years and Marie was now allegedly the new love of his life, which was more than fine with her.

'I'll come down,' he said again. 'I've got to come down.'

'Can you afford it?' she asked.

'I guess I can manage the train fare but somewhere to stay will be more difficult. I remember when I came down with the band, we slept on blow-up mattresses on the floor in the rehearsal rooms most of the time. Do you remember the pictures you took for us, sitting on a fire escape?'

Kate hesitated. She remembered very clearly Dave Donovan's dispiriting attempt to break into the big time himself and his ignominious return home. She did not want Dave Donovan back in her life but she had known him since school and she had to believe he was desperate to find out where his girlfriend had gone.

'I might be able to fix you up at Tess's place,' she said. 'For a few days at any rate. But I'll have to talk to her about it first.'

'I thought you were sharing with Tess,' he said sharply. 'That's what your ma thinks, anyway.'

'And let's leave it that way,' Kate said equally sharply. 'Call me back later this evening when I've spoken to Tess to see if she'll put up with you for a bit. Though I don't hold out high hopes. My boyfriend thinks you're on a hiding to nothing if she doesn't want to be found and he knows about these things.'

'I suppose he would, being a bizzy?'

'And he's a Londoner born and bred,' she said. 'He should be able to help.' Although she wondered how willing Harry would be to get involved with anyone from Liverpool after his recent experiences there.

'Anything,' Donovan said. 'I'll never forgive myself if I don't chase up this bastard manager who seems to have taken her for a ride. What's that all about?'

'I've no idea,' Kate said with a sigh. 'He seems completely disorganized, though when I went back to get a lead on Kevin Dunne he did say that some record company was interested in Marie's demo tape after all, a bit late in the day, but she's not been back to see him yet. Call me back later and I'll let you know what Tess said about the spare bed at her place. Technically it's still mine but I need to check it out with her first. I'll talk to you later.'

She glanced at her watch. Barnard would be home later than usual and she guessed that with all that seemed to be going on in Soho he might be later still, so cooking would be a waste of time. They could go to the local Italian later. But she knew that Tess Farrell, with whom she had shared a flat in west London when three girlfriends from Liverpool had arrived in the capital to seek their fortunes several years ago, would already be home from her job teaching English at Holland Park School. She might well be up to her eyes in marking but it was probably too early in the evening for her to be out with the history teacher Kate suspected she was seeing regularly these days and, sure enough, when she dialled Tess picked up the phone quickly.

'How's things?' Kate asked cautiously.

'All right, stranger,' Tess said. 'You've been keeping very quiet lately. You're not planning to come back to claim your bed, are you? Have you finished with your detective?'

'Certainly not,' Kate said. 'What gave you that idea?'

'It's just that I keep on wondering what your mam will say if you decide to marry him, let alone if she discovers you're already living together. We'll hear the explosion in Shepherd's Bush, I should think.'

'She's met Harry already, when we went up to Liverpool to cover the Beatle's film premier,' Kate said defensively.

'But I bet you didn't introduce him as husband material, did you? All primed and ready for the chat with the parish priest and ready to convert? You're not that brave – or optimistic – are you?'

'Not quite,' Kate admitted. 'I'm not sure he is that anyway – husband material, I mean. But my mam's not as daft as you think. She might have worked it out for herself when I went home, la.

Anyway, I think she knows that she's not going to have any say in what happens in the end. She should have ditched that idea when I left Liverpool.'

'You'll be lucky,' Tess said. 'So what about coming over for a meal soon, la. It's time we caught up.'

'Yes, that would be good. But the reason I rang was not so much about us as about Dave Donovan. You remember Dave and his slightly off-key band . . .'

'I thought he went home? He wasn't exactly Ready Steady Go material, was he?'

'He did, and the band's still alive in Lancashire apparently. But he's coming to London for a few days. He seems to have mislaid his girlfriend who came down to see an agent about a singing career. She's seen the agent but hasn't got back to him or to Dave and he's going frantic. I wondered if you'd mind if he had my room for a few days while he tries to track her down.'

'Are you sure she wants to be tracked down?' Tess asked waspishly. 'I'm not sure I would from what I remember of your friend Dave. And I'm not sure my boyfriend will approve of me having a lodger – especially a musician from Liverpool.'

'Come on, Tess, do me a favour. It's my bed, after all. You can tell Dave how long you'll put up with him if you want. It only needs to be a few days. He wants to see the manager she went to see, and I'll get Harry to talk to him to persuade him how impossible it is to track down one person on the information we've got. He won't want Dave hanging around for long either. He's never thought much of Liverpool and he thought even less of it after our trip up there.'

The silence at the other end of the phone told Kate how seriously reluctant her friend was to agree to the arrangement.

'Three nights,' Tess said in the end.

'I can tell him that?'

'Tell him my sister's coming to stay after that and she'll need the room,' Tess said.

'You're quite an inventive liar when you try,' Kate said, laughing. 'I hope you don't miss anything out at confession.'

'I got quite good at that when we were at college and we started to want to go to the Cavern. We had a parish priest who seemed to think John Lennon threatened our immortal souls.'

'There were quite a few of those around,' Kate said. 'He wasn't the only one. More to the point, are you sure Dave doesn't know you don't have a sister?'

'Pretty sure,' she said. 'I hardly knew him when we were at college. I met him down here when he was trying to get his group off the ground and we were living in the Notting Hill flat.'

'OK,' Kate said. 'I'll get back to him and tell him the conditions.'

'Ask him to phone me and let me know when he's arriving,' Tess said. 'I'll tell him how to get to Shepherd's Bush on the Tube.'

It was almost ten o'clock and the first clients were beginning to filter into the Late Supper Club before Sergeant Harry Barnard decided to call it a day and go home. He had waited for Mercer to turn up and then corraled him in his office to go through the records of who had been in the club at any time on the night of the unknown young girl's death.

'There's no record that I can see of anyone signing the girl in,' Barnard said. 'I'll want to talk to everyone who was on the door that night. I want them to look at her description to see if it rings any bells. And try to recall if and when the door was left unmanned and someone could have brought her in without anyone noticing. Are the same people on duty tonight? I'll probably need to talk to the waiting staff too, to see if they noticed her and anyone she was with.'

Mercer consulted his lists and nodded reluctantly. Barnard scowled at him. It was incredible how detached the man remained after a young girl on his premises had died, whether by accident or design.

'Can you organize them to talk to me – one at a time, please – so I can check what they can remember? It will be even more messy if I have to take them to the station. Easier for you if I ask the questions here.'

'Anything else, Sergeant?'

Barnard could see the question was almost dragged from Mercer's lips, he was so uncomfortable with this interrogation.

'Yes, there is,' Barnard said. 'You talked about attracting well-known people, rock stars and such, models, actresses, I suppose.'

'Here today and gone tomorrow,' Mercer snapped.

'But I don't see anyone like that on your guest lists for that night. Do they sign in at the door like everyone else or do they have special privileges?'

'I suppose you could call it that,' Mercer admitted, stony faced. 'We don't expect them to run the gauntlet of the overexcited slappers, the girls who gather outside in the street wetting their knickers. The very first week we were open half a dozen kids got hysterical when two of the Beatles turned up. So we put in a private door at the back where taxis could drop VIPs out of sight.

'But you keep a record of who comes and goes that way? Your licence demands that.'

'We have one member of staff on duty there, to be of assistance.'

'I'd like to talk to him,' Barnard said. 'And were any of your VIPs here on the night this unfortunate girl fell?' Mercer's hesitation was so slight that afterwards Barnard wondered if he had imagined it.

'I will be talking to some of your clients too,' Barnard said quickly. 'They would be likely to notice if there were any big stars here. They do use this room, I assume? They don't have their own private quarters?'

'Some of them we reserve tables for,' Mercer said. 'They have their favourites, mainly at the back. Jason Destry was here for a while that night – Jason Destry of the Rainbirds – with some friends. They have a new record out. I don't know if you follow that sort of music.'

'That's the lad who struts about in a red velvet jacket?'

'That's the one,' Mercer said with a shrug

'And when did they leave, what time exactly?'

'They didn't stay long,' he said.

'Well, of all your clients he should be one of the easiest to track down,' Barnard said. 'And I understand clients can use a room you've got on the top floor, which is where this girl fell from. Is that right? Can you show me that, please? I understood she fell from this level but if she was higher that could explain the severity of her injuries.'

Mercer opened his mouth to say something but then closed it again, which Barnard regarded as a sort of victory. If the manager had learned nothing else from his questions it must be that he wasn't going to be deterred from trying to find out what exactly had happened to the underage clubber and who was responsible, and that he would speak to whoever he chose.

'Can you get your staff to talk to me, the door staff first? If I can't finish tonight I'll come back tomorrow. It would be helpful if you could ask clients coming in if they were here the night of the death as well. We can track them down from their details in your registers but if they happen to be here tonight that will make the process quicker. I'm sure we'll all benefit from that, sir, don't you?'

Mercer got to his feet, red-faced and breathing heavily. As he was working in his own time Barnard did not worry about any complaints from DCI Jackson for wasting police time. He just hoped that Mercer himself was not a commissioner's best mate. He knew that there was something very wrong about the young girl's death – her presence in the club, her lack of identification and anyone who claimed to know her, the drugs the test results confirmed she had taken and the fall itself – but he was not at all sure that Mercer might not be able to gag any useful witnesses among his staff and get back-up in high places to close his own inquiries down if that's what suited him or if he felt personally threatened by the investigation.

In the event, Mercer seemed to have decided to capitulate, at least for the time being, and a succession of staff members and a handful of clients approached Barnard with more or less ill grace and answered his questions. But not one of them could offer any information that would help identify the girl or any companion she might have been with, and least of all any information on any illegal substances she might have consumed. And he now understood why no one admitted to seeing her fall – because she had been a floor higher up the building, away from most of the clientele. When he had finished he approached Mercer again, knowing the manager had been watching his every move.

'I'll call it a night now,' he said. 'Thanks for your cooperation. I find it hard to believe that a kid as young as that didn't raise some questions in somebody's mind over the course of the evening. And I'd like to know who took her up to the top floor. It doesn't sound very likely that she found her own way up there.'

'The place was packed and half the population of the West End look like schoolchildren these days,' Mercer said contemptuously. 'Skirts halfway up their buttocks and so pumped up with booze or dope or sex that they're off their heads. Throw in a few rock stars and it can soon go out of control. You should know that working round here, Sergeant.'

'Not many young girls go head first out of windows,' Barnard said. 'That's a first.'

'I want it cleared up. It's not doing my business any good. There's only half the punters here tonight.'

'Well, I won't bother you again, sir, unless I have to, but let me know if anything new crops up,' Barnard said. 'Otherwise, I'll have to track down some of your notable clients myself. Should be an education.'

Kate was already in bed reading when Barnard finally got home.

'Sorry,' he said. 'I went back to the club where the girl fell. I didn't have time earlier as the brass are more interested in the murder at the Grenadier. It is a murder investigation now. Did you know the barman died? This afternoon? They think a gang war's going to break out although nobody's got a clue who's going to be fighting who. Nobody's talking, so either they don't know – which seems unlikely – or they're too scared. I've never known anything quite like it.'

'And nobody's identified the dead girl?'

'She's not cropped up among the missing persons reports so far and as there's no chance of a picture given the state she's in we can't circulate more than a written description. I went to the club in my own time to see if I could find out a bit more, but nobody admits to knowing anything about her.'

'That's very sad,' Kate said.

Barnard nodded gloomily. Sad, he thought was an understatement.

'So how was your day?'

'Ah,' she said. 'A bit complicated.'

'That sounds ominous,' he said. 'Let me get a drink and then you can tell me the worst.'

'Dave Donovan? Three nights?' Barnard asked finally when he was settled on the side of the bed with a large Scotch in one hand

and the other round Kate's shoulder.

'That's all Tess will put up with,' Kate said with as much reassurance as she could muster.

'And he won't come here?'

'I don't think he'd dare,' she said, leaning round to kiss him. 'But no, Tess and I will keep him out of your hair.'

'You're too soft-hearted,' he said. 'But I like it.' He returned the kiss with interest.

'But I will have to talk to him, if only to tell him that I haven't got anywhere,' Kate said.

'It looks as if I'll have to talk to a few musicians myself, as it happens,' Barnard said. 'I discovered that Jason Destry was at the Late Supper Club the other night when the girl fell, celebrating his new record, as it goes. It wouldn't be surprising if his party got a bit out of hand.'

EIGHT

D S Harry Barnard knew that he had almost certainly put more than one foot wrong as soon as he went into the CID squad room just after nine o'clock to find it full of officers and an oppressive silence. The reason was obvious. DCI Keith Jackson stood at one end of the room, a chalkboard on one side and a plainclothes officer Barnard did not recognize on the other.

Jackson looked pointedly at his watch. 'You're late, Sergeant,' he said.

'Sorry, guv,' Barnard said, hanging up his coat and sitting down at his desk. 'I didn't know there was a meeting.' He glanced at the stranger standing beside the DCI and raised an eyebrow.

'If you had been here a little earlier you would have heard me introduce DI Brian Jamieson, who is one of the officers involved in the Yard's plans to set up a specialist drugs unit. DS Barnard has considerable experience with gangs in Soho and their increasing involvement in the growing drugs trade. I'm sure you will be of mutual assistance once the unit is up and running.' The two younger men eyed each other warily and certainly not warmly before Jackson pressed on and Barnard concluded that assistance from Scotland Yard was not necessarily what his boss was looking for in the present situation. Drugs might be involved but the struggle which had broken out in Soho to such a deadly effect went much wider than that. It was about power and control. Ray Robertson's absence had left a vacuum and Barnard knew that sooner rather than later that vacuum would be filled. He just hoped that there would not be too much blood spilled in the struggle.

He turned his attention back to DI Jamieson who, in jeans and leather jacket, with tousled hair touching his collar, stood beside Jackson who was immaculate as ever in a well-pressed suit, high-gloss shoes and short back and sides, a whole generation and lifestyle apart. And, of course, it was Jamieson who knew most of what there was to know about the rapidly proliferating drugs scene. It was not yet quite an epidemic but usage and the variety of substances on offer was increasing and senior officers at the Yard were infuriated by the high-profile young users, many of them musicians, who did not make any secret of their illegal habits. Barnard had no doubt that retribution from the top of the Met was on its way and that if he wanted to survive he would have to adjust to the likes of DI Jamieson and his colleagues just as the increasingly bold dealers and users would. He listened to Jamieson's A to Z analysis of the growing market, which told him little that he did not know already, and when the DI offered to take questions he asked him how much an ounce of cannabis would cost on the street as if he wasn't sure, which raised a few eyebrows among his colleagues.

'In the region of seven pounds,' Jamieson said. 'That'd be in the West End. You'd get it cheaper in Notting Hill, especially if you were a darkie, know what I mean? So it's a lot more expensive than a pint of beer but it doesn't seem to do much more harm. But what's more dangerous is LSD, and that's turning up more and more. It can do real damage. It can take people days, weeks even, to get over a bad trip on LSD. Perhaps a lifetime, I'm told.'

'Can it kill you?' Barnard asked.

Jamieson gave him a long look. 'Not directly,' he said. 'It doesn't poison you like an overdose of heroin does, but it can do your head in. Some say they have a lovely time on a trip, like a Technicolor dream. Can't wait to have another go. Others go off their heads and spend hours in some sort of hell, the worst sort of nightmare. They draw the short straw, have a dream they can't get out of. Some of them never get to recover.'

'They say some people think they can fly?' Barnard ventured.

'I've heard of things like that but I've never met anyone to confirm it,' Jamieson said. 'Maybe they don't survive and the medics say there's no easy way to test for LSD in the body – it disperses very quickly. And there's no way of knowing how strong the tablets are or what's a safe dose anyway.'

Barnard nodded, aware that the DCI was watching him closely. 'Thanks for that, guv,' Barnard said as Jamieson glanced at his watch and then at DCI Jackson himself.

'I need to be off, sir,' Jamieson said to Jackson. 'I hope that was useful and I'm sure we'll all be seeing each other again in the near future. We'll probably be living in each other's pockets when the drug squad gets up and running properly. The problem's getting worse and the top brass are determined to sort it out.'

The two senior officers made their way to the squad room door but as DCI Jackson followed DI Jamieson out he glanced back. 'My office, Barnard,' he said over his shoulder.

Barnard drew a sharp breath. 'Sir,' he said, and followed his boss down the corridor as Jamieson peeled off and took the stairs down to the ground floor two at a time. The look in Jackson's eyes spelled nothing but trouble and Barnard was sure it wasn't just because he had been late for the meeting. The DCI placed his papers meticulously in the centre of his desk, squared them off neatly and sat down.

'The first thing which happened to me this morning – before I'd even finished my porridge – was a call from the Yard, Sergeant. Someone – they didn't even have the courtesy to tell me who the complainant was – had objected to your inquiries last night at the Late Supper Club, which I had to admit that I knew nothing about as you didn't bother to tell me you were going there. But from the general tenor of the complaints, I guess it must have been the manager – what's his name? Mercer? Captain Mercer, he was calling himself, so I suppose someone at the Yard knows him and he's taking advantage of his contacts. What is going on? I thought I told you we were concentrating on the murder at the Grenadier. You know the barman didn't regain consciousness before he died? This is now murder and murder with all sorts of implications for Soho which you must be aware of.'

'Yes, guv, I know. I was with DI Watson at the pub until well after seven. He reckoned that some of the regulars who hadn't heard what had happened might turn up and we could pick up some useful background. Personally I thought he didn't know how efficient the grapevine is among that clientele. I reckoned they would already know enough to stay away. In the event, one or two arrived and found the place closed but we didn't get much that was useful out of them when we hauled them in. They were people who hadn't actually heard anything about the attack. If they had I guess they wouldn't have turned up either. DI Watson decided to call it a day before eight but as I was passing by the Late Supper

Club on my way back to the car I thought I might see if I could pick up anything useful there. I was on my own time, guv.'

'And did you? Pick up anything useful?'

'Not really, except that the latest rock idol, Jason Destry – he's the one in the red velvet coat – was in there that night, but according to Mercer not for long, and he left before the girl fell.'

'Is he another pervert?' Jackson asked, not hiding his distaste for the red velvet.

'I've no idea, guv, but the little girls seem to love him anyway.'

'So is there any progress on the dead girl's identity that I don't know about?'

'Not that I know of,' Barnard admitted reluctantly. 'I was passing last night and thought it might be worthwhile chatting up some of the staff there. Some were already on duty. That's all.'

'It's a waste of time and energy, Sergeant,' the DCI said. 'And it's causing upset and nuisance at the club for no useful purpose. Do you not understand? Our priority is to find out who trashed the queer pub and killed the barman Stevenson. That's what the Yard wants, that's what the new drug squad, when it eventually gets itself off the ground, will want because they're sure drugs are involved in this. And that's what I want too. Clear?'

'Yes, sir,' Barnard said. 'Quite clear.' He hesitated. 'Do you want me to keep looking at the missing person reports, guv, for the girl who died?'

Jackson took a moment to reply. 'Ask uniform to do that. We've got more than enough to do in Soho without worrying about what's a suicide or a drunken accident and without even the name of a victim. You concentrate on your own patch and find out who's behind this outbreak of violence there. That's what you are supposed to know about. I'm still not convinced Ray Robertson's not behind what's going on. Maybe he thinks he's been away long enough now and needs to make a big comeback to re-establish himself. Isn't that a likely scenario? They always had a foot in two camps, the brothers. Well, that's over now. It may be Georgie who's locked up but Ray's credibility is gone too with all his glamorous friends. No more black-tie events at the Delilah Club; no more lords and ladies accepting invitations to boxing galas. That's all finished. If he wants a role again it's going to have to be a criminal one. The other doors are tight shut. I'll talk to DI

Watson and tell him I'd like you to find out where he is and what he's doing. And don't tell me he's the gangster with the heart of gold, no drugs, no toms, helps old ladies across Whitechapel High Street out of the goodness of his heart because I don't believe a word of it. He's as bad as his brother, just a wee bit smarter, and it's time he was behind bars. Do you understand me, Sergeant Barnard? Do I make myself clear?'

'Yes, guv,' Barnard said. 'I'll get on to it.'

Kate was still in the office without an assignment when the phone call came.

'Is that Kate O'Donnell?' It was a man's voice which sounded as if he was standing at the Pier Head gazing across the Mersey with the wind behind him. For a moment, the accent sent a tremor of homesickness through Kate's chest – but only for a moment.

'Who's that, la?' she asked.

'Kevin Dunne. You left a message for me.'

'I did,' Kate said. 'I thought you might be able to help. I'm looking for a Scouser called Marie Collins who's come down to London to try to break into the music business, though her manager has decided to call her Ellie Fox, so she may be using that name. She's a singer and her boyfriend hasn't heard from her for weeks. He's dead worried.'

'Who's the boyfriend? Do I know him?'

'I think so,' Kate said. 'He seems to know you. It's Dave Donovan.'

'Oh, yes,' Kevin said without much enthusiasm. 'I do remember him, la. Didn't think much of his group, to be honest. I wasn't surprised when he scuttled back home with his tail between his legs.'

'You don't need to be his best mate,' Kate said irritably. 'I only want to know if you've seen this girl around the scene. Have you come across her at all?'

There was a silence at the other end of the line. 'I don't think so,' Dunne said. 'Are you sure this Marie hasn't just dumped him?'

'She could have done, I suppose, but he's coming down to London for a few days to look for her, so I thought if I could track her down it would help.'

'Where are you? Do you fancy a bite to eat? The band's meeting at our manager's office to sign some stuff at twelve but I could buy you a drink and a bite after that. What do you say? I could ask Pete as well. He plays drums and comes from Southport. They're giving him a trial.'

'Great,' Kate said. 'What time?' And she agreed to meet him at the Charlotte Street office of the Rainbirds' manager at one.

This time she waited outside and soon after the hour five young men came hustling out of the door. She immediately recognized Jason Destry even without the signature red velvet jacket he had abandoned today in favour of a dark duffel coat which Kate supposed was some sort of disguise. Young girls were not yet swarming after the Rainbirds like they did for the more established groups, but she guessed that was almost certainly coming down the road fast.

Even so, Destry hesitated for a moment and gave Kate a nod. 'Are you waiting for me, pet?' he asked.

'No, for Kevin,' she said.

'Shame,' Jason Destry said. 'Lucky Kevin, though I can tell you're from his neck of the woods by the accent. Is there something in that Mersey water that produces so many musicians?'

'Must be in their mammy's milk; Mersey water's pretty mucky,' Kate said and Destry laughed.

'Get Kevin to bring you to my next party,' he said. 'I've got this new house out in Surrey. You'd have a good time, I promise.'

'You'll have to tell me how to get there,' she said.

'Come with Kevin. He knows the way,' Destry said. 'Next Saturday night? OK?'

'OK,' Kate said, feeling slightly breathless and wondering what Barnard would make of an invitation in which she guessed he would not be included. The last members of the band out of the door were definitely looking for someone, she realized, and she stepped forward with a smile.

'Kevin?' she asked. 'I'm Kate O'Donnell.'

'So you must be, la,' the shorter, darker of the two said with a grin. 'A bobby-dazzler like you could only come from the Pool.' He waved a hand towards his companion. 'This is Pete Jones. Plays drums in a Liverpool band and is down for an audition with Jason Destry.'

'Right,' Kate said as the other three musicians turned away and hurried towards Oxford Street where they hailed a taxi. 'It's good of you to spare the time. Dave can't understand what's going on.'

'Who did you say her manager was?' Jones asked.

'Jack Mansfield,' Kate said.

'I know him,' Jones said. 'I came down here six months ago and did a trawl round the managers because Brian Epstein wasn't taking people on in Liverpool any more. He was too tied up with the so-called Fab Four and all the touring they'd been doing.'

'That's why Marie came to London, apparently,' Kate said. 'She thought he didn't want any more girls once he'd taken Cilla Black on. Anyway, when I went back to Mr Mansfield to find out who your manager was he said he had eventually had some interest in Marie Collins' songs so there's another reason to track her down if I can, not just poor old lovelorn Dave Donovan who she may not be very interested in any more. She might actually stand a chance of making a record after all.'

'What did you say her recording name was?' Kevin Dunne asked as he guided Kate into a scruffy-looking pub called the Three Horseshoes she had never noticed before down one of the narrow side alleys which linked Soho's main streets and which themselves linked Oxford Street, with its department stores, to Leicester Square and Theatreland.

'Ellie Fox,' Kate said, glancing round the almost empty bar. Harry Barnard always said his patch was no more than a square mile and even in these out-of-the-way corners she reckoned there was very little that escaped his notice. He would know this place and its reputation, which she could not imagine was very high.

'Ellie Fox: can't say I've heard of her,' Dunne said. 'Have you, Pete?'

'Don't think so,' the drummer said. 'What are you drinking, Kate?'

'Just a half of shandy.' She glanced at her wristwatch. 'I have to be back at work in about half an hour and I don't want to breathe too many fumes over the blokes in the office. They're easily shocked. They haven't got used to the idea of a woman with a camera yet. They twitch every time I walk through the door or demand some time in the dark room.'

'Like rock music doesn't do girls on guitars?' Kevin said.

'Vocals the lads can just about get their heads round, maybe. We'll have to see whether Marie gets shunted back to Liverpool like Dave Donovan did.'

'Is he easy with it?' Pete asked. 'He won't get jealous if she makes the big time? Maybe our Cilla is easing the way. Her bloke seems to put up with playing second fiddle pretty well.'

Kate took her shandy from Pete Jones who had a plate of fairly desiccated sandwiches in his other hand.

'Sorry, Jason said to keep a low profile,' he said, waving the plate in Kate's direction. For want of any alternative she took one and nibbled it cautiously.

'He thinks the new record will be a big hit and he's worried about the fans,' Pete went on. 'He didn't really want to come into London this morning. He's so made up with the new house he's planning a house-warming party for the weekend.'

'He invited me,' Kate said with a grin. 'Said you could show me the way, Kevin.'

Kevin looked slightly surprised at that suggestion but Pete nodded cheerfully.

'I'm sure we could manage that,' he said. 'I'll give you a phone number if you really want to go. It's an amazing house though it's not finished yet. The builders are still all over the place.'

'Yeah, anyway, our manager insisted we come in today, said there was stuff we all had to sign. So here we are and I'm bloody starving.' For a few minutes they worked their way through the ham and cheese and slabs of dry bread but none of them were impressed with their Soho lunch and were already getting ready to leave when a tremendous crash startled them. Shards of broken glass fell around their table.

'Holy Mother,' Kevin Dunne said, but that was all any of the three of them had time to say before four or five men, with scarves pulled up to their eyes, burst into the bar, turning over tables and chairs, pushing the few customers into the corner close to the toilets and throwing drinks across the counter where the barman had been reading the *Daily Express* moments before but now cowered close to the floor with his arms protectively over his head.

'Tell your boss that no is not an option. Understand?' the scarved man closest to the bar shouted. The barman was visibly shaking and did not reply until the burliest of the five intruders jumped over the counter and grabbed him by his collar, pulled him to his feet and pushed his face into the mess of spilled alcohol and broken glass on the bar counter.

'Are you listening to me? Did you hear me, mate?'

'Yeah, yeah,' the barman said as blood mingled with the spilt beer.

'If he can't afford it tell him to put his prices up. All right? So you pass it on, yeah?'

'Yeah, yeah,' the barman said again more faintly. The intruder vaulted back and all five men had disappeared through the smashed door and away into the lunchtime crowds before the terrified punters in the pub could draw breath.

Kate went over to the barman, who was bleeding heavily from cuts around his face and head.

'There's a phone there. You'd better call the police and an ambulance,' she said to Kevin Dunne, who licked dry lips and picked up the receiver with a shaking hand.

'This is worse than Scottie Road on a Saturday night,' he said. 'And in broad daylight. Lunchtime. Jesus wept.'

By the time Kevin put the phone down Kate had made her way to the back of the bar and was trying to staunch the blood which had covered the barman's face with not very clean tea towels that had been lying by the sink.

'The police say to stay here,' he said, at which the handful of other customers in the bar made a beeline for the door and disappeared into the lunchtime crowds outside. 'They'll want to talk to us.'

'Get that lad round here to sit down,' Pete said, and took one of the barman's arms with Kate on the other side to slide him into one of the few chairs with arms which looked as if it would prop him up.

'What's your name?' Kate asked him.

'Tony,' the barman said, taking one of the tea towels and pressing it hard against what looked like the worst of the cuts on his forehead as he began to shake uncontrollably.

'They said an ambulance will be here in ten minutes,' Kevin said just as a uniformed constable ran through the door and stopped dead, obviously taken by surprise at the scene of chaos which faced him. But before he could even ask what had happened he was elbowed aside by DS Barnard who, Kate reckoned, was the officer she least wanted to see. The words he clearly intended to utter died on his lips as his eyes met Kate's and he turned away.

'Detective Sergeant Barnard,' he said, addressing himself to Kevin Dunne, who had wet another tea towel and was trying to clean some of the blood off Tony's face. 'Is anyone else hurt?' Barnard asked as he took in the barman's injuries. 'Have you sent for an ambulance?'

'Ambulance is on its way,' Kevin said. 'And they didn't touch anyone else, I don't think, though there were some other people in here who scarpered as soon as they could.'

'Right,' Barnard said. 'We'll see if we can find them later, but I'll want you all to make statements . . .'

Kate suddenly found that her legs were giving way beneath her and she sat down next to Tony and propped herself up on the single wooden table which was still upright.

'All right?' Barnard asked, brushing her shoulder almost imperceptibly with his hand.

'Just about,' she said, feeling as if her voice was coming from the bottom of a deep well. 'I'll be all right in a minute.'

Barnard looked as though he wanted to say more but at that moment they heard the sound of the emergency vehicles arriving outside and the bar quickly filled with uniformed men, medical staff and police, and Barnard's attention was wholly taken by a heavy-set, grey-haired man in plainclothes who made it obvious that he expected to be in charge.

'Another one?' he said angrily to Barnard. He glanced at the barman who was being attended to by the ambulancemen. 'We're not going to have another death, are we?'

'I wouldn't think so, guv, it looks like nasty cuts and bruises,' Barnard said quietly to DI Watson. 'Some of the punters turned tail and ran but I've told these three we'll need witness statements. They saw everything that happened.'

'And descriptions of the gang,' Watson snapped.

'Scarves over their faces apparently.' Barnard shrugged. 'We'll be lucky to get an ID.'

'Right, you go to the hospital with fellow-my-lad here and take his statement and push him for anything we can identify these bastards by. And get him to tell you what he knows about what the gossip is as you don't seem to have a clue in spite of all your so-called contacts. The Yard will want chapter and verse as well as DCI Jackson. I'll get a DC to process the witnesses here. Look sharp.'

'Sir,' Barnard agreed, risking no more than a quick glance at Kate, who was still sitting in her chair looking shell-shocked. Damn and blast, he muttered to himself as he turned away and pushed his way to the door. As far as he could compute there was no possibility that Watson could link him with Kate O'Donnell and that could only be for the good. But he wasn't sure what Kate would say in the state of shock she looked to be in. He really did not want his private life the talk of the squad room at the nick and even less an open book to senior officers. He turned back for a second as he pulled the door open but he could not catch her eye and he started the walk to the hospital casualty department again in a state of some anxiety.

But this time the news from the casualty doctor was encouraging and he waved Barnard into a cubicle where the barman Tony was sitting up against pillows with a bandage around his head wound and a nurse cleaning the more superficial cuts to his face and neck.

'Police,' he said, flashing his warrant card and pulling out his notebook. 'DS Barnard. And you are?'

'Tony Mason,' the patient said, and from the tremor in his voice Barnard realized that he was not quite as unscathed by the assault as the doctor had implied. The physical effects might be relatively minor but the experience had unnerved the young man in other ways.

'You got away lightly then?' Barnard said, trying to reassure him. 'That's good. So do you feel up to giving me all the details on what happened there?'

Mason nodded uncertainly. 'They came in so suddenly, it was a quiet lunchtime, only a few people in,' he said. 'And it was all over after a couple of minutes. I hardly knew what was happening, it was so quick.'

'Well, I've seen what they did to the bar,' Barnard said. He took down his details and the details of the pub's owner. 'So if you just go over it for me, as far as you can remember. And what I'd especially like is anything you remember about what the attackers looked like.'

'They had their faces hidden,' Mason said. 'They had scarves up to their eyes and a couple of them had hats pulled down.'

'Yes, I understand that, but think about what you can remember about what they were wearing – coats and jackets, for instance. Or anything you could see of their hair or eyes. They couldn't hide themselves completely, could they? So we have to rely on what you could see, what was still visible.' But the description Mason offered was sketchy and no doubt they had intentionally dressed to make themselves look as anonymous as possible. They could have been any group of men out for lunch in Soho's pubs and cafes until they chose to hide their faces.

'And how many were there of them?'

'Four, I think, or maybe five. They were moving around fast, chucking stuff about, and for some of the time I dodged down behind the bar. That annoyed them. That's why one of them jumped over to get to me. I thought for a moment he was going to kill me.' Mason started shaking more convulsively and the doctor began to look more concerned.

'He's had a nasty shock and lost quite a lot of blood,' he said. 'Maybe you should leave your questions till later.'

'Are you going to keep him in?' Barnard asked the doctor.

'Overnight probably, to be on the safe side.'

'OK, I'll come in again in the morning to see if you can remember anything else when you've got over the shock,' he said to Mason. 'A decent night's sleep might help. Is that all right?' Mason nodded vaguely and closed his eyes as Barnard turned away with a feeling that he had probably got all he could realistically hope to get out of the injured barman today. And that it would be nowhere near enough for DI Watson.

Barnard drove past Kate O'Donnell's agency when he finished work in the hope that he was early enough to pick her up, but the offices were in darkness when he stopped outside and he had driven on into Camden Town, up the hill to Highgate and parked outside his flat in a frustrated frame of mind. To his surprise the flat was also in darkness and he had gone inside and poured himself a whisky before he remembered that this was the evening Dave Donovan was supposed to be arriving in London and he guessed that Kate had gone to Tess's flat after work to talk to the musician from Liverpool about the inquiries she had made for him. Inquiries he had been talked into as well, he thought irritably. He hoped at least that she had got over the shock of the attack on the pub at lunchtime. Kate was nothing if not resilient, but she was also impulsive and he did not trust Dave Donovan to take care of her or even attempt to hide the fact that she was his girlfriend. As her ex he might well think he could gain some advantage by annoying or embarrassing Barnard.

Barnard took another slug of the neat spirit and smiled wryly. He knew Kate would accuse him of being jealous at the arrival of her former boyfriend but he knew that was not really true. The root of the problem between them, if there was one, was his own difficulty with commitment, his reluctance to being pinned down, the conviction that there was always something, or someone, better round the next bend in the road. If he and Kate split up the fault would be his and his alone and he hoped that the arrival of Donovan would not be too obvious a reminder for her that there were other fish in the sea, although he reckoned this one would not prove very tempting after all that had passed between them.

It was after ten when Kate finally got back to find Barnard asleep in his favourite spinning chair with an empty whisky bottle on the floor beside him. She was hot and tired after walking up the hill from the Underground station, thinking it would not be very tactful to call him and ask him to pick her up. She took her coat off and went into the kitchen to make a drink, but before long she felt rather than heard him behind her.

'Have you had anything to eat?' she asked, without turning round.

'I'm not sure,' he said, dropping his empty glass into the sink. 'I flaked out when I got in.'

Kate turned towards him. 'You look worn out,' she said. 'Sit down and I'll make you something quick. Tess made spaghetti for me and Dave while we talked. He was a bit desperate when he heard that I hadn't made any progress. We're going to see Marie's manager tomorrow lunchtime to see if he can get more out of him than I did.'

'Right,' Barnard said. He leaned against the breakfast bar feeling exhausted and fuddled from the neat spirit.

'So what were you doing in the pub that got trashed? Who were the blokes you were with, for God's sake?' He tried to keep the irritation out of his voice but he knew he was failing miserably.

'That was Kevin Dunne and another lad from Liverpool who wants to play with the Rainbirds. Dave asked me to try to contact Kevin. I told you about that. I arranged to meet them at lunchtime to ask him if he had run into Marie. Anyway, it was another dead end because he hadn't seen anything of her. She seems to have disappeared off the face of the earth. So it sounds as if we've both had a bad day. I couldn't believe it when those men started smashing up the pub. Is the barman all right?'

'They've kept him in hospital overnight but he's not badly hurt,' Barnard said. 'You gave a statement about what happened?'

'It didn't seem very adequate,' she said. 'It all happened so fast and to be honest I was terrified. Kevin pushed me behind him, so I couldn't see much . . .'

Barnard put an arm round her, which was as close to an apology as he felt able to go. 'That was good of him,' he said.

'What's going on, Harry?' she asked, anxiety gripping her again. 'It's like a war out there.'

'It *is* a war out there,' Barnard said. 'And at the moment I don't think we're winning.'

NINE

Primed with aspirins and three cups of strong coffee before he left home, DS Barnard was first into the squad room the next morning, although only by a hair's breadth. DI Fred Watson followed close behind him and immediately demanded to know where the night shift was hiding. Kate had watched Barnard get out of bed with eyes that were anxious and dull. Neither of them had the inclination or energy to talk and even when Barnard had walked slowly up the stairs at the nick and had hung up his coat he was even less inclined to answer Watson, although he knew he must.

'They usually go to the canteen around about now for breakfast,' Barnard said, wondering if it was ever any different in any nick among coppers who had been up all night.

'Leaving the phones unmanned?' Watson complained. 'You go and get them back down here and I'll listen out for the phones until the place is properly staffed.'

'Guv,' Barnard said, thinking that would give him the chance of taking another cup of coffee on board before he had to concentrate on the morning's instructions. He found his colleagues halfway through their full English breakfast and not best pleased to be summoned before they had finished. His own habit of taking a leisurely stroll around Soho before reporting for duty seemed to be on hold while Watson was around. Nothing was said but his preferences were made clear enough. Watson was in charge of the murder case and what he wanted from Barnard was obedience.

'Fred Watson is not best pleased,' he told them as he queued for his coffee. 'He obviously thinks the DCI runs a sloppy ship – which is a joke – so I wouldn't hang about if I were you. This latest attack on a pub wasn't quite as violent as the one on the Grenadier but it wasn't pretty.' He added three heaped teaspoonfuls of sugar to the drink, which he reckoned had no right to be called coffee at all and stirred it hard before following his grumbling colleagues back downstairs. DCI Jackson seldom arrived

before nine and was generally happy with a written report of the
night's events. DI Fred Watson was evidently built of even sterner
stuff although quite why the south coast – was it Brighton or
Hastings? Barnard wondered vaguely – should require a firmer
hand than the West End of London he was too fuddled to work
out in his hungover state.

At least the scorn Watson poured on the heads of the hungry
night shift distracted the DI from Barnard for a while and gradually the coffee worked its magic so that by the time Watson turned
in Barnard's direction the sergeant felt moderately able to face the
working day. The sergeant was aware that he was being watched
closely by some of his colleagues who would be happy enough
to see him fall flat on his face. They glanced away as Watson
turned back to Barnard.

'Right, Sergeant,' he said. 'I want you to go back to the hospital
and go over every word of the barman's statement. They don't
discharge people early in the day as a rule, so you'll catch him
before he leaves when the doctor gets around to giving him the
all clear. Then report back here. I'm going to check all the statements and see what similarities we've got between what happened
at the two pubs. So far, we're just assuming this is the same people.
My guess is that it is, but it's only a guess. I want to know how
many people are involved and who should have some idea of who
they might be and who they might be working for. And that includes
your input. I want to know everything you know about your famous
– or is it infamous? – square mile and then some. Understood?'

'Understood, guv,' Barnard said, putting his coat back on with
some relief. He celebrated by taking the stairs two at a time to
make his way back on to the busy shopping streets around
Piccadilly Circus and then crossed Regent Street into the narrow
lanes of Soho, which did not seem to have woken up yet. It was
here he felt most at home, although even as early in the morning
as this he felt a tension in the air which had not been there just a
few weeks previously. Something he did not understand was going
on and he found it slightly unnerving.

As he expected, Tony Mason was still in the hospital ward
where he had left him the previous night, fully dressed and with
his bandage replaced by a large plaster which had reduced the
dominance of the cut he had sustained from the broken glass and

which had needed stitches. But he still looked pale and Barnard noticed that his hands were shaking. The shock of what had happened to him might take much longer to mend than the cuts and bruises, and he wondered if he would go back to his pub job at all.

'You look as though you're on your way home,' Barnard said. 'I don't suppose you'll be at work for a bit though. Our forensics people will still be rooting through the debris to see if they can pick up fingerprints or anything else which might identify these people.'

'The bastard who grabbed me was wearing gloves,' Mason said gloomily, confirming Barnard's feeling that what was going on was threateningly professional. Someone out there had a plan and, so far, on what he thought of as his home turf, he had not a clue who it might be or where the plan was heading or who was in charge of it. The Robertson brothers had never made much of a secret of what they were up to in Soho, relying on the fact that the police would want to be very sure they had a cast-iron case against them while they were in their pomp, close to so many well-connected friends. The Maltese were secretive and maintained a cast-iron discipline on their operatives which the Met found difficult to break and the Italians found it hard to maintain that sort of discipline when many of them had only a sketchy hold on the English language. This latest violent campaign did not fit easily into any of the patterns he was used to. His attention turned back to the traumatized young man who had sat down on the edge of his bed as if he had difficulty standing for long.

'Did you remember anything else in the middle of the night?' Barnard asked Mason. 'Anything unusual they were wearing? Anything unusual in the accents? Anything in the way they walked? It's sometimes possible to pin people down through quite small things.'

But Mason shook his head and instantly looked as if that was a step too far. 'I told you, I dodged down below the bar and couldn't see much. That annoyed the tall bloke. He probably wouldn't have hurt me if I hadn't done that. I suppose he must have been the leader. He behaved like the boss, telling them what to do. And maybe he did have an accent. He wasn't a Londoner, not a Cockney . . .'

'Scottish, Irish, Welsh, Northern English . . .?'

'No, and not foreign either, but a bit different,' Mason said uncertainly. 'I might recognize the accent if I heard it again. Or the voice.'

'Were you not worried after the trouble at the Grenadier?' Barnard asked. 'Did you not worry that they might come for you too?'

'Not really,' Mason said. 'The boss thought they got hit because they were all shirt-lifters in there. He didn't think anyone would bother us.'

Barnard nodded, grim-faced. 'I suppose people might think that,' he said. 'But there have been other incidents. Hadn't you picked up on those?'

'The landlord might have, I suppose. But I'd not heard about anything else. I don't live round here.'

'OK, we've got your details,' Barnard said. 'I'll get someone to pop round to your place in a few days to see if you've managed to put your finger on anything more definite when the shock's worn off a bit. We've got the customers who hung around to talk to as well, though not all of them did. I'm sure one of you will come up with something. What are you doing now?'

'Waiting for the doctor to discharge me and then the landlord is coming in to run me home in his car. I don't fancy going on the Tube looking like this.'

'Well, we'll be in touch again,' Barnard said before turning away feeling even more deflated than he had been when he left home. His route back to the nick took him past Evie Renton's house and he was surprised to see a couple of women he knew deep in conversation outside the door at a time at which most ladies of the night would be fast asleep.

'You're up early, girls,' he said as he approached, but the smiles they usually offered back to a good-looking man, even at this untimely hour of the morning, were not forthcoming today.

'Do you know where Evie is?' the taller of them asked.

'I saw her the other day,' he said as a worm of concern grabbed him fiercely in the stomach. 'Is she in trouble?'

'We don't know, do we?' the second girl offered, and Barnard could see that whatever was worrying them was serious.

'She's not answering her door,' the first girl said. 'We arranged to go together to sign on with a doctor. There's not many who will take us on. They reckon we put most of their patients off. But there's a new woman doctor . . . Anyway, Evie's not here and she promised to come with us.'

The worm in Barnard's stomach was rapidly turning into something much bigger and more vicious.

'Do you want me to see if I can get inside? It's not like her to take any risks, is it? If you're reporting her missing I'd have a legitimate reason to look at her place.' He did not need to spell out to these girls the risks the toms took every night.

'Go and have a look,' the tall girl said quietly. 'There's funny stuff going on. A murder at the Grenadier and something else yesterday. The Italian cafe trashed. Everyone's scared silly. And now Evie. It's not like her to forget anything important. But I know she was worried about people coming round and demanding money.'

'Did she pay?' Barnard asked.

'I don't think so. She doesn't like being bullied.'

'It's probably nothing,' Barnard said, though he knew his voice didn't have the conviction that it should have had. 'She may have gone to see her daughter. Maybe the kid's ill. But I'll have a look. Do you have a key or do you want me to force the door?'

'The outside door's open. We tried it, but her room's locked.'

'OK,' Barnard said. 'You wait here and I'll see what I can do.' He did not want the two women anywhere near the scene if Evie had come to any serious harm and that fear haunted him as he made his way up the stairs alone to her door on the first landing. There was, as the two women had said, no answer to a knock and the door was firmly closed and secured with a mortice key. Before he had time to have second thoughts, he put his shoulder hard to what turned out to be a flimsy lock and found himself looking into what still seemed to him like a familiar room, although it was years since he had spent any significant time here.

The curtains were still closed and Evie's belongings were strewn untidily about, but there was no sign of Evie herself. Angrily he pulled the curtains open to let more light in and began a search, although he had no idea what he was looking for, and he was on the point of giving up when he found it. Close to the unmade bed, beneath a sheet which was hanging low to the floor, smeared on the rug and pooled on the linoleum which surrounded it, was a small patch of blood. He stared at it for a long time, telling himself that she could have cut herself and gone to get help at the chemist, but found that impossible to believe. Evie had lived in Soho for years and had enough friends like the two who would by now be waiting impatiently outside the front door below not to have to go far for assistance. The toms tried to look after each other because they believed, quite rightly, that no one else would.

Barnard sat down on the edge of the bed, breathing heavily. He had to report this as soon as he could, though he still hoped against hope that there was an innocent explanation for the tiny pool of rusty red on the floor. He had no doubt at all that it was blood. He put his gloves on and began to trawl through the papers in a battered school satchel which looked as though it was where Evie kept her official documents – her rent book, receipts and records of fines for soliciting – but he found nothing to tell him where her mother and daughter lived. It would have to be done through official channels, and if Evie could not be found the two women downstairs would very likely have to be questioned as witnesses and his own credibility on the streets would be shattered.

He went downstairs slowly and found Evie's friends smoking and still looking stressed outside the front door.

'I don't know,' he said with a shrug. 'She's not there. It looks as if she slept there but she must have gone out early for some reason. I'll report her as possibly missing and we'll track down her mother to see if she's gone there first and I'll get someone to come round and make her door secure again. Did she seem as if she was worried about anything in particular?'

'No more than anyone else,' one of Evie's friends said. 'Nobody knows what the hell's going on around here at the moment.'

'Has anyone approached you for protection money?' Barnard asked.

'Not yet,' the woman said. 'But I'm sure someone was hassling Evie. She told them to go to hell.'

'Right,' Barnard said with a sinking feeling in his stomach. He could imagine how fiercely Evie would resist that sort of demand and what the reaction of the violent men who were effectively terrorizing the neighbourhood would be. 'I'll see what

I can find out. Give me some details where I can contact you later if we find there's some reason for serious worry and I need to talk to you again.'

They gave him addresses and hurried away towards Oxford Street looking anxious while Barnard continued back to the nick, aware with every step that he took that the air was thick with a threat he could almost touch. The usual anticipation as cafes and shops opened their doors to the new day was not there and nor were the customers and clients, mainly legitimate at this time of day on the rain-washed morning streets. Conversation was brief and muted if it happened at all and some passers-by who evidently recognized him moved to the opposite side of the road as if to avoid him. If someone was trying to bring terror to Soho's square mile they were doing a pretty good job, Barnard thought angrily, and the police were having rings run round them very efficiently indeed.

Kate O'Donnell met Dave Donovan in Denmark Street at lunchtime outside Jack Mansfield's office.

'I think it would have been better to phone first,' she said as they waited for a quartet of musicians to struggle down the stairs and out of the building with their instruments, bickering angrily as they went.

'He would have turned me and the band down,' Donovan said. 'I came across him when I was down here, la, and we didn't exactly hit it off.'

'You always were a seriously awkward devil,' Kate said unsympathetically. 'Not that Mr Mansfield inspires much confidence. Anyway, let's give him another try. He did say he's raised some interest in Marie's music so he might be a bit more motivated to help find her.'

'She's got a seriously good voice, though she doesn't always choose the right songs. But then Cilla didn't at first either, did she? Brian Epstein wasn't interested the first time he heard her.'

'Really?' Kate said.

'You'd gone by then. But Ringo was pushing her at the Cavern. He wasn't with the Beatles then but they all knew each other. We all knew each other,' he ended slightly plaintively, and Kate was aware of how deep the divide now was between those who had

won the platinum records and much, much more besides and those
who had not, when all had started out with the same high hopes
just a few years back. She sighed as she pushed the door open
and set off up the stairs.

'Maybe if I go first he'll let you in as well,' she said. 'You
really shouldn't annoy people so much, you know. You have to
smile and make friends to find things out.'

'Is that what your boyfriend does?' Donovan said, his expression sulky. 'He'll be the first bizzy in history to make that his
selling point.'

Kate glanced back at Dave and then shrugged. This was neither
the time nor the place to get into that sort of an argument with
Donovan, who was never going to forgive the Londoner who he
believed had stolen his girl. He was the type who wallowed in his
grudges. She stopped outside the door to Mansfield's agency and
put her finger to her lips.

'Calm down,' she said. 'Let me do the talking; you just back
me up. OK?'

'OK,' Donovan muttered and followed Kate into the outer office
where the same young woman who had been behind the typewriter
the first time she had come was leafing her way through a copy
of the *New Musical Express* with the Rolling Stones on the cover.
She showed no sign of remembering Kate when she finally turned
her attention to the visitors.

'You got an appointment?' she asked. 'He's going out to lunch
in ten minutes.'

'Ten minutes will do,' Kate said. 'Shall we go through?'

'Oh, you're that grotty bird from Liverpool,' the receptionist
said, waking up to what was happening only when Kate pushed
Jack Mansfield's office door open to find the man himself leaning
back at his desk with a bottle of Scotch on his desk and a half
full glass at his lips.

'Who the hell . . .?' he began but he got no further as Donovan
pushed Kate aside and took the glass out of the manager's hand,
spilling spirit over the papers on the agent's desk.

'I've come all the way from Liverpool to talk to you, whack,'
he said. 'I want to know where the hell Marie Collins is. You
already told Miss O'Donnell here that you saw her, you made a
tape with her and now you say there's been some interest in her

songs. Now what I don't understand is why you're not following that up with an audition. How the hell have you lost track of her? And if she's really gone missing, why haven't you reported it to the bizzies?'

'She wasn't at the house she said she would be at,' Kate said loudly, pulling Donovan back across the desk before he hit Mansfield. 'And the phone number she gave Dave isn't being answered. Shouldn't one of us report her missing to the police?'

'What I don't get is why you haven't done that already,' Donovan said, his voice thick with emotion.

'I'm not a bloody nursemaid for these kids,' Mansfield said angrily. 'Your Marie was only one of the dodgy girls who come down from the sticks and think they can follow in Cilla Black's footsteps. I only gave her the time of day because when I heard her voice I thought she really did have what it takes. But it would take a lot of hard work and I wasn't convinced she'd put that in. Most of them that come through that door are a waste of bloody space. And it's getting worse. I should have known better with your girlfriend, mate. She came in breathing alcohol all over me. Forgot to suck her peppermints, did she?'

'Marie? Are you saying she was drunk? I've never seen her drink more than a Babycham.'

'Well, maybe she's made some new friends down here,' Mansfield said. 'I know for a fact that there's a lot of booze drunk by these kids and there's more and more using drugs as well. If you ask me the whole scene's getting out of hand. Anyway, I'm not going to waste any more time on Marie. If you want to report her missing to the police feel free, but don't involve me.'

'We'll do that, but if we do they'll come asking you questions a lot more fiercely than we have,' Kate said, grabbing Donovan's arm tight and steering him towards the door. But she stopped before she reached it.

'She must have left you some details,' she said. 'Address, phone number? How were you supposed to get in contact with her if you had some news?'

'My girl will have kept all that stuff – ask her. Though remember I had her down as Ellie Fox. And I reckon she said she would come back to check out what happened to the reel. I'm sure I asked her to. But we've not heard from her. They're all unreliable

little toerags, these musicians, all out of control. I don't know why
I bother. Ask my girl if she kept any details or got a phone number
she didn't tell me about.' But when it came to it and they asked
the receptionist to help, she was unexpectedly sympathetic but not
very informative.

'I've only been here two weeks and he seems to go through
temps like there's no tomorrow,' she said. 'I'm going to tell the
agency I don't want to come back here next week. I reckon he's
going bust. He's kidding these kids who come in, telling them he
can get them auditions. I don't think he bothers half the time.'

'Can you give us the details you've got?' Kate asked. 'We could
go round and see if she's there at least. Dave will feel we've done
our best then, won't you, Dave?'

Donovan grunted his assent and the receptionist wrote down an
address and phone number that was not the same one Marie had
given Dave before she left Liverpool.

'I never got a reply on the phone so I sent her a letter a couple
of days ago asking her to ring here but she hasn't done that either.
It's only in Camden Town. She could walk down here. Remember
she's calling herself Ellie Fox now. At least the boss thinks she
is. Maybe you'll have better luck tracking her down. We've pretty
well given up.'

'It sounds as if "his girl" is running the place pretty much
on her own,' Kate said as they made their way back down the
stairs without extracting anything more useful after she had
made a token search of what seemed to be a filing system in
complete disarray. She had given Kate nothing last time they
had met and she had done only a little better this time. Outside
on Denmark Street, they stood and looked at each other for a
moment in near despair.

'We'll have to keep trying this number,' Kate said. 'Or you
could go round to the house yourself. Camden Town's not far on
the Tube.'

'I suppose you want to get your bizzy involved,' Donovan said.

'Only if you do too,' Kate said. 'He's helped me try to find her
already by driving me to Wimbledon but that turned out to be a
complete dead end. I think you'll have to make it official now if
you want the police to help. They've got a murder case in Soho
and Harry's very much up to his eyes with that.'

'But the police at home just tell me she's an adult person and she's got a right to disappear if she wants to. I've got no claim on her and we've got no evidence that there's been a crime. I talked to a bizzy I know back home in Anfield. He more or less said there's nothing I can do. I've got no status.' His shoulders slumped and he staggered slightly against a tall passer-by carrying a guitar case.

'Sorry, whack,' he muttered.

'More Liverpool talent?' the stranger said with a grin and an arm to help Donovan to get his balance back. 'It's a bloody northern invasion.'

'You'll just have to work harder down here,' Donovan said irritably. 'Anyway, the Rolling Stones are doing OK. And this new lot, the Rainmen. They're mainly Londoners, aren't they?'

'And the Kinks,' the stranger said. 'I'll tell you something for nothing though. If you're thinking of talking to Jack Mansfield I'd say don't, especially if you're as pretty as this lady here. It's all hot air and empty promises with that bloke. Making tapes and promising auditions but all he really wants is to get the girls into bed. All he ever offers in the end is a few invitations to parties and the risk of an unwanted bun in the oven. Steer clear is my advice.'

'Yeah, we've already discovered he's not exactly reliable,' Donovan said.

'You don't know how unreliable,' the stranger said. 'He's a con man, is Mansfield. I wouldn't let him near my great auntie Mabel.' He glanced at his watch. 'I'm early for my session,' he said. 'Come and have a coffee and tell me about this girl you're looking for. I heard you talking about someone missing. I may have come across her. Or know someone who has. Name is Steve, by the way.'

'I'm Kate and this is Dave,' Kate offered reluctantly. She reckoned that what Steve had offered them on Mansfield's reputation was little more that she would have been able to uncover herself in time and after the encounter with the other nosy stranger in the Blue Lagoon she was reluctant to share anything with anyone else she didn't know. She looked suspiciously at the coffee bar on the corner of the street that he led them to and followed the two musicians through the door warily.

'What's the matter?' the man with the guitar asked as he propped his instrument carefully against a chair. 'You look as if you've lost a fiver and found a ha'penny.'

Kate shrugged. 'I had a nasty experience in a pub round here yesterday,' she said. 'The place got trashed while I was there, and there's been a murder at another pub.'

'I heard about that,' Steve said. 'Nasty. What will you have? Cappuccino?'

'Are you in a band?' Dave asked, still with a touch of aggression in his voice.

Steve shook his head. 'No, I'm just a session player. We fill in the background when it's needed.'

Dave nodded. 'The Beatles are using more backing now,' he said. 'It's not something the Liverpool groups are big on, to be honest. Or maybe we just can't afford it. We're the poor relations. Everyone who's anyone gets sucked down to London. Liverpool will end up just a backwater.'

'Come on, Dave,' Kate said. 'It's not as bad as that.'

'Isn't it? Could you find a good job at home when you finished at college?'

'Taking baby pictures in a local photographers, or school photos, sure, but I wanted more than that, just as all you lads did,' Kate said. 'The *Liverpool Echo* didn't want me. And you boys in the bands were just as bad when girls wanted to join in the fun. How many of you gave the girls a chance? All you wanted the girls to do was get their knickers in a twist and take them off when you felt in the mood. Cilla was a very lucky girl.'

'And so were you by the sound of it,' Steve said, looking somewhat stunned by the turn the conversation had taken. He turned to Donovan. 'Anyway, tell me about your girlfriend and I'll see if I can find anyone who's seen her – or heard her, maybe. If she's landed an audition she must be pretty good. But that's only if you can believe a word Jack Mansfield says.'

Kate sipped her coffee for a moment until she noticed a passer-by she thought she recognized.

'Give me a minute, boys,' she said, pulling her camera out of her bag, dodging on to the pavement outside and through the hurrying crowds until she was sure that the person in her sights really was Ray Robertson deep in conversation with a man she did not recognize. Without getting close enough to attract their attention, she took a couple of shots that she knew Harry Barnard would be glad to see but as her quarry headed in the direction of the Delilah Club, which she guessed would be their destination, she dropped back. Just as she had easily recognized Robertson she knew with a sense of real foreboding that he might recognise her too. And that was a possibility she did not want to risk.

TEN

Kate knew that what she planned might not end well. She had asked Dave Donovan to meet her when she finished work, hoping that Harry Barnard would also turn up to collect her and she could persuade the two men to sit down over a drink and talk to each other, and also fill Harry in on her sighting of Ray Robertson. She just hoped that they would not come to blows. She had mentioned to Dave the unsolved mystery around the death of the girl at the Late Supper Club, and although she insisted that the victim of the fatal fall was much younger than Marie Collins, Dave had not totally believed that. He insisted that the fact that an unidentified body lay in the hospital morgue had to be checked out. And she reckoned that Harry might regard the possibility that he could identify the body at last as a reason to talk to Dave even if he only ended up insisting that the girl who fell could not possibly be Dave's missing girlfriend.

'Harry will only tell you what he's told me,' Kate had argued.

'I want to hear it from him,' Dave said with an obstinate look which Kate recognized from old long-dead arguments, 'I want to ask him some questions.' So they waited over coffee in the Blue Lagoon from where it was possible from a window table to see the door which led to the Ken Fellows Agency, and it was not long before Kate saw the familiar figure turn into Frith Street and take up a waiting pose by the door, glancing up at the still illuminated office windows above him.

'Stay here,' Kate said to Donovan. 'I'll persuade him to come in for a coffee. I don't suppose he'll be too pleased to see you.'

Barnard looked surprised when she approached him from an unfamiliar direction and his expression darkened when she explained why.

'There's no way I should be discussing details like that with him,' he said. 'It's a stupid thing to set up, Kate, and could get both of us into trouble.'

'It'll take two minutes to tell him it's nonsense,' Kate said. 'And it won't do anyone any harm. We're just having a friendly drink after work, la, nothing heavy at all.'

'One cup of coffee then,' Barnard conceded. 'I really came over early to tell you I'd be late home tonight. I've not finished with DI Watson yet and then I need to check someone out who seems to have gone missing unexpectedly. It shouldn't take too long but don't cook for me. I'll pick something up on the way back. Come on, Kate. I haven't got much time before Fred Watson starts missing me.'

The sergeant followed Kate into the Blue Lagoon and bought himself a coffee at the counter before nodding to Donovan with a chilly smile and sitting down across the table from him.

'I thought maybe you'd like a bevvy,' Donovan said. 'Something stronger?' but Barnard shook his head quickly.

'I've not finished work,' he said. 'I don't want to be breathing fumes over my boss. I've got enough trouble with him already. So what is it you want to know? I assume Kate's told you what happened to this girl we can't identify?'

'You've still not identified her?' Dave asked.

'No, but it's not your girlfriend, I can assure you of that,' Barnard said. 'The pathologist reckons she's no more than sixteen, if that, about five foot three, slim build. She was badly injured in the fall, she went head first, so we don't have much chance of an ID from her face. I've even got someone trying to find out if it's possible to reconstruct her features so we get a reasonable likeness, but that's a very long shot. There are people who can apparently do it but it seems unlikely they'll bother. It would be expensive. We'll have to rely on an artist's sketch from what people can recall of her face when she was alive. What we do know was that she was on drugs and must have been as high as a kite, and she carried nothing which would give us a clue who she was and we haven't had any missing person reports to indicate where she came from. It's unusual but kids seem to be doing increasingly unusual things these days.'

'What colour's her hair?' Dave asked.

'Blonde,' Barnard said.

'Natural blonde or bottle blonde?'

Barnard hesitated for a moment. 'Natural, I think, but I wouldn't be totally sure,' he said.

'With Marie it was natural, though she was talking about dying it red. A lot of the girls want to look like Cilla. Can I see her, just to make sure?'

'No chance,' Barnard said. 'The coroner's office would go spare. I shouldn't even be here telling you any of this. This is not your friend Marie. Believe me, it's not her.'

Dave nodded, fighting back tears.

'I'm sorry,' Barnard said. He reached out to touch Kate's hand briefly. 'I'll see you later, honey,' he said, and was gone even before she could respond. She realized that she had not told him about seeing Ray Robertson. She would print the photo for him this afternoon.

'What next?' Dave asked.

'You could go round all the music studios on the off-chance she's tried looking for a better manager than that waste-of-space Mansfield,' Kate suggested. 'If you've got a couple of days here you'd have time to do that maybe. I can't take time off work to help you but you could get round a few of the major players while you're here.'

'Maybe,' Dave said, but before either of them could work out a concrete plan they were approached by a tall man in a duffel coat who Kate half recognized.

'Hello again,' he said, sliding into the chair Harry Barnard had just vacated. 'So is this the boyfriend you were telling me about the other day? I'm Bob, by the way,' he said, turning to Donovan. 'We shared a table in here when it was packed out the other lunchtime. I hope you don't mind me chatting up your girlfriend.'

Kate flushed slightly, annoyed by a familiarity she did not think the man had earned.

'It's nothing to do with me, whack,' Donovan said. 'And she's not my girlfriend, as it goes.'

'Oh, sorry,' Bob said quickly, and Kate realized that although he was smiling his eyes were cold. 'I thought you must be the boyfriend. My mistake. Though you obviously come from Liverpool too.'

'Have you got a problem with that?' Dave asked, and Kate was aware of the seething frustration beneath his calm exterior. Dave Donovan wanted to hit someone. She recognized the signs and hoped that Bob did too.

'No, no,' Bob said. 'Not at all. I love the Beatles as much as anyone, though I'm probably too old to be a proper fan. I've a daughter who's begging me to take her to see them but she's only nine. Too young, I think.'

'Yeah, well, we all love the Beatles but some of us might wish they left a little bit of attention for the rest of us.'

Kate could still see this encounter ending badly and glanced at her watch. 'I have to go. I'll have a think about what we were talking about before, Dave, and I'll ring you later at Tess's place, OK?' she said, pulling on her coat and making quickly for the door. Bob watched her go in silence and, as Donovan stood up and picked up the bill for their coffee, he gave the musician a crooked smile.

'She's still with her copper then, is she?' he said. 'That can't be much fun with all the mayhem that's going on round here just now.'

'I wouldn't know about that,' Donovan said, and turned on his heel and followed Kate out on to Frith Street, but she had already disappeared. He glanced at his watch and wondered if there was time to catch a train back to Lime Street tonight. For the first time he felt the sheer size of London bearing down on him and he understood how remote the chance of finding Marie was if she really did not want to be found.

On the way back to the nick to pick up his car, Sergeant Barnard strolled past the Late Supper Club and decided to make a quick detour. The doors were not locked and he found Hugh Mercer talking to the kitchen staff upstairs. He did not hide his annoyance at seeing Barnard and waved his chefs and waiters, all impeccably dressed for the evening service, away to their quarters irritably.

'What can I do for you, Sergeant?' he asked.

'We've still made no progress in identifying the dead girl and I just wondered if your staff had found any unclaimed items which might have belonged to her?' Barnard said, ignoring the manager's obvious irritation. 'She's not likely to have arrived here without some sort of a bag or even a coat and as we've not been able to identify her any other way it's becoming more urgent that we track down her belongings. I'm sure you understand that, sir. They should give some indication of her name or where she had come from before she arrived here. Even a Tube ticket would help.'

'As you requested, Sergeant, I've passed that message on to all my staff,' Mercer said. 'You can be sure they've got the gist and don't need constant reminders from you, any more than I do. And my clients certainly don't need to be told that there was an unfortunate accident here the other night that was nothing to do with them. We are taking much more care on the doors now so there is no possibility of a repeat intrusion by anyone who is not a legitimate client. So if that's all, Sergeant, I hope we won't see you here again any time soon.'

'I hope so too, Mr Mercer,' Barnard said. 'But you can be sure that if we need to talk to you or your clients again we will be in touch.' He could have said more but he knew that whatever he did say would be relayed to whoever it was he guessed the manager knew at the Yard, so he turned on his heel and made his way quickly downstairs to the street. He knew that the search for the dead girl's identity was being pushed down the list of priorities at the nick by the mayhem which had broken out on the streets, and that he was unlikely to be able to change that. Even in his own mind, the possible fate of Evie Renton already loomed much larger than the frustrating hunt for the name of the girl already past saving or even, it seemed, past returning to her family for a decent burial. He knew that she would languish in the mortuary's freezer indefinitely if she was never identified and eventually be consigned to an anonymous grave.

He drove fast out of London to the west where the Chiltern hills eventually rose up ahead and the roads to the north of the A40 became progressively more constricted and winding. The last lap took him down a lane so narrow that it was difficult to work out how two cars could pass between the steep banks on each side, but there was no other traffic to be seen and eventually the road widened out to run alongside a village green, past a Victorian school and eventually down a steep hill to where a cluster of stone cottages stood on each side of the road. Number 11 stood on the left and the curtains were already drawn at the windows against the dusk. He had found Evie's mother by checking court records and finding her details noted as next of kin. He parked and knocked on the front door, which was opened surprisingly quickly by a plump, grey-haired woman who was closely followed by a small, skinny girl in pyjamas clutching a book in one hand and a biscuit in the other. She stood half hidden by the woman Barnard assumed was her grandmother, who was looking anxious, but there was little doubt that she was Evie Renton's daughter.

'I'm not even sure what to call you,' Barnard said. 'But are you Evie's mother?'

The woman glanced at the child, whose bright eyes watched both adults with a certain grave suspicion. Barnard guessed she must be about ten years old, which would fit with what Evie had very occasionally revealed about her child. The woman stooped down to give the child a hug.

'Go and have a little read by yourself, petal,' she told her. 'I'll be indoors in a minute and we can read a couple of chapters together.' She came out on to the doorstep and pulled the door shut behind her.

'Is Evie all right?' she said sharply, already looking years older than she had when she had opened the door. 'Who are you? Are you from the police?'

'Yes, but off-duty,' Barnard said carefully. 'My name's Harry Barnard. And you are?'

'Mrs Renton, Nancy Renton.'

'I've known Evie a long time, Mrs Renton, and she seems to have gone missing. I'm worried. I wondered if you had seen her recently?'

'Not for a couple of weeks, and I thought there was something wrong then. She often comes out on a Sunday to see Rosie, but she didn't come last week and she usually rings me if she's not coming. She paid to have the phone put in here so she could contact me and talk to the child. And she sends me money for Rosie's keep if she can't get here herself. She's a good mother.'

'When did she first go to work in London?' Barnard asked.

'After the baby was born. There was no future for her here. There's no work for a girl in her situation and a lot of spite and bullying. She was a young mother so I'm a young grand-mother – and a widow – and I reckoned I could cope with the baby. Evie sends money every month. It pays the rent. She must have a good job.'

Barnard could see the fear in the woman's eyes and guessed that she did not know for sure how Evie earned her money and probably did not want to know. But she obviously had her suspicions.

'Has she mentioned any reason why she might want to go away somewhere? A new boyfriend maybe, or anyone she might be frightened of?' Barnard persisted. 'Or anything else she might have been worried about, anything that's changed recently?'

Mrs Renton shook her head and her eyes filled with tears. 'I'm not a fool, Mr Barnard,' she said. 'I can guess what Evie's doing in London but she has always looked well and happy. She still had the lovely smile she had when she was Rosie's age and Rosie has it too. But the last time I saw her she looked poorly, very pale and anxious, and I guessed there was something wrong. But she didn't say anything about it. She wouldn't say anything to me, would she? She'd know it would only worry me. She got the bus back to Amersham as usual. That's where you can get on to the Underground and go to London. And that's the last time I saw her.'

Barnard knew that smile too and had seen it fade, but that was something he dare not share with Evie's mother.

'If I give you a phone number, will you ring me if you hear anything from her?' he asked. He rooted through his coat pockets, pulled out an old envelope and wrote down the numbers of the nick and his flat. By now Rosie had pulled the door open again and was looking anxious.

'Ask for Harry Barnard,' he said.

Mrs Renton glanced at the child. 'Go indoors, sweetheart,' she said. 'You can take another biscuit out of the tin.' She turned back to Barnard, took the envelope and the pen out of his hand, wrote another number down and tore off the corner she had written on.

'That's my number,' she said. 'When I saw you on the doorstep I thought you'd come to tell me she was dead. I hope you never have to do that, Mr Barnard. I hope and pray you find her safe.' Nancy Renton had tears in her eyes, but she turned away without a backward glance, her shoulders rigid, and closed the cottage door behind her.

Barnard sat in his car outside the cottage for five minutes before he started his engine. He had thought that seeing Evie's daughter and seeing that at least she was safe and well would make him feel better, but the opposite had proved to be the case. The sense of dread which had been sparked when he had seen the single smear of blood beside Evie's bed was only reinforced by this idyllic rural landscape such a short drive from the city. He drove back into London at a more sedate pace than he had left and was relieved to see that the lights were on in his flat when he pulled into the parking place below the windows. He found Kate in the kitchen with the fridge door open.

'Have you eaten?' he asked, and when she shook her head he closed the fridge door for her.

'Come on. We'll go out. It's the least you deserve.' He put his arms round her and kissed the back of her neck.

'I hardly ever see you,' Kate said, her frustration suddenly boiling over.

'I know, but you know why,' he said. 'Someone is running rings round us. I've never known anything as ruthless as this before. Ray Robertson in his pomp was a pussy cat compared to whoever is behind this new campaign.'

'Are you quite sure it's not him trying to prove he's still a force to be reckoned with?' she asked as she put her coat on. 'I know how ruthless he can be when it suits him. He almost got me killed, Harry. You can't forgive him for that.' She pulled a couple of photographs from a folder lying on the kitchen table.

'I saw him today,' she said. 'Look.'

Barnard looked at the shots she had taken and put his arm round Kate's shoulder.

'Are you sure he didn't see you?' he asked urgently.

'Pretty sure,' Kate said. 'It was very busy. But you did say you thought he was still around. I thought you might like some evidence.'

'I would,' he said. 'But I have to convince the DCI as well. I'll never forgive Ray for what he did to you, I promise. But exactly what we can pin on him, if anything, I'm still not sure. I'll take these pictures in to work tomorrow but I don't think anyone there will be trying very hard to find him while we've got all this other violence and murder on the streets. That will take priority. And there's no evidence he's involved in that. All we've got is vague sightings. But the pictures will prove he is actually around. We're not imagining it. And if the DCI approves we can take it from there.'

ELEVEN

Barnard left his car at the nick and took his time walking through the narrow Soho streets towards the Grenadier. It was early and most of the night-time haunts and some of the shops and cafes were still closed up. He stopped for a moment at Evie Renton's front door and pressed the bell, but no one answered and the curtains at her window were still drawn exactly as he had left them. He would check again later in the day, he thought, but the hollow feeling in his gut told him that the longer she was missing the less likely she was still to be alive. It was the same rule which applied to missing children, he thought, but the desperate search they caused was almost always absent in the case of the working girls. Street girls got swept away like flotsam on the beach, picked over for anything useful and discarded and forgotten as the tide went out.

As he approached the queer pub, which was still draped with police tape and had a bored-looking uniformed constable outside, he noticed the familiar figure of Vince Beaufort loitering on the opposite side of the road, slightly more inconspicuously dressed than usual, his take on a low profile, Barnard guessed, and he also guessed that he was waiting for him personally. He crossed over and offered Vince a cigarette, which he took eagerly and drew on deeply.

'So what's new?' Barnard asked. 'Have you been keeping an eye out for me?'

'There are two new kids on the block, apart from the bog-standard thugs who are doing the terrorizing but don't look in the same league as these two,' Beaufort said, glancing around the still, quiet street anxiously, his voice barely audible above the noise of a delivery van dropping off groceries at the Italian delicatessen a few doors down from the pub. 'I told you about a dark-haired bloke, tall, swarthy? Looked a bit Spanish, though not in a bad way. Remember?'

Barnard nodded, also recalling that Beaufort had said he

fancied him. 'You didn't make a pass at him, did you, and get thumped?'

'Not as such,' Beaufort said coyly. 'Just a little encouraging look, but it wasn't appreciated. I did pick up his name, though. I was told he calls himself Minelli, which sounds Italian. He's around a lot and I saw him watching when the bastards who are threatening people were busy trashing the bookshop by Soho Square yesterday. Why is there never a copper about when you really need one? He took a very close interest, though not so close that you could say he was actually involved. Wore a dark raincoat, black trilby, leather gloves. Very trad.'

'Could he be Maltese, do you reckon?'

'Could be, I suppose, somewhere down south in the sunshine anyway. But I haven't heard him speak so I don't know about a language or even an accent.'

'OK, and the other man?'

'Younger, heavier, dressed more casually in jeans and a duffel coat, not so dark but not exactly a blond. Longish hair, though, not short back and sides. I've seen him a couple of times in Frith Street but he doesn't seem to work anywhere, just drifts about, stopping for a coffee or a pint, sitting around a lot watching the scene go by. Sitting too long, I reckon, as if he's watching for something or someone.'

'Right,' Barnard said. 'No chance of a name, I don't suppose?'

'Not that I heard,' Beaufort said. He glanced up and down the street, which was slowly beginning to come to life.

'I'll get out of your way, then,' he said, glancing at the Grenadier where the obligatory bobby seemed to be beginning to take an interest in their conversation.

'Just one other thing,' the sergeant said quietly. 'Have you seen Evie recently?'

Beaufort stood stock-still for a moment, his eyes blank, and then shook his head. 'Not recently, no,' he said. 'Is there something wrong?'

'Maybe,' Barnard said. 'If you do see her, ask her to get in touch with me, will you?'

Beaufort nodded. 'You were close once, weren't you?'

'A long time ago,' Barnard said. 'When I first came to Soho.'

'Those bastards have been hassling the working girls,' Beaufort said, looking appalled. 'I do know that. They seem to want to take control of pretty well everything that makes a bit of cash, no exceptions tolerated.'

'I know,' Barnard said, and turned to cross the road and face the demands of DI Fred Watson while Beaufort watched him go with a look full of anxiety. Suddenly for him, what had seemed a reasonably settled life had filled with unpredictable risks and dangers just when he had expected the change in the law to make life easier for men like him. He spun on his heel and headed out of Soho towards Oxford Street, wondering if he could afford a holiday.

Back at the nick at lunchtime, Barnard was wondering if he could take time out to see Kate as he had often done before murder erupted so violently on his home turf, when he realized he had caught the eye of the DCI, who looked surprised to see him in the squad room.

'Sergeant,' he said. 'A word in my office.' Barnard cursed under his breath but had to follow the DCI along the corridor where he left him standing in front of his desk while he sat down and rooted through a few out-of-place documents on his normally pristine workplace.

'I'm glad I caught you,' Jackson said. 'I know DI Watson is keeping you fully occupied but there was something I wanted to ask you about.'

'Guv,' Barnard said, feeling his mouth dry.

'I know I asked you whether you knew where Ray Robertson is concealing himself so discreetly at the moment, so I imagine the reason you went to Bethnal Green to talk to his mother was a result of my interest and with the aim of flushing him out. And I suppose the fact that you haven't reported back to me on those inquiries is a result of DI Watson keeping you so busily occupied, but I would like to know whether those inquiries bore any fruit or were a complete waste of police time.'

'Not a complete waste of time, sir,' Barnard said quickly. 'But all they told me was that Mrs Robertson is still fighting the local council, which is planning to demolish her street, and claims to be getting no help from Ray to stave that off or to find somewhere decent for her to live. They're threatening to put her into an old folks' home of some kind and she is not best pleased. I had a look at Ray Robertson's gym as well while I was down there and that's due to be pulled down soon too. It's empty and pretty well derelict. There'll not be much of the old East End left in a year or so and Ma Robertson is spitting blood.'

'She has no idea where Ray is? Is that what she told you?'

'Yes, sir. That's what she said. And I could see for myself that he's not using the gym any more.'

'And you believed her story?' Jackson snapped. 'Don't you think she might have been covering up for him?'

'She's a very old woman, guv, and she doesn't look well. I don't think she's capable of inventing a complicated set of lies in the circumstances and probably wouldn't have thought she needed to lie to me anyway. I've known her most of my life. I think she's frightened to death of what's about to happen to her down there and needs Ray more than she's ever needed him before. My take on it is that she doesn't know how to contact him or she'd have done it already, and he doesn't know the trouble she's in or one way or another he would be there for her.'

'So if we set up surveillance we might just have a lucky break? He might turn up at his mother's. This is the strength of the East End family, is it? And I thought that was just a fairy story.'

Barnard shrugged wearily. 'I suppose he might,' he said. 'He's definitely been in Soho though. My girlfriend saw him near Denmark Street and took a photograph of him yesterday. You remember she's a photographer? And she knows Robertson. I've got a copy for you on my desk.'

'Leave it with me, Barnard. I'll see what the Yard thinks about setting up surveillance at his mother's. And I'll get the necessary authorization to insist the manager at the Delilah tells us how he keeps in touch with Robertson. He's running rings around us at the moment.'

'Sir,' Barnard said.

'And Barnard, next time you go on some freelance enterprise like your trip to Bethnal Green without telling me or reporting back to me I'll have you on a disciplinary charge before your feet touch the ground. Understood?'

'Understood, sir.' But as the sergeant made his way back to the squad room he was thinking hard and wondering who had followed him to east London and reported back to the DCI so very promptly. And if that surveillance was so efficient, might someone be

following him round Soho as well? Like, for instance, the embry-
onic drugs team which DI Jamieson had already assured the West
End's assembled detectives was about to spring into being? Life
looked like getting even more complicated very soon.

'Have you still got Marie's picture?' Dave Donovan asked Kate
O'Donnell as they walked with Kevin Dunne through the busy
area around Leicester Square where cinema and theatre crowds
were pouring on to the streets seeking Tube trains and buses and
last orders in the pubs. Dave had visited the address in Camden
Town Marie had given Mansfield's secretary but had got no reply
when he rang the doorbell or tried a phone call.

The two men had rung Kate halfway through the evening when
she had realized that Harry Barnard was unexpectedly late home
again and that she felt increasingly aggrieved. The men had
persuaded her against her better judgement to change into something glamorous, although she told them that she had little to wear
which could claim that description. Then they said enthusiastically
that she should get the Underground back into the West End to
come to the Late Supper Club with them, where Kevin Dunne
reckoned he could talk his way in to join Jason Destry who was
supposed to be still there celebrating the success of his new record
in the charts, and while they were there Dave could use his photograph of Marie check if anyone in the club recognized her.

'Jason won't mind,' Kevin Dunne said. 'He rates this club because
it keeps out the little girls. They're quite strict on the door now, so it
keeps Jase out of the way of people who want his autograph and the
girls who wave their knickers around. There's a bit of privacy.'

'They didn't manage to keep out the girl who fell out of the
window, though, did they?' Kate said.

'Yeah, I've no idea how she got in. They were either very care-
less or someone turned a blind eye.'

'I don't think they've even managed to identify her yet,' Kate said.

'People can disappear in London evidently, la,' Donovan said
heavily. 'Easy as pie.' Even in the short time he had been in the
city, his optimism seemed to have drained away and he looked
increasingly stressed as he came to terms with the fact that it was
very unlikely that he was going to track Marie Collins down. It
was time, Kate thought, that he went back to Liverpool and gave

up on what looked increasingly like a wild goose chase. She caught his eye as they walked up Greek Street and stopped in front of the door to the Late Supper Club.

'OK?' she asked, but his nod was perfunctory.

'I suppose, la,' he said. 'Let's do it. Can't hurt, can it?'

Kevin Dunne led the way up the stairs to the main entrance and told the doorman that they were joining Jason Destry. The man looked sceptical but when he checked, Destry himself came to the door and signed them all in without a problem and led them to a table at the back of the room, slightly apart from most of the other drinkers and diners.

'Good to see you,' he said, although Kate realized that his greeting was directed particularly in her direction rather than towards his fellow musicians. When they had all been served with the champagne Destry ordered he took the seat next to Kate and leaned close.

'I like your dress,' he said in her ear with his gaze on the emerald green satin, which was as close to glamorous as she had been able to provide. 'You're going to come to my party on Saturday, aren't you? I'd really like that.'

'I'll see what I can do,' she said, moving a little further away. She had known enough musicians in her time while the Merseybeat took off and swept through Liverpool not to be dazzled by this new version. For a while they enjoyed the drinks that Destry apparently put on his bill, refilling the glasses at will, and he browsed the menu and encouraged the others to do the same, although Kate claimed that she wasn't hungry, which was true enough. She was beginning to think that this expedition might have been a mistake as Destry filled her glass for the second time and she removed a wandering hand from her knee.

Across the room, she was surprised to see a face she recognized. The man who had chatted her up in the Blue Lagoon was close to the bar and deep in conversation with a man in black tie and dark suit who she guessed must be working at the club.

'You see the man talking to the one all dolled up in a black tie . . .'

'Black tie? That's Hugh Mercer, the manager,' Destry said. 'Or Captain Mercer as he likes to be known. They do like their titles, don't they, these toffs? He's not old enough to have been in the war, is he? My dad was a captain in Normandy and was lucky to

survive. That one probably ran the cadets at a grammar school in
Surrey just like the one I went to, all part of pretending to be a
minor public school. Anyway, no, I don't know who the other
fellow is. I've never seen him before.'

'There's a lot of pretending to be something you're not that
goes on down here in the south,' Kate said mildly, wondering for
a moment whether what she was saying made sense as her head
began to ache. 'In Liverpool you're either a left-footer or a Prod
and you don't get a choice – you're born into one tribe or the
other. And if you want to cross the line all hell will break loose.
Mixed marriages are only spoken of in whispers. Cilla Black
found that out. Someone on one side or the other is going to
complain, all claiming God is on their side.'

'Jesus wept,' Destry said. 'Does that go for you too?'

'My mam would like to think it does,' Kate said, giving the
singer a wicked grin and a giggle as her vision unexpectedly
fragmented for a moment. 'But we're a long way from the Pier
Head. I don't reckon they can hear me from here.'

'They don't look as if they're the best of mates, do they,
those two?'

'I'd say they were having a blazing row in whispers,' Kate said.
'Whatever they're on about, Mercer doesn't want his precious
clients to overhear. The other man told me he was called Bob
when he chatted me up the other day.' They watched as Mercer
edged Bob backwards towards the door as if anxious to get him
off the premises.

'Never mind them – I'm starving and the food here is pretty
good.' But before any food was ordered, Dave Donovan got to his
feet impatiently, pulled his photograph of Marie out of his pocket
and took his picture from one table of diners to another, asking
them in turn if they had ever seen Marie in the club. None of them
seemed to be very pleased to be approached, though whether it
was the photograph or Dave's broad Liverpool accent that annoyed
them most, it was impossible to tell.

'You'd better stop him doing that,' Destry said to Kevin Dunne
quietly. 'They're very twitchy since the accident the other night.'

'So they should be,' Kate said sharply. 'That was awful.
Apparently she was high on drugs before she fell.'

'They've tightened up their security since then,' Destry

said. 'That's fine by me. Mercer's got a new man looking at the arrangements.' He glanced around the crowded club and focused on a dark-haired man with an olive complexion who was eating a meal alone but was already apparently beginning to take an interest in Dave Donovan's tour of the tables.

'I remember the girl vaguely from that night,' Destry said. 'Apparently she was called Jackie. Do the police know that?'

'I don't think so,' Kate said. 'I don't think they have a clue who she was. Some family somewhere must be completely desperate. She was only a kid.'

'Of course, you're the one who has a copper for a boyfriend, aren't you? That seems a bit of a waste when you could have me.'

'Dream on,' Kate said and saw a moment of irritation cross Destry's face.

'I'll have to be a bit careful with you anyway,' Destry said. 'I don't want my bad habits coming to your boyfriend's attention, do I? It did get a bit wild that night. I don't know where some of the stuff came from to be honest. There was a lot of it about.'

'What you take is up to you,' Kate said angrily. 'But for someone to give drugs to a young kid, that's dreadful.' But she was not sure that her protests were making sense any more.

'I agree with you,' Destry said with an edge to his voice now. 'I haven't a clue who she was or who brought her in here. So let's move on shall we and get something to eat?' Still watching what was going on across by the bar, Kate felt Bob's eyes lock on hers for a moment before he pulled away from Mercer and moved towards the door.

'Do something about your Liverpool friend, Kev,' Destry said.

Dunne got to his feet abruptly and followed Dave Donovan to the other side of the busy bar where the burly man in evening dress Kate had been watching was approaching Donovan with obviously aggressive intent now he was free from the man who had been lambasting him verbally. They arrived one each side of Donovan at the same time and with a firm grip on each of his arms.

'Is this a friend of Mr Destry's?' Hugh Mercer the manager asked Dunne, barely able to choke down his fury. 'And if so, what the hell does he think he's doing?'

Dunne took the photograph out of Donovan's hand. 'Sorry about that,' he said. 'He's looking for his girlfriend who came down from Liverpool and seems to have disappeared. I told him she was not likely to have been in here even though we know she's been in Soho. We were invited here by Jason Destry, but Dave here seems to have taken advantage a bit. I play bass in the Rainmakers.'

'So are we supposed to be the haunt of every waif and stray in the West End?' Mercer hissed. 'That's not what I had in mind when I opened this place. You had better believe it.'

'Not good enough for you southerners, are we, us from up north?' Donovan jeered taking the photograph back and trying to straighten out the crumples. 'Not posh enough? I met enough of you lot when I did my National Service to last a lifetime.' On the far side of the room the dark-haired man was getting to his feet and heading in the manager's direction.

'And I dare say they treated you appropriately,' Mercer sneered, still in the stage whisper, which was supposed to shield the clients who were by now avidly watching the proceedings, cutlery halfway to their mouths.

'But you haven't got the MPs lining up behind you now to protect your backside, have you?' Donovan said, and suddenly threw an ungainly punch in Mercer's direction, which caught his arm and which he returned instantly, twice as hard and a hundred per cent more accurately. Dunne caught Donovan's arm and kept him upright with difficulty.

'Get that stroppy little northern bastard out before I call the police,' Mercer said.

'There's no need for that,' Dunne said quickly. 'We'll take him away and leave you in peace.' Mercer hesitated for a moment.

'Well, my instinct is to throw the lot of you out but I'll have a word with Mr Destry. I don't want to lose valuable members like him.' He waved the man who had left his table away impatiently. 'But at this rate I'll never live down that stupid girl and all the fuss she caused.'

'I take it the police haven't made any progress yet then?' Dunne said, trying to defuse the situation.

'Not that anyone has told me,' Mercer said dismissively. 'Now will you ask Mr Destry to sort his friends out if he wants to remain a member here?'

'Don't worry, I'll take this one home,' Kate said, her voice slightly slurred. 'I think he's going back to Liverpool tomorrow so you won't see him again, la. He's nothing to do with the Rainmen or Jason anyway. He's just passing through.'

'Well, make sure he knows he's not welcome to pass through here again,' Mercer said, and went back to soothing the ruffled feathers of the diners, some of whom had been present and taken offence at the sight of the dead girl in the street and the rapid emptying of the club a couple of nights ago. This time they looked fairly determined to get their money's worth one way or another. When they got a rumpled Donovan back to Destry's table, the singer raised an eyebrow.

'I guess we're not in Captain Mercer's good books?' he said.

'Well, Dave isn't anyway,' Kevin Dunne said. 'Mercer'll want you to hang around because he seems to reckon you're the next big thing.'

'The next John Lennon, no less,' Destry said with a slightly shamefaced grin.

'I'll take Dave home,' Kate said again. 'He's staying with an old friend of mine in Shepherd's Bush.'

'I've got a car outside and a driver,' Destry said. 'He can drop you both wherever you want to go.' He looked at Kate and pulled her towards himself.

'Don't I get a goodbye cuddle?' he asked and did not wait for her permission to plant a kiss on her lips. 'Don't forget the party on Saturday,' he said. 'And don't be late. We'll be kicking off about ten and there'll be breakfast if you want it. If you've any appetite left after I've finished with you, that is. Kev will fill you in on the arrangements.'

She pulled away angrily but said nothing, wary of reigniting the club manager's anger before they had got Donovan off his premises. She would settle with Jason Destry another time once she felt better. This evening had not gone well as far as she could tell, although she was not quite sure why. The drinks, she supposed, had been stronger than she was used to and she could not wait to get some sleep now. If she went to Destry's party she would have to be more careful.

TWELVE

DS Harry Barnard had been about to leave the nick for home at about six when a message came from the control room that there had been a report of dead body discovered in a little used passageway linking streets not far from Oxford Street. Barnard knew he must have been there at some time since he had come to Soho, but he could recall little about it except that it seemed to be such a narrow backwater that it was often clogged with rubbish which the bin men ignored. He was not very keen to launch himself into another murder case but he thought perhaps he ought to show willing as he was not regarded as the most cooperative link in the chain by his bosses and the arrival of DI Watson seemed to have made his life even more difficult. He parked his car under the trees on Soho Square where the evening's revellers had not yet arrived in numbers and walked down Carlisle Street to the alleyway, which so far boasted only one uniformed officer at the entrance, whose brief seemed to have been merely to keep passers-by away.

'What have we got?' Barnard asked the constable. 'Another murder?'

'Dunno, Sarge,' the copper said. 'They just told me to mind the shop until the big boys arrived. Are you one of them then?'

'Not really,' Barnard said. 'I just picked up the shout at the nick and thought I'd better have a quick look as there was no one else around. This is my patch and it could be someone I know. I'll take a look. You keep anyone else out until CID turn up in force.'

He stood for a moment peering into near darkness, wishing he had brought his flashlight with him from his car.

'Lend me a light, will you,' he said over his shoulder, and the constable handed him a torch, which he directed at the ground as he began to walk slowly forward through heaps of accumulated garbage under a light scattering of dry leaves which must have blown in from the gardens in Soho Square. The alley took a right-angled turn and it was only when he went round the bend that he knew that whoever had called in a body had been right. The sudden, panicked scurrying of rodents and the smell only confirmed the worst. He took a deep breath and directed the beam on to the huddled bundle which lay right across the narrow footpath, though he had seen enough already to know that there was no way he should so much as lay a finger on it. It was obvious that not only was life extinct but it had been so for some time.

In no time at all, he knew, the massed ranks of police and doctor and forensics officers would be arriving and it would be easiest if he himself were safely out of their way. But as he turned and made his way out of the narrow passageway again, handing the constable his torch back, one fear almost clotted the blood in his brain. He was sure that the body lying on the ground behind him, not tall, not heavy and mostly covered by some sort of blanket, was Evie, and if so she must have been thrown away in a dark corner like a discarded toy. It was possible that she had simply been unlucky with a punter who did not know when to stop. But given what had been happening over the last few weeks, it was much more likely that Evie had drawn the short straw in someone's complicated criminal game. She was the warning to the other working girls that they should fall into line, do as they were told and pay their dues in the new Soho that was being established with ruthless and indecent haste.

He walked slowly back towards Soho Square and took refuge in the public bar of a pub and ordered a pint. He drank it very slowly and then retraced his steps to the alley which was now surrounded with police cars and vans and crammed with officers almost falling over themselves in the confines of its high brick walls. DI Watson had arrived and glanced in his direction before he extricated himself from the melee with a scowl.

'I heard you'd been here already,' he said.

'I was on my way home when the call came in and thought I'd better stop and have a look as no one else was around.'

'Did you recognize anyone or anything?'

'I borrowed the uniform's flashlight but I couldn't get an ID. It looks like a woman but I thought it could be a child. I didn't want to touch. There wasn't any doubt she was dead.'

'You'd better get in there now and have a closer look if you think you might recognize her,' Watson said begrudgingly.

Barnard nodded, took a couple of deep breaths and worked his way into the scrum to where the police doctor was crouching close to the body. There was never any way you got used to this, he thought as he met the doctor's eye when he glanced up at Barnard and pulled what appeared to be the tattered scraps of a blanket away from the battered remains of a face. Barnard nodded, made himself inspect what was revealed but then stepped quickly away before the nausea which seized him took over so quickly it prevented his saying anything at all coherent to DI Watson.

'Evie Renton,' he mumbled when he got back to the hovering DI. 'One of the toms. She's been working around here for years. One of her friends told me she was missing.'

'You'd better go back to the nick and put everything you know about her down on paper,' Watson said. 'Chapter and verse.'

'Guv,' Barnard said, and it was not until he was walking slowly back to collect his car that he realized there were tears running down his face. 'Hell and damnation,' he said to himself. 'Is there no end to this?' But he knew there would not be an end any time soon. If there was one group of people in the West End who came even lower down the pecking order than homosexual men it was prostitutes, male and female. Watson would go through the motions but unless there was clear evidence that Soho had acquired its own Ripper – and Barnard was not quite sure how many deaths that might take to qualify – Evie's death would be shunted to one side and her killer was very unlikely to be caught. There was an accepted hierarchy of victims and she was at the bottom of the heap.

Barnard finally got back to his flat halfway through the evening, leaving his summary of all he knew about Evie Renton on DI Fred Watson's desk. At least, he thought, someone from the local force would inform her mother about what had happened, but she would be left alone to tell Evie's daughter. All he could do himself to keep the investigation alive he would do, but he had no high hopes of success in keeping the case active or of finding whoever had killed her.

He was surprised to find his flat empty but he supposed that Kate was still playing nursemaid to Dave Donovan and he hoped that the musician would soon be on the train back to Liverpool. He was a distraction they could both do without, he thought. He poured himself a large Scotch followed by several more and eventually fell asleep in his chair.

It was almost midnight when Jason Destry's driver dropped Kate O'Donnell off at Barnard's flat and she opened the front door as quietly as she could because she expected Harry to be in bed asleep. But once again he was still fully dressed and slumped in his revolving chair, just about awake and gazing at her with half-closed eyes and a bemused expression.

'You're late,' he said, his voice thick, and she could not tell whether he was complaining or relieved.

'I got a lift back in Jason Destry's car,' she said. 'Kevin Dunne took me and Dave to the Late Supper Club because Dave thought his girlfriend might have gone there. Destry was there holding court. But Dave's completely obsessed and made such a nuisance of himself that in the end we got thrown out. With a bit of luck he'll be going back to Liverpool tomorrow and he'll be out of my hair.'

'Thank God for that,' Barnard said with an intensity which startled Kate. She sat down heavily on the sofa. 'I think I had a bit too much to drink,' she said.

'Not a good idea,' Barnard said. 'You need to keep your wits about you when you're dealing with these musicians. They're into all sorts of dangerous stuff. You know that.'

'You really were jealous, weren't you?' she asked in surprise.

He shook his head irritably. 'Not really,' he said. 'It's just there's a lot of pressure at work. There's stuff going on that no one seems to have a clue about, like the attack in the Three Horseshoes you got caught up in. I was going to ask you something about that. The barman thought that the man who seemed to be in charge had an accent, not necessarily an English accent. Did you notice that?'

'No,' Kate said. 'I was too terrified to notice anything very clearly, to be honest.'

'And there's been another killing,' Barnard said quietly, wondering where he was going with this information.

'Not the barman from the Three Horseshoes? I didn't think he was badly hurt?'

'No, not him. He's all right. But the body of one of the street girls was found this evening dumped in a dark back alleyway.' He hesitated for a moment and then shook his head with a sigh. Kate might have been brought up to believe in the value of confession but he knew that he had to stop well short of that.

'I must get some sleep,' he said.

'Both of us,' Kate said, picking up the whisky glass which was lying on its side by his chair.

'One thing Jason Destry told me that will interest you,' she said. 'He saw the girl who fell from the window and thought her name was Jackie. Does that help?'

'It might do, Barnard said, although there was not much enthusiasm in his voice. Kate looked at him critically, taking in the dark shadows under his eyes and the hands which were shaking slightly. He was, she thought, pretty much at the end of his tether and she was not exactly sure why, but she knew that she had to find out soon.

When Kate woke the next morning Barnard was already up and dressed and eating breakfast in the kitchen. She followed him and fed bread into the toaster while she took a closer look at him. He did not look much more refreshed than he had the night before and she felt similarly hungover. She put her arm round his shoulders and gripped him tightly.

'Are you going to tell me what's wrong?' she asked.

He shrugged. 'Nothing I can put my finger on,' he said. 'I've never been top of the pops with the DCI, but I seem to be getting more and more hassle, ever since I had that little disagreement with the Liverpool police. And suddenly I've got DI Watson brought in from the seaside with sand between his toes to breathe down my neck, questioning every move I make. And Jackson is still obsessed with Ray Robertson and convinced I must know where he is when I haven't a clue. What's more, I don't even want to know. I'd be quite happy if I never saw Ray Robertson again in my life.'

'There was a chap in the Late Supper Club last night who I'd seen before,' Kate said. 'He chatted me up one day when I was having lunch in the Blue Lagoon by myself. It was very busy and he claimed a seat at the table I was at, all very polite, bought me a coffee as it goes. But it didn't feel quite right, la. He was a bit too intrusive and he ended up by asking what my boyfriend did for a living.'

'Did you tell him?' Barnard said sharply, suddenly interested.

'No,' Kate said. 'It seemed a question too far. He reminded me of those secretive bastards who bullied us into protecting people who should have gone to jail.'

'Did he speak to you again?'

'No, he was talking to the manager for quite a long time and he knew I was there. I saw him looking in our direction but he didn't say anything to us. And he left before Dave began making a nuisance of himself and it all got a bit agitated. Dave made the mistake of hitting the manager and the manager hit him back – hard, knocked him over and then threw us all out. All except Jason Destry. He was obviously too useful to the club to put out on the street.'

'Is Dave going back to Liverpool today? He's not safe on the streets down here.'

'I'll see if Tess and I can persuade him to go,' Kate said. 'But he's not easy to persuade. And Jason invited us all to a party at his new house at the weekend. I thought that might be interesting if he will let me take some pictures. The boss would go for that and Jason's so full of himself that he might agree. They try to avoid the little girls who chase after them but if it's an article about their new car or their big new house they'll go along with it.'

'They're all full of themselves, these rock and roll stars. They sneer at businessmen making lots of money but if they make it themselves prancing around a stage in a red velvet jacket then it's all fine. They behave like the new royalty.'

'They certainly get treated that way,' Kate admitted. 'But you won't persuade the fans to hold back. Jason Destry's just another dedicated follower of fashion like the Kinks and he's beginning to sell records like them too. Not quite the Beatles but heading in that direction.' Barnard pulled on his coat and clamped his hat to the back of his head.

'So you think Donovan might be heading north today?'

'I hope so,' Kate said.

'If you can get rid of him I'll take you out for a meal tonight then,' he said before he gave her a kiss and went out, looking, Kate thought, just as stressed as he had the night before.

* * *

Barnard knew that the briefing on the latest murder would be difficult. And it threatened to be even more difficult when DCI Keith Jackson arrived soon after DI Fred Watson and just as Barnard himself was beginning to go through his summary of information on Evie Renton, which he had prepared for the DI the night before. This level of interest from senior officers surprised him. He had expected Evie's death to be low priority given the level of violence which was stalking the streets of Soho and the clear threat of some sort of involvement by organized gangs of apparently unknown origin.

'In your experience, who's been running the girls?' Watson asked. 'Fill me in.'

'It used to be mainly the Maltese,' Barnard said. 'The Robertsons concentrated on protection when they weren't prancing about doing a bit of social climbing. But that came to an end when Georgie decided to try his hand at robbery and murder and Ray more or less retired as far as we can tell. But now we have this new outfit and I've not heard anyone with a satisfactory explanation as to where they've come from or who's running them. What's obvious is that they are very determined and very violent and seem to want to use protection to take a cut of pretty well every criminal and legitimate activity in the square mile.'

'So how does prostitution fit into this?' the DCI asked with his usual expression of puritanical distaste. 'Didn't all the girls already have pimps?'

'Most of them,' Barnard said. 'But a few of them managed to organize themselves. They have to be careful or we'll have them for running a brothel if they share premises, but Evie Renton had her own place. She seemed to attract a different type of client, older men mainly, and she kept out of the clutches of the men who occasionally tried to take over her life. She's been in Soho longer than I have. I've always thought she knew how to look after herself.'

'Right, well, what interests me is whether she's another victim of the gang which is trying to set up a protection business again,' Watson said. 'Is the death of the tart a way of getting the rest of the girls to fall into line and pay their dues? You can follow those leads, Sergeant. Go to the post-mortem, and then talk to the toms and their pimps and find out if they're being intimidated and who by, if anyone knows.'

'Guv,' Barnard said, almost overwhelmed by a feeling that this could only end badly.

'And don't rule Ray Robertson out, Barnard,' the DCI added. 'I've got the name of his lawyer out of the club manager so you can have a go at him too.' He handed the sergeant a sheet of paper with the name of a legal firm and its address in Holborn written on it. 'Don't let him pull the wool over your eyes either. We need to interview Robertson and we'll issue a warrant for him if we have to. Right?'

'Right, sir,' Barnard said, and made for his coat and hat. Interviewing Ray Robertson's lawyer might be difficult but it was a walk in the park compared to attending Evie's post-mortem which would come first. It was almost as if Watson knew that his relationship with Evie was closer than it ever should have been, although he could not imagine where he had gleaned that embarrassing information. He was not the only cop in central London who had his own arrangement to tax the local criminals in one way or another. He decided to leave his car parked close to the nick and walk to the hospital as much to clear his head as put off the inevitable. This post-mortem would be seriously unpleasant even if he had not known the victim as well as he did. It would take iron self-control to protect himself from letting the pathologist and his technicians see how vulnerable he was.

Taking several deep breaths, he pushed open the swing doors which led him from the barren basement corridor to the mortuary and greeted the technicians who were already preparing the body. He turned away to take off his coat and turned back slowly to absorb the shock of seeing Evie's naked body heavily smeared in dirt and bloodstains from what looked like several deep stab wounds around the neck and face. Barely able to draw breath himself, he could see that her death had not been quick or painless. It had been, he realized, merciless, and he was sure that was quite deliberate. It had been intended to be a very public and utterly ruthless statement to ensure compliance with the will of whoever was orchestrating the campaign of terror which was under way. He turned away from the table again with relief to greet the pathologist who had come into the room and was pulling on his gown and moving to the table to check his array of instruments.

'Do we know who we've got here this time, Sergeant?' the doctor asked.

Barnard took up an observation point as far away from the table as he decently could without betraying himself. 'A prostitute who made a mistake,' he said through bone-dry lips. 'It happens.'

'Indeed,' the doctor said. 'Though strangulation is more common than a knife.'

Barnard listened as the doctor began to dictate the multiple external injuries visible on Evie's body, and it was not until he picked up his scalpel for the first time to make an initial incision that the sergeant lowered his eyes and avoided looking directly at what was going on in front of him. He hoped that the doctor and the technicians were concentrating sufficiently hard on the task in hand not to notice how strenuously he was fighting to remain calm and control the bile which was threatening to overwhelm him.

'Bit of a hangover this morning, Sergeant?' the doctor asked with a sympathetic smile as he removed Evie's internal organs and handed them to his assistants for weighing. Barnard nodded, not trusting himself to speak. 'You can get away shortly,' the doctor said. 'She was killed with three stab wounds here, here and here, deep wounds and a lot of bleeding.' He pointed to the sites of the knife thrusts. 'There's no damage to the head that I can see so you don't need to witness any damage there. There's some sign of rodent damage . . .'

'I saw rats at the crime scene,' Barnard said, his voice sounding very far away.

'She's been dead anything up to forty-eight hours,' the doctor said. 'Out of doors perhaps two nights, relatively warm, bound to be rodents. Surprising how secluded some of these alleyways in Soho are, isn't it? So close to the main shopping streets. Makes it tricky looking for witnesses, I expect, that she was in such a secluded spot.'

Barnard nodded and turned away to pick up his coat and hat.

'I'll get back to the nick then,' he said. 'I'll pass on your initial findings.'

'You'll have my full report as usual as soon as it's typed up,' the doctor said. 'I'll call you if I find anything more unusual.'

Barnard turned away quickly and made for the lavatory halfway down the corridor to the front doors, locked himself in a cubicle and vomited until nothing remained in his stomach except bile. Then he sat on the pedestal shaking uncontrollably for a long time with his head between his knees. For once in his life, Flash Harry Barnard did not know which way to turn.

It was fortunate that he had been given plenty of leeway to take in an interview with Ray Robertson's lawyer before he needed to report back to the nick. When he had recovered he picked up his car and drove the short distance to High Holborn where lawyers' chambers clustered around the inns of court. He parked close to Lincoln's Inn and found the offices of Sinclair and Stewart a couple of blocks away from the Tube station and used his warrant card to demand immediate access to the senior partner Abraham Stewart.

'We understand you are acting for Mr Ray Robertson, the owner of the Delilah Club, supervising the day to day affairs, I assume, as he still owns the place,' Barnard said when he was ushered into the solicitor's office.

'Who told you that, Sergeant Barnard?' Stewart asked. 'It is not our practice to discuss our client's affairs with the police except under the most controlled circumstances. We don't expect detectives to walk in off the street unannounced. We expect appointments to be made and records kept.'

'Then I'm afraid you'll find your client the subject of an arrest warrant,' Barnard said. 'Scotland Yard is very anxious to ask him some questions and I don't think they are willing to take no for an answer.' Stewart took a deep breath and steepled his fingers in a way which reminded Barnard of DCI Jackson's contemplative pose when something faced him that he disliked.

'Can you give me any indication of exactly what these questions concern?' Stewart asked. 'My client has a great many interests, not just at the Delilah and not just in London. I would be happy to discuss your request with him if you can give me more detail of what you want to know.'

'And how exactly will you communicate this information to him? Do you have an address and phone number? Is he even in the country? I spoke to his mother recently and she thought he might have gone abroad. Do you know if that's likely?'

'I've no information about a foreign trip,' Stewart said. 'But I do have an ex-directory number for him. You said you had already spoken to his mother. Do you know Mr Robertson personally? Or have you just had what one might call professional contact with him?'

Barnard hesitated, not quite sure how to interpret that question. 'Strange as it might seem, we went to school together,' he said. 'We were both East End boys but we went our very different ways later.'

'Are you saying that Mr Robertson might be more willing to talk to you personally than some other officer?'

'It could be,' Barnard said cautiously. 'Do you want some time to get an answer to that question?'

'Possibly,' Stewart said. 'Leave it with me.'

'I need an answer today,' Barnard said. 'Don't string me along. We've had three deaths in Soho within a week and Scotland Yard is getting very impatient.'

'I understand, Sergeant. Leave it with me. I'll get back to you before the end of the day.'

Barnard glanced at his watch as he left the solicitors' offices and picked up his car. Mention of Ray Robertson's mother reminded him of her poor health and made him wonder whether or not that had persuaded Ray himself to venture back to Bethnal Green. He had time, he thought, to check up again with the old lady on the off-chance that she had heard from her son. The traffic was unusually light and he parked outside her house twenty minutes later only to realize immediately that he had probably wasted his time. The doors and windows were now boarded up and it was obvious that Ma Robertson, in spite of her defiance, had been moved away. He got out of the car, taking his flashlight with him this time, and realized that all the houses were in the same condition. The demolition men would not be far behind and he had apparently come too late. Idly he glanced at what looked from a distance like secure boarding over the front door and was surprised to discover that it was not as impregnable as it at first appeared. Someone had loosened the fixing and made it possible to treat the boards like a door which could be pulled far enough to give a slim entrance to what remained of the house. Barnard glanced up and down the narrow street and could still see no sign of life, so he made a narrow entrance for himself and slipped inside. He guessed that if Ma Robertson had been removed unwillingly the house might not have been cleared very thoroughly and something of interest might remain.

Once inside, though, it was obvious that someone else had gutted the place. There was no furniture left and a thorough search seemed to have been made in every room and every cupboard, with doors off their hinges and even the fireplaces partially disman-tled and soot pulled out of the chimneys to create a level of chaos that Barnard had not seen since he and Ray and his brother Georgie had rooted around in bombed-out houses during the war. The plunder then was bomb fragments and the remnants of people's lives and deaths. Whatever had been sought here he could not imagine, but someone was looking very hard for something.

He shrugged in frustration and turned back towards the front door when he realized that there was a car outside and the sound of a door slamming. Within seconds the boards covering the door had been wrenched roughly aside and a heavyweight figure was shielding the daylight which now filtered through.

'What the hell are you doing here, Flash?' the familiar voice of Ray Robertson asked as he played a bright light into Barnard's eyes and pulled the woodwork more or less closed behind himself. 'What are you looking for down here?'

Barnard put his hand up to shield his eyes. 'I could ask you the same question Ray,' he said. 'I came to see your mother, as it goes. I didn't expect to find you here. Last time I saw her she was complaining that she never saw you.'

'Yeah, well, life's full of surprises as you know,' Robertson said. 'My mother's in hospital and not likely to come out except in a box so I came to visit her, took her some grapes, as you do, and then decided to check on the house. That's all. So you can feck off back to Soho and mind your own business.'

'The Yard wants to talk to you about what's going on in Soho,' Barnard said cautiously.

'There's a surprise,' Robertson said. 'I don't think that's an invitation I'm going to take up any time soon. What do you think?'

'I think I should radio for some backup and take you in anyway,' Barnard said. 'That's what the Yard will expect me to do.'

'Only if they know I'm here and there's only you knows that so far, I take it,' Robertson said, his voice hardening. 'I knew you were here when I saw your car. People will notice your bright red job but they know mine as local so if anyone comes down the street they'll hardly even see it. This is my ma's house after all.'

'So you won't come back with me to Soho?'

'I don't think so, Flash, do you? But you weren't kidding were you when you said you'd turn me in if you had to?'

'You left Kate alone with those bastards. She nearly died,' Barnard said as the anger he had felt that night on the Essex marshes took hold again with unexpected force and he lunged at Robertson and caught him a glancing blow to the chin. But the older, heavier man had always been a fighter and he did not hold back. He struck Barnard efficiently with three quick blows to the face and the sergeant crumpled to the floor.

'I was always streets ahead of you in the ring,' Robertson said. 'I thought I'd taught you everything I knew but it doesn't seem to have stayed with you.'

Barnard tried to get himself up from the floor but Robertson put a foot on one arm and made it impossible for him to lever himself upright.

'Listen to me, Flash,' he said, leaning down to push his face into Barnard's. 'And remember what I say. The only interest I have in Soho these days is the Delilah Club and I only hang on to that for old times' sake. Call me sentimental if you like but I'm not interested in doing it all again in the West End apart from the club. It's all drugs and tarts and noisy music these days. I know what's going on. I keep an eye on things and if they come looking to tax the club I'll deal with them, but otherwise I'm not getting involved. I'm retired, if you like, so leave me be.'

'Evie Renton's been killed,' Barnard said. 'You remember her? Stabbed to death in a back alley.'

'Misjudged a john? That's a shame.'

'More likely punished to encourage the other girls to fall into line and pay their dues.'

'I'm sorry to hear that,' Robertson said and took his foot off Barnard and helped him up. 'You must be too.'

'Yes,' Barnard said.

'But it makes no difference. I'm not involved and not planning to get involved.'

'So you say.'

'But you're still with your Liverpool bird, are you? That's OK?'

'Yes,' Barnard said again, and picked up his hat off the floor and dusted it down.

'I'll go first,' Robertson said. 'I know once you get in that car you'll be tempted to use your radio. Don't waste your time. You won't find me.'

'They won't stop looking,' Barnard said.

'And I don't suppose you will either,' Robertson said and when Barnard didn't respond he pulled the makeshift door open and glanced back at him.

'I don't suppose it matters if the door's nailed shut again,' Robertson said. 'My ma says they're bringing the wreckers in within days, the ball and chain gangs, going to do what Hitler never did. End of an era for the Robertsons and for you too, as it goes, I suppose. But we know where we stand now, Flash. There's no going back.'

'No,' Barnard said under his breath, but he did not hurry back to his car. He stood for a moment by the partly demolished door taking in the boarded-up houses where he remembered boys in short trousers and socks around their ankles racing up and down the street with their arms out wide making aircraft noises and shooting off imaginary machine guns while the girls kept well out of the way. He had heard men who had fought in reality admit slightly shamefacedly that the war had been the most intense and exciting time of their lives and he could believe it. And he knew many only a bit older than Ray who openly regretted just missing the excitement of the biggest event of the century. National service which he had experienced himself was no substitute for fighting Hitler. But he was old enough to recall even more vividly the price some of the warriors had paid. Ray's father had not come home and many of those who had survived never fully recovered. This street had escaped the bombs which had devastated East London early in the war and had resulted in Barnard and the Robertson brothers being thrown together as evacuees on a farm, and the forging of a relationship which still had consequences which he knew might derail him. Hitler's malign shadow was still there under the surface and pulling down these houses would not eradicate his presence. Not yet. More than twenty years on the memories were still too raw for some.

He would report his visit to Bethnal Green back at the nick but not his encounter with Ray Robertson. No one else in the Met would believe what Ray had said but almost in spite of himself Barnard did. He would let it be for now although he knew that eventually he and Ray would have to settle their differences one way or another. There was no alternative.

THIRTEEN

'I reckon that's quite a good idea,' Ken Fellows said cautiously after listening to Kate O'Donnell's suggestion that she take some photographs in the Soho clubs. 'Do you really think that the Delilah and the Late Supper Club would go along with it? Aren't they rivals?'

'Yes, I suppose they are,' Kate said. 'But if we offer them free publicity together rather than on their own they might go with it. We could throw in some of the others as well. One of the jazz clubs would do – some of them have been around since before the war so that might be interesting.'

'It's got possibilities,' Fellows said. 'I'll run it past one or two of the picture editors and see if anyone bites. You can talk to the managers and see if they'll go for it. But what about this murder in the gay pub? I suppose the fact that the criminals are still active might attract more interest rather than less.'

'It's odd that the Late Supper Club was launched just when there was an outbreak of violence and murder. Was that bad luck or good luck? You could argue it either way,' Kate said. 'Soho's getting a lot of publicity but not necessarily the good sort.'

'Go and talk to what's his name? Mercer? If he won't go for it it's not really a runner. We need the Delilah and Mercer's place, the old and the new to set it up.'

'Well, I went to the Delilah in its heyday when everyone loved the Robertson brothers and flocked to their boxing galas,' Kate said. 'You remember?'

Ken nodded. 'I do,' he said. 'You looked a bit gobsmacked, as I recall. But you also came back with some good pictures. That was a bit of a test to see what you were made of when I first took you on. I had a lot of the blokes telling me it was a huge mistake to take on a girl. They wanted to know how you would cope if you had to cover some sort of violence, a riot, or even a war.'

'I'm sure you did,' Kate said recalling only too clearly how

suspicious her male colleagues had been when she first arrived in
the office. 'And how many wars had they covered?'

'When I counted up only Eddie and I were old enough to have
seen active service and we weren't shooting pictures back then.
We were shooting Germans.'

'Ha,' Kate said. 'Anyway, that's all water under the bridge
now. But seriously I don't think the Delilah is doing nearly as
well now Ray Robertson's taken his eye off the ball and his little
brother is in jail. Anything which might give them a bit of
publicity might go down well, especially with the Late Supper
Club man breathing down their neck and taking their clients
away. But first I'll look through the archives and see what we
still have from those days.'

'Then you can see if it stands up with the clubs themselves,'
Ken said. 'See what their reaction is. And I'll see if I can find
someone who would use it. If it lived up to expectations.'

Kate spent the rest of the morning trawling through the agency's
substantial backlog of photographs, many of them dating back to
the interwar period when Ken's father had established a photo
agency in a couple of rented rooms off Oxford Street, which had
survived by taking portrait photographs of people visiting London
who did not own even a Brownie Box camera but wanted a souvenir
of themselves standing outside Buckingham Palace or the Tower
of London in their Sunday best. The agency had closed during the
war and Ken Fellows had taken over from his father afterwards
and moved the enterprise into Soho and in the direction of news
pictures in the heyday of the magazines which told the post-war
story before the blossoming of TV.

She found her own pictures of one of the Robertson brothers'
glamorous galas at the Delilah, invitations to which were happily
accepted by the great and the good. Then she picked out a handful
of other clubs, dark and smoky, especially on the rare occasions
when American musicians managed to penetrate the strict limits
on foreign performers imposed across the Atlantic by the American
unions and reciprocated in Britain. When she had enough she went
back to Ken Fellows and showed him what she had trawled out
of the files.

'I think there's enough here,' she said.

Ken flicked through the prints and nodded. 'Enough to see if you can get the Delilah and the Late Supper Club on board then,' he said. 'It will only stand up if you get them both.'

'Fine,' Kate said. 'I'll see if I can get in after lunch. There should be somebody there by then who can say yes or no.'

She walked up to the Blue Lagoon just before one o'clock, which was the time she and Harry Barnard often met for lunch not really expecting him to be there as the newspaper billboards were announcing another murder in Soho. But as if that were not an ominous enough message, the sight of Barnard already at a table filled her with horror.

'Whatever happened?' she asked, taking in the swollen bruises on his jaw. He shrugged and tried to play it down but she could see that he was still shaken.

'Not a lot,' he said. 'A difference of opinion with a contact who was very annoyed and considerably bigger than me.'

'Did you arrest him?'

'Not much chance of that,' Barnard said. 'I was on my own and ended up on the floor. I'm all right, Kate. It looks worse than it is. Promise.'

'And the *Standard* says there's been another murder. Is that the one you mentioned last night?'

''Fraid so. One of the street girls. We knew she was missing. We'd been looking for her, though not very energetically. They don't come high on the list of priorities with the brass, the so-called ladies of the night. But this time it went completely pear-shaped. We found her dead. But it will be a one-day wonder. They'll forget about her tomorrow.'

'How well did you know her?' Kate asked, picking up on the fresh tension in Barnard's voice.

'I'll tell you about her tonight. I haven't got much time now. DCI Jackson wants me back at the nick to explain how I got thumped and who by. I haven't quite worked out the answer to that question myself yet. I don't know how he found out.'

Kate looked at him sharply. There were times, she thought, when there did not seem to be much to choose between the hunted and the hunters and an image of Ray Robertson flashed across her mind's eye.

'I'm going to be working on some pictures in Soho myself if all goes well,' Kate said, but Barnard looked more worried than impressed.

'Are you sure you want to do that just now?' he said. 'Soho's out of control. It's not a good time or place to be making yourself noticeable with a camera. It could be dangerous. Anyway, tell me about it this evening.'

'I might know if it's a runner by then,' she said. 'Sounds as if we've got a lot to talk about tonight. But this idea of mine is only an idea at the moment. It will take some organizing. And then some time.' Barnard stood up abruptly, shrugged his coat on and pulled his trilby low over his eyes to cast a shadow over the bruises.

'I'll see you later,' he said. 'But I don't reckon I'll be home early. Sorry.' Kate wondered what exactly the apology was for.

She went to the counter and ordered herself a sandwich and a black coffee. She still felt hungover, her head ached and her memory of what had happened at the club the previous night seemed curiously patchy now. Almost as soon as Barnard had moved out of sight and she had barely started her lunch, she saw the door open and the man she knew only as Bob came into the cafe.

'I thought I might find you here,' he said, taking the chair beside her without asking permission.

'Soho's a small world,' she said. 'I saw you at the Late Supper Club last night. Did you enjoy it?'

'I wasn't really there for fun,' he said. 'I work in security and was trying to sell him something to keep the place safe. He doesn't seem to have been bothered by these attacks yet but I'm sure he's in someone's sights. But like a lot of these ex-army types he seems to think he can look after himself.'

'Right,' Kate said, thinking that there had been an unusual level of heat in Bob's conversation with Mercer and that she did not quite believe him.

'Did you enjoy your night out with the musicians?' Bob asked. 'You need to watch out for them. In films you get a part via the casting couch, don't you? In the music world I'm sure there's an equivalent. Maybe it's just sleeping with your agent if you want to get on.'

'Or the leader of the band,' Kate said with a laugh. 'I'm not even in the music business but I reckon I'm going to have to watch out for Jason Destry if I go to his party at the weekend.'

'He's having a party, is he?' Bob asked.

'At his new house in the country.' Kate finished her sandwich and pulled on her coat.

'Is he that dangerous?' Bob asked.

'Not really, I don't think,' Kate said. 'He just likes to think he is.' She grinned. 'Don't you all?' she asked.

'Some of us are as innocent as the driven snow,' Bob said, but Kate knew that he was not that.

'Must go,' she said. 'I've got a lot to get through this afternoon.'

'I'll see you around no doubt,' Bob said, and Kate wondered if she was imagining a note of anticipation in his voice.

'The boss is looking for you,' one of Barnard's colleagues relayed to him as soon as he had set foot in the CID office.

'Right,' Barnard said. 'I need to report back anyway.'

'And DI Watson wants you at the Grenadier. Must be nice to be so popular, Sarge.'

That was not exactly how Barnard would have described his current status and he knocked on the DCI's door with some trepidation and was not surprised when his boss looked shocked at the state he was in.

'What happened to you, Sergeant?' Jackson snapped.

'Just a stupid accident yesterday, guv,' Barnard said. 'I missed my footing on stairs and nearly knocked myself out. It had been a very bad day.'

'Well,' Jackson said. 'Did you get anything out of Ray Robertson's solicitor?'

'He's agreed to contact him,' Barnard said. 'He obviously has some knowledge of where he is and will get back to us today.'

'Give him until three this afternoon. If we haven't made any progress by then I'll talk to the Yard and see what they want to do next. Do you gather Robertson is still in the country?'

'I think so, guv,' Barnard said carefully. 'I took the time to go back to the East End to talk to his mother again but I was too late for that. She's apparently in hospital, possibly dying, and his old gym and his mother's house are due to be demolished imminently, which is no doubt why he's suddenly back in circulation, but there was no one around who would even know who I was looking for. The war started the demolition and the local councils are finishing it off.'

'Not before time,' Jackson said sourly. 'But it seems highly likely that someone who has run a protection racket in Soho in the past might try to start it up again and there are two deaths now probably linked to the campaign of violence which is going on. I've decided to put DI Watson in charge of both inquiries as it seems they may well be linked. And as you know more about Robertson and the area than anyone else, you can work with him on a continuing basis. We'll have the press breathing down our necks if we don't make some progress. The *Evening Standard* is already screaming blue murder about people being at risk in Soho and the others won't be far behind. The pubs and clubs and legitimate activities are already in turmoil and now the less acceptable trades will start to panic too given this new murder of the tart. Scotland Yard is not happy, as you can imagine. Make getting Ray Robertson into an interview room your priority and keep me in touch. We can't go on like this.'

'Sir,' Barnard said.

'Let me know as soon as you hear back from Robertson's solicitor, please. He's had long enough under the radar. We need to ask him where he's been and what he's been doing and whether or not he's working with anybody else to relaunch himself in Soho. If it takes a warrant to bring him in I'm sure the Yard will go along with it.'

'Is he a murder suspect?'

'He is if I say he is,' Jackson snapped.

'Right, guv,' Barnard said with what he hoped was enthusiasm, although he was relieved that the DCI's obsession with Robertson might prevent anyone inquiring too closely about Evie Renton's relationship with him. As far as he knew no one had remembered that and he devoutly hoped it would stay that way.

'And while you're about it you can ask the manager at the Delilah to let us know the next time he hears anything from his boss,' Jackson said. 'It must be possible that we can track his boss down through the club instead of his lawyer. I refuse to believe that with all that's going on Robertson won't put in a personal appearance sometime soon.'

'I'll get down to the Grenadier and talk to DI Watson,' Barnard said.

'Report back to me at the end of the day,' DCI Jackson said. 'I'll have discussed the cases with the Yard by then. They are looking for a quick result on this now. There's been enough mayhem on the streets. It's got to stop.'

Kate ventured cautiously into the dimly lit Delilah Club halfway through the afternoon and found it empty apart from three men in shirtsleeves sitting round a table close to the bar with drinks in front of them. Her memory of the place was fading slightly, but from the night of the gala she had attended, she recalled it as full of light and life and animated conversation, easily enough to impress a young woman not long out of college in the provinces and with little idea of how the upper reaches of London society lived. She had been blown away by the unexpected attentions of tall men in full evening dress, stunned by the elegance of the women in silks and satins and the glitter of jewellery, which she realized was highly likely to be genuine, and by the sheer volume of noise generated by wealthy Londoners at play. The pictures that she had browsed through in the agency's files from that evening had reminded her of the occasion, but they were in black and white and so the colour and sparkle of the event were missing; so too was the sheer intensity of the social atmosphere that had preceded the boxing match with its lavish overconsumption going on around her as soon as she had stepped through the glass doors.

She stood just inside the door of the club now taking in how dark and dingy and rundown the place looked when it was almost empty with the lights out in the middle of the day. If this had really been Ray Robertson's pride and joy when he had been riding high, it had certainly fallen out of favour. The men by the bar took no notice of her for a while, but eventually one man got up and crossed the floor towards her.

'Are you looking for someone, petal?' he asked, putting a hand on her arm. 'Is it a job you're after? Waitress, is it? They like the prettiest girls on the tables.'

'No, thanks,' she said. 'I'm looking for the manager.'

'Well, he's in his office,' the man said. 'What's it about then? I'll tell him if you like.'

'I'm a photographer and my boss wants me to take some pictures of the club. Publicity for this place and some of the other clubs in Soho, looking at how they've changed over the years, their history and all the well-known people who've used them. And this place has got more history than most.'

The man looked at her, she thought, as if she had turned into some sort of an alien species. If she had come in to ask about a job as a waitress or a cleaner he might have been able to handle it, but he was completely thrown by the fact that she might be capable of doing anything different.

'You only have to press a button to take a picture,' she explained, as if to a five-year-old. 'I actually did it a couple of years ago at one of the Robertson's boxing galas.'

'And they came out all right, did they?' he asked, still dubious.

Kate sighed in frustration. 'They did actually,' she said. 'Can I talk to the manager? I'm sure I can't do anything without his OK. I can show him some of the photographs I took back then at the gala. They appeared in several magazines and the *Daily Mail* when the Robertsons were all over the newspapers. I've brought some of them with me.'

'Well, I'll ask him if he's got time to talk to you. But I don't think he'll want to be bothered.' The man turned away and disappeared through a narrow door beside a low stage, leaving Kate standing close to the doors for so long that she eventually sat down at one of the tables until two men finally emerged. One was dressed mainly in black and Kate thought she vaguely recognized him – he headed quickly to the main door and left. The other man was in shirtsleeves, headed in her direction and took a seat opposite her.

'So what's all this about photographs?' he asked. 'I'm Derek Baker, the manager. I expect we do need some up-to-date publicity pictures, as it goes. The ones we've got are beginning to look a bit old fashioned. Is that what you want to do?'

'Not exactly,' Kate said. 'It's more a sort of picture history of the Soho clubs, going back to before the war when a lot of them got started and ending up with new ones like the Late Supper Club. They've always pulled in more than their fair share of famous people: writers, artists, actors and now rock stars . . . And some of the clubs themselves, like the Delilah and Ronnie Scott's, were famous themselves. I expect if you wanted to buy some pictures from my agency to use yourself that would be OK once they'd been used in a magazine or a newspaper. It would all be good publicity for you anyway.'

'I could only do this if Mr Robertson approved,' Barker said.

Kate took a sharp breath and realized that there was a flaw in her plan if Ray Robertson was not as far out of the picture as Harry Barnard seemed to believe. She was relieved that she had not told the manager her name.

'Right,' Kate said carefully. She took an agency business card out of her handbag and handed it to him. 'This is the agency I work for,' she said. 'Maybe you can talk to my boss there, Ken Fellows, if you want to know any more detail. He can explain better than I can, especially about how you could get hold of some of the pictures once they've been published. Now I'd best get on. I've got to work my way round quite a lot of places this afternoon. You don't have to join in. There are plenty of places to choose from.'

'I'll talk to your boss,' Barker said, and Kate recognized the frequent reluctance she met when men were faced with talking business with a woman.

'Yes, that will be fine,' she said, feeling relieved as she pulled her coat back on and got to her feet. 'Let Ken know what you decide.'

That, she thought as she pushed the doors open, was very nearly a disaster, and she determined that there was no way she would come back to take photographs here. In fact, she wondered if she could even risk telling Harry what she had done. He would not be pleased. But, she thought, he should have told her if Ray was back in London. She really did not want to meet him unexpectedly round some street corner.

She decided to go to the Late Supper Club next but as she walked towards Greek Street she noticed that the dark-haired man in a black coat who had left the Delilah not long before she did was heading in the same direction a few yards in front of her. She had been aware that she had seen him somewhere before and suddenly it came back to her. He had been in the Late Supper Club the night Dave Donovan had got himself thrown out, looking relaxed over dinner alone and apparently exchanging pleasantries with the manager, Hugh Mercer. Whoever he was, he seemed to be heading back to Mercer's new enterprise, and Kate decided that it might be sensible to postpone her visit until tomorrow and choose somewhere else to direct her inquiries this afternoon. In the meantime, she would take a quick shot of him to see if she could identify who he was. Barnard might know. Dodging into a shop doorway to disguise what she was doing, she waited for him to half turn in her direction, then spun on her heel and headed for Ronnie Scott's as an alternative and less contentious option. And there was another jazz club called the Marquee, which she had not been to before. The Late Supper Club could wait.

FOURTEEN

By the time Kate got back to Harry Barnard's flat that evening she was beginning to feel distinctly uneasy. She had reported back to Ken Fellows on the clubs she had visited but she had to admit that her reception had been at best lukewarm. She had heard nothing back from the Delilah's manager and the other three where she had outlined her project had not given the idea much of a welcome. She got the distinct impression that the problems in Soho caused by the increased criminal activity had already caused the managers sleepless nights and they did not much feel like drawing attention to themselves.

'I think we'll pass on that then,' the manager at a club in Wardour Street that she had never heard of said. 'In a couple of months maybe, when the police have got on top of what's going on. But not now. It would be a wasted effort. People are scared, which is exactly what these thugs intend.'

'I think he's right,' Ken Fellows said. 'It's a good idea but maybe not the right time. The fact that there's been another murder isn't good news. We'll keep it in mind and see how things stand after Christmas. OK?'

'I'd never heard of the Marquee Club,' Kate said. 'But they've had the Rolling Stones there and the Who and a lot of other rising stars, according to the manager.'

'He started off just promoting jazz at a place in Oxford Street,' Ken said. 'I used to go there in the fifties when they still had a lot of jazz bands around. Then he moved round the corner and seems to be going from strength to strength. It would be a good one to include if we do get this idea off the ground.'

'I didn't know you were a jazz fan.'

'I don't bother so much these days now rock and roll has taken over but the Marquee had all the trad jazz bands for a while – Chris Barber, Lonnie Donegan and Skiffle, even a few Americans as well when they managed to sort the musicians' unions out, and now he's moved on to the big rock and roll groups and the hit parade lads. It's a big place and pulls in big crowds.'

'Right,' Kate had said reluctantly, and put her pictures of the Delilah in its pomp back into the files. 'We'll have to wait for the clubs then.' It was up to Harry Barnard, she thought, to make the Soho clubs a safer proposition.

'Meanwhile, see what you can set up with these people,' Ken said, handing her some publicity about a new chain of fashion boutiques which were about to launch themselves from a base in Carnaby Street into shopping centres in other large cities. 'It's not urgent. You can leave it until after the weekend. But they're aiming at young men as well as the girls. Might be quite fun. A change from the mods and rockers.'

She set off for home early, knowing that Harry Barnard seldom had the time to pick her up after work with the current state of tension in Soho. She was happy enough to have some time to herself to cook a meal that she hoped he would be home in time to eat. She was annoyed to be approached by her persistent follower Bob as she left the office and even more irritated when he fell into step beside her as she headed for the Tube station at Tottenham Court Road.

'You again,' she said without slackening her pace.

'I saw you coming out of the Delilah earlier,' he said. 'Whatever were you doing in there? It's a pretty dodgy place these days.'

'Is it?' she said, quickening her pace. 'Why's that?'

'Surely you know about its history,' Bob said. 'It used to be run by two gangsters who made a big thing of throwing lavish parties and raising money for charity, or so they said. One of them's in jail now and the other's disappeared so it's anybody's guess where all the proceeds went.'

'I remember all that,' Kate said. 'I was here then. I took some photographs at one of their parties as it goes, la.'

'Really?'

'Yes, really,' Kate said, not hiding her irritation at his tone. 'That's what I do. I told you all this.' She had quickened her pace as she turned into Oxford Street and hurried through the crowds towards the Tube.

'I need to get home early tonight,' she said as she joined the queue to buy a ticket.

'Waiting for you, is he?' Bob asked. But he hesitated and then shrugged, though she was very conscious that he was still watching her as she set off down the escalator to the Northern Line. The man was becoming more than a nuisance, she thought.

'I'll see you around,' he said, and Kate could not tell whether that was a threat or a promise.

DS Barnard had already put his coat on thinking he might get home at a reasonable time after a run of late nights when the summons came to report to DCI Jackson's office. He cursed under his breath as he knocked on the door and knew as soon as he opened it that the presence of DI Fred Watson standing behind the DCI spelled nothing but trouble.

'Sir?' he said.

Jackson turned to Watson. 'I think this is your call,' he said. 'It concerns your case.' Watson's face was flushed and his expression unforgiving. 'So, Sergeant Barnard, could you tell me what the hell you think you are doing covering up the fact that you've been screwing this tart who's lying in the morgue?'

Barnard felt his mouth go dry and his heart rate speed up. 'That was a very long time ago,' he said carefully.

'So you don't deny it?' Jackson snapped.

Barnard shrugged. 'It happens,' he said.

'And you didn't worry about the conflict of interest when you marched into the crime scene when I had no idea you'd been in the sack with her?' Watson came back hard.

'I had no idea who the victim was at that point,' Barnard said. 'I should have told you when I realized. It was stupid of me.'

'Stupid? Or criminal?'

'Stupid, sir,' Barnard said quietly. 'I've known Evie Renton ever since I started working in Soho, ten years or more. I liked her. And I slept with her now and then. Show me a copper working in Vice who hasn't done that. But not recently, and once I recognized her I wanted to stay on the case. I wanted to know who did that to her.'

'And cover your own tracks?' Watson pressed.

'Because I knew her and she didn't deserve what happened to her,' Barnard said.

'You turn up here having obviously been in some sort of a

fight. How do we know that wasn't something which involved Evie Renton?' Watson snapped.

Jackson and Watson looked at each other for a moment and then Jackson nodded.

'Go home, Sergeant, and stay there until Monday. Then I want you in here at nine for a formal interview. I won't suspend you now but I will if I am not happy with what you tell me then.'

'And you can consider yourself off the Evie Renton murder case and likely to be facing a disciplinary at the very least,' Watson said.

Barnard looked at the two senior officers and could see no glimmer of sympathy there. He felt very tired and wondered how he was going to explain all this to Kate.

'Sir,' he said and spun on his heel, anxious to leave the remnants of his career securely shut behind Jackson's office door for now. The trouble he faced in Highgate loomed even larger than the crisis here and he did not think he would survive that either.

When he parked his car outside the flats, with very little recall of how he had got there, Barnard saw that the lights were on in his windows and there was no way of avoiding Kate or the necessity of explaining what had happened. Over the few years they had been together, they had had differences of opinion and Kate had on one occasion moved out and gone back to the flat she technically shared with Tess in Shepherd's Bush, but he knew that his present problems were in a different league from anything which had gone before. The decision he had taken when he recognized Evie's body had been professionally inexcusable, but the fact that he had maintained even a casual relationship with Evie while persuading Kate to sleep with him he knew she would find unforgivable. He might hang on to the vestiges of a career but he and Kate would be finished. She would not forgive him and he would not forgive himself.

She met him at the front door with a smile which faded quickly when she saw the expression on his face and how pale he was, the bruises he had acquired earlier in the day standing out in Technicolor across his cheek.

'What happened?' she asked. He turned away and hung up his hat and coat and she could see that his hands were shaking. 'Tell me,' she said, leading him into the living room and pouring him a drink. 'Whatever it is, tell me,' Kate said again.

Barnard sat down and took a slug of the neat spirit followed by a deep breath. 'The roof fell in,' he said. 'And it's all my own fault.'

'And?'

'I told you about the prostitute I knew being found dead?'

Kate nodded. 'You found her, you said.'

'DI Watson let me see if I could identify her when she was just a body lying in a dark alley.'

'And you did? Identify her?'

'Yes, and I knew her well enough to want to work on the case. Which I shouldn't have done because I knew her too well.'

Kate froze, her face as pale as his now and her breathing shallow. Barnard wanted to stop but knew he couldn't.

'Not often, not recently even, but I slept with her sometimes. It's not that unusual. But now she's a murder victim and the DCI and DI Watson are all over me like a rash. I've to be back at the nick on Monday morning for a formal interview and I guess I might be lucky to have a job at the end of the day. Or I might be a murder suspect . . .' He shrugged, looking as dispirited as Kate had ever seen him.

'Have you any idea who told your boss?'

'Have you any idea how long the list of people who hate my guts is?'

'Not least Ray Robertson,' Kate said. 'Why didn't you tell me he was back in London? It gave me a shock to see him in the street like that, and I saw the man he was with at the Delilah today.'

Barnard looked at her as if she had slapped his face, which he reckoned she was entitled to do, but not for the reason she seemed to have in mind.

'What's Ray got to do with this? Why were you at the Delilah anyway?'

'You're not the only one who's had a bad day,' Kate said bitterly. 'I persuaded Ken Fellows to let me research a picture feature on the Soho clubs – the new ones like the Late Supper Club and the ones that have been around for years like Ronnie Scott's and the jazz club in Wardour Street which I didn't even know existed.'

'Not a good time to launch that idea,' Barnard said.

'And the Delilah. I even took some pictures there when I first came to London. You remember?'

'Did you go there?' Barnard asked urgently. 'Was Ray there? Today?'

'No, no, he wasn't, but the manager said he's going to let him know what I'd like to do.'

'And that you're looking for him?'

Kate nodded. 'Though by the end of the day Ken had decided not to go ahead with the idea. None of the clubs were very willing to draw attention to themselves just now.'

Barnard took hold of her by the shoulders. 'Thank God for that,' he said. 'Listen, Kate. I did know Ray was back in London. I bumped into him at his mother's house and we had a blazing row. Where do you think I got these bruises? He's still good enough with his fists to put me on the floor. But I didn't want to frighten you by dredging that man up again after what happened the last time you saw him. If it was just the picture you took of him he might never find out about it but by now he'll know from the club manager you're looking for him through the agency so he'll assume I am too. Worse, he knows you're living here. You can't stay here any longer. You need to get out straight away. Ring Tess and tell her you need your bed back. It's an emergency and if that deadbeat Dave Donovan is still there he'll have to get on a train to Liverpool or sleep on the sofa tonight.'

He put a finger on her lips as she made to argue as he knew she would.

'The other stuff we'll have to sort out later,' he said, kissing her cheek. 'I'm sorry.'

'I'm sorry too,' Kate said with tears in her eyes.

'Pack what you need to take and I'll run you into town and get you a cab to take you to Shepherd's Bush. I won't take you all the way in case anyone is watching. My car's too bloody notice-able at times. I'll have to buy a Mini.'

'I'm not sure that's quite you,' Kate said with a faint smile.

'Will Tess be home now?' Barnard insisted.

She looked at her watch and nodded. 'She does her marking when she gets in and then sees the boyfriend later,' she said. 'I'll pack my stuff.' And she turned away with her eyes brimming with tears.

*   *   *

Kate woke up early, aware of every lump in the single bed in what had been her room when she and Tess had moved into the Shepherd's Bush flat. Dave Donovan had somewhat sulkily moved to the sofa in the living room, promising reluctantly that he would find out the times of trains to Liverpool in the morning. It was obvious that he was unwilling to leave and effectively give up on his search for Marie or his invitation to Jason Destry's house party that night. Kate lay on her back staring at watermarks on the ceiling, which had the appearance of a map but one full of meandering avenues that seemed to lead nowhere. Like her life, she thought, as the events of the previous night flooded back. Harry had parked his car in Soho Square and walked her back up to Oxford Street, which was still crowded with late shoppers and cinemagoers. He had hailed a taxi, put her suitcase beside the driver and hesitated with the passenger door open and an arm round her waist.

'I'm sorry,' he had said. 'Really, really sorry. One way or another, Ray Robertson will get his comeuppance. I promise.' And he had steered her into a seat, closed the door and given the driver Tess's address. 'I'll call you,' he had said to Kate through her open window, tempted to say more but knowing he had run out of credible promises. Kate very soon lost sight of him in the crowds.

She could see through the gap in the curtains that it was still early but she was dehydrated after crying herself to sleep and she soon got out of bed and searched through her hastily packed suitcase to find her dressing gown before venturing into the living room. Dave Donovan did not stir as she opened the kitchen door and filled the kettle. She rooted through Tess's cupboards but could only find instant coffee, so opted for a tea bag and a substantial mug with plenty of sugar, which she carried carefully back to her bedroom. It was half past seven and she guessed that neither Dave nor Tess would be very energetic on a Saturday morning.

By the time there was a tap on her door she felt more in control and had decided what to do with the weekend which Harry had made very clear was not to include any contact with him or Soho or – most importantly – Ray Robertson or any of his enterprises.

'Is that you, Tess? Come in,' she called, and her friend put her head round the door.

'You got tea, I see?'

'Harry's weaned me on to coffee, but it has to be real coffee, Italian style.'

'And how am I going to wean you off Harry?' Tess came back quickly and seriously. 'You know I always thought it would end in tears.'

'Don't let's do "I told you so",' Kate begged. 'It won't work because I honestly don't know what's going on. But if he thinks I'm at risk, he's in a position to know what he's talking about and I'd be a fool not to listen to him.'

'But why should you be at risk?' Tess came back angrily.

'You know why,' Kate snapped back. 'You were at risk yourself when we lived in Notting Hill, or have you forgotten the flat which got set on fire? There are some seriously bad people in London just like there are in Liverpool. It's just that Harry Barnard has to deal with them every day. He has to get close to them just like I'm close to him – or was.' Kate looked on the verge of tears again. Tess sat beside her on the bed and put an arm round her.

'And how long do you think you can stay close to Harry? It sounds as if he's in a load of trouble himself now.'

Kate sighed and did not reply directly. 'I'll stay out of the way over the weekend. We'll go to Jason Destry's party tonight if you like,' she said. 'He won't mind you coming too. He invited me and Dave. And we'll be well out of Harry's way. But on Monday I have to go to work in Soho so Harry will have to get used to that idea. There's no alternative, is there?'

'If he seriously thinks you're in danger it's up to him to get his mates to keep you safe,' Tess said in an uncompromising tone. 'If he can't manage it himself it's up to him to call in the troops, isn't it? It's what they're there for.'

'Maybe,' Kate said, knowing that it was more complicated than that. But she didn't want to fill Tess in on Harry's other problems and she was pleased to hear a bellowing noise from the living room where Dave Donovan had apparently been sleeping soundly in spite of the conversation in the next room.

'He's awake,' she said.

'Evidently,' Tess said. 'I expect he thinks we'll get him some breakfast. But he'll be unlucky. I'm all out of bacon and eggs and black pudding. That may be what his mammy lays on for him but I don't have much more than cornflakes myself. What about you?'

'Cornflakes would be fine,' Kate said with a grin.

'I'd really like to get him on a train back to Lime Street today if I could,' Tess said. 'I said three nights and he's had those now. He's only half civilized.'

'Not up to Wirral standards, then?' Kate mocked, knowing the insult had less bite here than closer to the Mersey.

'My mother wouldn't give him house room,' Tess admitted.

'Well, I don't think you'll stop him staying for Destry's party. He'll need something to tell the other members of the band when he gets home. Especially if he goes back without Marie.'

'The mysterious Marie,' Tess said. 'Do you think she's real or did he just make her up so he could come down here and find out what we were getting up to? He always carried a torch for you, Katie. Maybe he just wanted to see you again.'

'I don't think my personality is as magnetic as that,' Kate said. 'No, I'm sure Marie is real, but where she's hiding herself, and why, I haven't a clue.'

FIFTEEN

Harry Barnard woke late and for a fleeting moment wondered why Kate had got up so early on a Saturday. Then he remembered that the empty place beside him harboured a bleak fact: he had sent Kate away, fearing a threat from Ray Robertson who was clearly in a mood to draw the worst conclusion from her incautious visit to the Delilah. Unaware of the risks, she had handed Ray a new way to get at Barnard – a way he would not hesitate to use if it suited him. How long, he wondered, would the Robertson brothers blight his life and threaten his career? The DCI obviously did not believe him when he told him he would not hesitate to arrest Ray if the opportunity arose, and Jackson probably never had believed him and probably never would. The major problem anyway with that scenario was that he guessed the opportunity was very unlikely to arise again. He had missed what might be his last chance to extricate himself from the assumption that he was in Robertson's pocket and had been ever since he was a kid.

Reluctantly he got up, had a shower and examined his bruises carefully in the mirror to work out how quickly they were fading and whether they would allow him to look reasonably civilized on Monday morning, to which the only answer could be not nearly fast enough. He brewed strong coffee to kick himself into life again, and by the middle of the morning he had driven into the West End, parked in Soho Square, well away from the nick, and was strolling down Frith Street as if he had not a care in the world, though with his trilby still pulled down low over his eyes to conceal the damage Ray Robertson had inflicted.

He soon felt the need for more coffee and he slipped into the Blue Lagoon where he and Kate often had lunch, and he wondered whether hanging around in territory they had shared so often was a good idea, but he signalled to the waitress at the counter to refill his cup. The place was almost empty, but even on a quiet Saturday morning the coffee was good and strong. He sat close to the window for a long time with his second empty cup in front of him, until eventually it dawned on him that he had limited time to play with if he was to present a credible case to DCI Jackson and DI Watson on Monday, so he abruptly got up to go, still not quite sure where to turn next.

Kate O'Donnell had pulled some clothes on quickly before joining Tess for cornflakes, wondering if she could persuade Dave on to a train heading north before the day was over. It was obvious from the tense silence round the breakfast table that Tess was becoming increasingly impatient at his obsessive anxieties about Marie and, although Kate was more sympathetic, she had little hope that they would succeed in tracking her down.

'I think we should go out, Dave,' she said. 'We could have one last try at Marie's agent to see whether she's been in touch and if not you could get a train from Euston and be home this afternoon.'

'You're forgetting we have a party to go to tonight,' Dave said, his expression determined. 'I'm not going to miss that.'

'Are you sure you want to bother?' Kate asked but she could see from Donovan's face that he had no intention of missing Jason Destry's housewarming, obviously looking forward to the name-dropping he could indulge in on Merseyside as some consolation for being dumped – if that is what had happened – by his girlfriend. Kate gave Tess a despairing look knowing that meant he would want to stay another night on the sofa.

'Come on,' she said. 'Let's go and see if Marie's made any contact with Jack Mansfield. He was supposed to have some news for her so maybe she got in touch in the end. If she was going to talk to anyone it would have to be him. It's worth checking.'

'I suppose,' Donovan said with the expression of a sulky toddler denied another ice cream which would probably make him sick.

'Give me ten minutes,' Kate said and, seeing the desperation in Tess's eyes, she was even faster than that. If she wasn't careful Dave's unwelcome presence would end a friendship which had lasted since she and Tess had been at college together and she did not see why she should be punished in that way over Dave Donovan's bad luck with women. Her own experience with him had shown her just how pig-headed he could be.

Barely speaking to each other, they took the Tube into the West End and by ten o'clock they had arrived at the now-familiar office in Denmark Street which Kate was relieved to find had lights on even on a Saturday morning.

'Someone's in,' she said, pushing open the door and setting off up the narrow stairs.

'Right,' Donovan said ominously and followed, but when they reached Mansfield's agency and pushed open the door, the receptionist's chair was empty.

'Someone's in the other office,' Kate said, aware of a voice she took to be the agent's beyond the frosted glass in the door. Donovan banged impatiently at the door and pushed it open to find Mansfield at his desk. He spun towards them and looked distinctly unwelcoming as he put his hand over the telephone receiver he was holding.

'You again,' he said. 'What do you want now?'

'The same thing we wanted the last time,' Donovan said, pushing in front of Kate. 'Is there any sign of Marie – Ellie, you're calling her – since we were here last? Did she get back to you to talk about her showreel? Did someone really like her stuff? She'll be made up if that's true. She's not likely to miss her chance.'

'Wait outside a minute while I finish this call,' Mansfield said reluctantly, though it was much more than a minute he took, and Mansfield was shouting down the phone and Donovan was becoming distinctly agitated on the landing outside before the agent finally opened his office door again and called them back in.

'So what's going on, whack?' Donovan said, not hiding his anger. 'Where the hell's my girl? You say you saw her and no one else has seen her since. I reckon the bizzies will be interested in that, don't you? Girls can't come to London and then just vanish into thin air, can they? That's no kind of a carry-on.'

Kate put a hand on Donovan's shoulder in the hope of calming him down as Mansfield's already flushed features reddened into an expression of fury.

'I'm not responsible for what these little slappers do in their own time,' he said. 'I listen to their music and tell them more often than not that it's rubbish and they go off to bend some other sodding agent's ear. But I didn't with this one – Ellie, Marie, whatever you want to call her – I told her she had potential and in the end I found a record label which agreed with me. She's the one who's sold us short, disappeared on us, so I look like a fool and the label won't bother to put my tape on the machine another time. If the artistes behave like that we all lose in the end.'

'So you've still not heard from her, Mr Mansfield?' Kate asked, trying to calm the discussion down.

'That's what I'm saying, girl,' he shot back.

'Then I think we really do need to report her missing to the police. Don't you think so, Dave? It's been too long?'

Donovan turned away from Mansfield with a look of pure despair. 'OK,' he said, his shoulders slumped. 'Let's do that.'

They left Mansfield delving into his desk drawer, pulling out a bottle of Scotch and pouring himself a serious glassful as they closed his office door behind them. The secretary's place was still empty but as they retreated down the scruffy staircase the girl who had been at the desk the last time they had been here met them halfway up.

'You again?' she said. 'Haven't you found Ellie Fox yet then?'

'No sign of her,' Kate said.

'She's probably decided it's easier to be a groupie than a singer, you get all the benefits of being one of the gang and none of the hard work. Unless you count taking your knickers off as hard work.'

'She's not a slapper,' Donovan said angrily. 'She was – is – ambitious. She wants to sing.'

'But how long would it take her to earn what one of the big groups like the Kinks or the Rainbirds are earning on her own? I did hear that Jason Destry puts himself about a bit. And some of his group are from Liverpool. Maybe she's joined Jason's big happy family.'

Donovan pushed past the two women and stormed out of the door into Denmark Street.

'He's in love,' Kate said with a grin, and followed him out.

'Come on,' she said. 'We'll go to Destry's party tonight and ask around. And if we don't have any luck there we'll report her missing to the police. I'll talk to Harry later and see what he thinks. But we'll have to take Destry up on his offer of a lift to his place.

It's somewhere way out in the country. We'll need to check it out. Is that a plan? Kevin gave me a phone number to ask where the car is going from. That makes sense, doesn't it?'

'I suppose,' Donovan said.

In the event it turned out that Barnard's place by the window in the Blue Lagoon gave him a ringside view of the passers-by who had not been deterred by the area's rapidly sinking reputation and the heavy policing by uniformed officers, and it wasn't long before he spotted Vince Beaufort walking smartly in the direction of Soho Square. He tapped on the window to attract his attention. Vincent spun towards him with unexpected nervousness and only relaxed slightly when he had peered through the glass and recognized the sergeant. He raised his hand in greeting and, after looking up and down the street, carefully pushed open the door.

'Flash,' he said. 'What are you doing here on a Saturday morning?'

'Trying to track down anyone who knows what's going on at the Delilah these days,' he said, glancing around the half-empty cafe and deciding it was impossible for anyone to overhear them with the coffee machine hissing vigorously.

'Really?' Beaufort said. 'It's a bit of a mystery, that place. People keep saying that Ray Robertson is still in charge but there's not much sign of it. It's getting very rundown. And now he's got competition from the new club just round the corner, that's pulling in a different class of punters with plenty of money to spend.'

'So I hear,' Barnard agreed. 'It's a cut above the Delilah in some ways but what's really the big attraction? Rock stars drinking there?'

Beaufort gave him a sideways look. 'They're not letting the young kids in any more, evidently, apart from the poor girl who fell out of the window. So it's what the rock stars get up to more likely,' he said.

'Drugs?' Barnard asked quietly, and Beaufort gave an almost imperceptible nod.

'Drugs and girls. You're not surprised, are you?'

'Not particularly,' Barnard said. 'The level of violence and intimidation that's going on has to be motivated by something substantial. There've been three deaths now, if you include the kid at the Late Supper Club. Someone's looking for a very big profit out of Soho that they're not getting at the moment. It can only be drugs, but I need some evidence and nobody is talking to me.'

'I was sorry to hear about Evie,' Beaufort said. 'But you can't be surprised no one will talk. It's as if these bastards are fastening on to every group, one by one, so everyone knows someone who's been hurt or threatened. Nobody's feeling safe. It's like the Italian Mafia. They take over whole villages and towns . . .'

Barnard froze. 'How come you know so much about the Mafia?' he asked.

Beaufort shrugged. 'My mother was Italian,' he said. 'From the south.'

'So, what about that tall, dark fellow you told me about who's suddenly appeared on the scene? Could he be Italian?'

'Minelli? He's dark enough, and the name's Italian,' Vince agreed. 'But what about the other face I told you about that I hadn't seen before? I've noticed he's been chatting your girlfriend up once or twice. Here in the Blue Lagoon, as it happens. You'd better ask her who he is. He looked quite attentive.' Beaufort gave Barnard a not very sympathetic smile as he got up to go. 'You're not making any progress on the Grenadier murder then? Len Stevenson was a good man. And poor Evie. What did she do to deserve that?'

'We're working on it,' Barnard said irritably, knowing that the attackers descended on innocent people like an armed platoon and withdrew just as quickly and anonymously, leaving no evidence of the slightest significance behind. Unless the police had information in advance there was very little chance of their being caught at all, least of all red-handed, and Soho would slide into a lawless jungle like parts of New York.

He watched Vincent Beaufort slide effortlessly back into the slowly increasing number of strollers drifting between the pubs and cafes and sex traders outside on the street as business began to pick up as the day went on, and decided that if there was to be any breakthrough on these cases which could conceivably make a difference for him on Monday morning, he would have to be more proactive. He finished his coffee and made his way to an unfashionable pub on the corner of a narrow mews close to Berwick Street Market, which drew in the punters from all over London looking for exotic food and drink that had not yet percolated to the suburbs, but which provided the staples for the disciples of Elizabeth David's popular Continental cookery books. His quarry, Joe Inglot, was sitting at a corner table with a couple of fellow drinkers who could have been his brothers or cousins so similar were they with their dark-eyed and sallow-skinned Mediterranean looks. Inglot looked up when Barnard walked in and did not look pleased to see him.

'A word, Joe,' Barnard said in a tone which did not leave any room at all for his quarry to argue. 'Outside, if you like.'

Inglot extricated himself with a scowl from the group and followed Barnard on to the pavement outside the pub where waste vegetables were strewn in the gutter.

'You will get me into bad trouble, Sergeant Barnard, if people think I am in your pocket.'

'In this case it won't damage your reputation, Joe, if you reckon you've got one, which I doubt. I want you to take a message to your boss.'

'The Man?' Inglot did not look the least bit reassured by that explanation.

'Your man, Falzon,' Barnard said. 'I need to talk to him. Can you pass that on? And get back to me as soon as you can? But not at the nick. I'll give you a phone number where you – or he – can contact me this evening. Tell him it's in his interests. A brief word, is all.'

Inglot was staring at Barnard as if mesmerized, but in the end he jerked his head in what Barnard took to be consent and took the piece of paper on which he had written down his home number. Barnard knew he was taking what was probably a ludicrous risk, but he could see no alternative. If something did not change soon there would be no justice for the murdered barman Len Stevenson, or for the nameless teenager who had fallen from the top window of the Late Supper Club, or for his old friend and former lover Evie, who had been viciously beaten and stabbed and dumped to die in a back alley apparently to encourage the other girls to do as they were told. If that was the future then he thought he might as well resign now as wait for DCI Jackson to sack him because the game was no longer worth the candle.

He turned back towards the busier streets, telling himself that what he was doing was no more than he used to do when times were more normal and violence sporadic but far less aggressive than the tactics being used by the marauding gangs who now seemed to want to take over the streets and businesses of Soho completely. Whoever was coordinating the campaign seemed to be using random murder as a weapon, and that Barnard had never seen before.

Approaching the Delilah, he abruptly slowed down and half turned to study the window display of a bookshop which he knew concealed its more blatant pornography underneath the counter. Ahead of him he recognized the tall, black-clad figure of the man people called Minelli pushing open the doors of the club and making his way inside. Barnard's first instinct was to follow him and take him by surprise, but he decided it might be more useful to tackle whoever he had gone inside to talk to, most likely the manager Derek Baker, who would not be too surprised that he was following up on his earlier inquiries about Ray Robertson's whereabouts. He took refuge in a cafe opposite the club, ordered yet more coffee and took a seat where he could watch the club doors easily.

He did not have to wait long. Minelli left the Delilah no more than ten minutes after he went in, and Barnard was through the doors almost before they had stopped swinging. He found Baker sitting close to the bar with a whisky on the table in front of him and a phone clamped to his ear. He was obviously annoyed to see Barnard and hung up quickly.

'What the hell do you want, Sergeant?' he asked incautiously.

Barnard took the chair across the table from him. 'I happened to see Mr Minelli coming out a few minutes ago and wondered what he was doing here. He seems to be putting himself about a lot at the moment and I wondered if he was working for Ray Robertson. Would that be a good guess?'

'It would be about as far from the truth as you're likely to get,' Baker said angrily.

'So can you tell me why he was here?'

'I think that's none of your business,' Baker said. 'But he wanted to discuss something with Mr Robertson and I had to tell him that's not likely to happen any time soon. Mr Robertson's mother has just died and I don't think he is likely to want to be discussing business propositions until after the funeral.'

'Aah,' Barnard said, 'I knew she was very ill in hospital.'

'Did you? That's more than I did. But then I'm just a dogsbody round here.'

'I know the feeling,' Barnard said with a wry smile. 'I'll send your boss a sympathy card.' But he knew he wouldn't, not least because he had not a clue where the elusive Ray Robertson was staying and while his solicitor probably did he would not be available on a Saturday morning. More to the point, even if he tracked him down the solicitor would be very likely to complain to the DCI or even to Scotland Yard about such an uncalled-for request.

He left Derek Baker refilling his whisky glass behind the bar and decided that now he had breached the defences of one club he might as well try another, especially as he recalled that Kate had seen Minelli looking quite at home having a meal at the Late Supper Club. It was a short walk down Old Compton Street to the new club and again Barnard was slightly surprised to find the club which he knew did not swing into action until relatively late in the evening already had its outer door open on to the street. He went up the stairs two at a time and pushed open the door into the reception area where to his surprise he found Hugh Mercer deep in what looked like a perfectly amicable discussion with Minelli himself. Both men turned in his direction with what could only be described as deeply unfriendly expressions.

'Sergeant Barnard,' Mercer said. 'What are you doing here?'

'I was just going over my notes last night and there were one or two supplementary questions I found that I need to ask you, sir.'

'Really?' Mercer said with every appearance of disbelief. 'They must be important if you've taken the trouble to come round on a Saturday?'

'I happened to be passing,' Barnard lied. He glanced directly at Minelli and nodded in recognition. 'We seem to be following each other from club to club. Are you in the entertainment trade as well, sir? You must be as worried as most people in Soho at the crime wave we seem to be experiencing.'

'I am sure the Metropolitan Police will sort it out,' Minelli said with an accent which Barnard identified immediately as Italian with a superficial overlay of East London. But it was distinctive and he was sure that if it had to be identified by witnesses it could be. But Minelli was obviously anxious to leave. He and Mercer shook hands and the visitor spun on his heel and hurried down the stairs to the street door without looking back.

'So what are these questions, Sergeant?' Mercer snapped. 'Could they not have waited until Monday? You haven't identified the dead girl, have you?'

'I'm a bit preoccupied on Monday, sir,' Barnard said. 'But one of your clients who was here the night the girl fell said she saw a small bag on a chair for some time that night – flowery satin, she said it was, mainly pink and slightly childish in style, she thought, given your clientele. She wondered if it had been found later and could belong to the girl who it's been suggested could have been called Jackie.'

'Jackie?' Mercer said. 'Who told you that?'

'One of Jason Destry's friends,' Barnard said flatly. 'I've also been told that the girl spent some time with him and his colleagues – musicians, essentially . . .'

'This all sounds like hearsay if not pure fantasy to me, Sergeant, don't you think?' Mercer snapped back.

'Not necessarily,' Barnard said. 'Somebody must have brought the girl in and I've no evidence on which to rule out Destry and his friends. Do you?'

'Do I what? Have evidence? No, of course I don't. If I had any clue who the girl was or who brought her in I would have told you days ago.'

'Right,' Barnard said, although the more Mercer protested innocence the less inclined he was to believe him. He was sure that any self-respecting and even barely competent club manager in Soho would have made it his business to find out for himself how such a devastating breach of security had happened, even if only to protect his licence from close scrutiny by the magistrates.

'Well, the other thing you might help me with is some background on the man you were talking to when I came in, sir. He calls himself Minelli, I understand, but I've not been able to find out what he does for a living. He looks pretty prosperous. Is he in the club business, or some similar trade? Yours isn't the only club I've seen him in recently.' Barnard saw Mercer wince at the word trade but he evaded the question.

'He was asking about the availability of tables next weekend,'

Mercer said. 'He wanted to bring a party but I couldn't accommodate him. We are pretty well fully booked for dinner, I'm pleased to say.'

'So he's merely a client?'

'He's merely a client, Sergeant,' Mercer said. 'Apart from his appreciation of my chef and my wine cellar I know nothing at all about him.'

Wondering if he had been wasting his time, Barnard made his way slowly back up Frith Street feeling very little wiser from his inquiries and certainly no more confident that he would survive his interview on Monday professionally unscathed. Not far from the Blue Lagoon he was stopped in his tracks by a cry which was much more of a scream than a shout. The voice was female and the outcry did not decrease. In fact, it intensified and became shriller as Barnard began to run towards it. Just beyond the Blue Lagoon he found a group of women surrounding another who was writhing on the pavement.

'What's happened?' he asked, grabbing one of the spectators whose face seemed familiar. 'Gracie, isn't it?' She nodded, her face white under its make-up and her eyes still horrified.

'Someone ran past and threw something over Marilyn,' the woman said. 'We were talking about Evie . . .'

One by one, Barnard recognized the women as some of the so-called working girls who had evidently assembled earlier than normal. Barnard knelt down beside the injured woman.

'Have you sent for an ambulance?' he asked, recognizing the telltale smell of bleach. 'Go into the cafe and get some cold water,' he said. 'And call an ambulance now. Use their phone. If this stuff has gone into her eyes she could be blinded.' Cursing under his breath, he grabbed hold of the jug of water someone thrust into his hands and tipped it over the woman's face and hair, making sure plenty of it washed out her eyes thoroughly by forcing the lids apart. Gradually her cries of pain diminished to wracking sobs. To his relief the ambulance arrived within minutes and he explained what had happened to the ambulancemen who rushed to assist. He flashed his warrant card and told them he would stay with the witnesses to find out whatever he could about the incident and watched as Marilyn was helped into the ambulance and driven away.

He turned quickly to the women who were still standing in an appalled group just outside the Blue Lagoon.

'Did you see exactly what happened?' he asked.

'Two men came hurrying towards us, walking fast,' Gracie said. 'I told you, we were talking about what happened to Evie. I wanted the girls to come with me to the nick to find out what was happening – of course you're a copper, aren't you? I thought I recognized you.'

'Saturday night's not the best time to talk to people at the nick,' Barnard said. 'They'll be busy. There was a big football game this afternoon. Anyway, I'll need statements from all of you after this. It's an escalation. I've not heard of anyone using bleach or acid in that way before, have you? Did you see their faces?'

'They had thick scarves pulled up.'

'Give me your names and addresses and I'll get someone to come round and talk to you all as soon as they can. In the meantime, I'll go up to Casualty, make sure Marilyn is OK and get the beat coppers to look out for the attackers.'

'Can't you do anything to stop these bastards? We can't go on like this?' Gracie asked, her voice shaking with emotion.

'I know,' Barnard said, wondering if that did not go for him as well.

Marilyn was still in Casualty when he pushed his way through the swing doors and tracked her to a cubicle where she was propped up on the bed, leaning against pillows with a young doctor examining the red burns around her eyes. Barnard introduced himself with his warrant card and the doctor glared at him as if he had thrown the noxious liquid himself.

'I've never come across anything like this before,' he said. 'She could have lost her sight. What the hell's going on?'

'The girls reckon it's a punishment because they're not willing to pay protection money to these thugs. They're not the only people being attacked. One girl has already been found dead.'

The doctor looked at Barnard in disbelief. 'She's lucky then, I suppose,' he said, nodding in Marilyn's direction. 'But I want to keep her in overnight to see an eye specialist in the morning. I'm not really qualified to discharge her off my own bat.'

'That's fine by me,' Barnard said. 'We'll need witness statements from all the women who were involved in the attack. There were half a dozen of them but whoever chucked the liquid wasn't a very good bowler. Marilyn was the only one he caught full-on.'

'Perhaps it was me he was aiming for,' Marilyn said, her voice hoarse as if she had breathed in whatever had drenched her. 'There's some mad bastards out there.'

'I'll get someone to come in to see you in the morning,' Barnard said. 'You'll be safe here for tonight.'

'I hope so,' she said, although she did not sound totally convinced, and Barnard knew as he turned away that his chances of getting a working girl serious protection in the West End on a busy Saturday night were practically non-existent.

SIXTEEN

I t was gone eight o'clock before Barnard parked his car outside his block of flats in Highgate and the darkness inside reminded him forcibly that Kate was not there although he guessed that she would probably be waiting for a phone call. After seeing Marilyn safely transferred to a ward to await more specialist treatment the next day, he had gone back to the nick and reported what he told the control room was an accidental involvement in the assault on the angry prostitutes in Frith Street and handed over all the details he had of their furious reaction to the death of Evie Renton.

'You're sure this was the gang which is smashing up the pubs and cafes?' the duty inspector asked. 'It wasn't just some disgruntled punter who didn't get what he thought he'd paid for off Marilyn?'

'The description of the men – two of them this time – sounded much the same as we've been told about at the Grenadier and at other crime scenes,' Barnard said impatiently. 'I told the women we would want witness statements and they didn't have any objections. They're seriously worried. Worried enough to ask for help for once.'

'Right, I'll see it's followed up,' the inspector promised. 'Throwing acid is certainly novel.'

'It could be lethal and it'll put the fear of God into the street girls, especially after Evie Renton,' Barnard snapped over his shoulder as he left feeling weary and anxious to get home. But when he got there he sat in his car for several minutes before turning off the engine and opening the door. He wished that he could have gone out to Shepherd's Bush to see Kate, but knew that would be a reckless move. And in a split second, as he fumbled with his keys at the front entrance to the building, he realized just how dangerous his life, and potentially Kate's, had become. A sliver of sound, no more than an incautiously indrawn breath just behind him, made him spin round just as something hard and heavy hit him across the back of the head and he fell forwards. After that there was nothing but darkness.

He came round with a thumping headache to find someone trying to pour what felt like neat alcohol down his throat. He was lying prone on a sofa in a comfortably furnished room which he did not recognize, and when he managed to focus on the two men who were effectively holding him still with his hands pushed behind his back, he did not recognize them either. He took a deep breath but lacked the energy to speak until he had succeeded in spitting out most of the liquor which had been forced into his mouth, almost choking him.

He felt rather than saw a door on the far side of the room open and a third figure come in. His eyes slowly focused and he was able to recognize who had entered the room. It was only then that he began to make sense of what had happened – and was still happening – to him. His instant relief began to slowly damp down the cold fear that had paralysed him when he first came round.

'Mr Falzon,' he said, his voice little more than a whisper. 'I would have come if your people had asked nicely.'

'Perhaps,' Frankie Falzon said, switching on the main lights and taking a seat in a comfortable armchair close to Barnard, crossing one careful leg over the other and adjusting the crease. His suit was fashionable, his silver tie immaculate and his shoes gleaming, and Barnard guessed that he must have been brought to Falzon's large house somewhere in Mill Hill. 'The Man', as he was generally known among the Maltese, looked older than when Barnard had last seen him in an angry exchange with Ray Robertson, and he sat down with what looked like an ill-concealed wince in a seat facing the sergeant, almost knee to knee.

'I doubt if you would have accepted my offer of a lift without a struggle,' Falzon said. He turned to the two men who had attacked Barnard. 'You can let him go now, just wait outside.' The speed at which they obeyed him said all it needed to about the Man's dominance.

The Maltese looked much as he had when Barnard had last seen him in the flesh. Not tall, maybe a little broader round the waist, his hair slightly more silver, a grandfatherly figure on the surface, his face benign apart from the eyes which were as cold, if not colder, than Barnard remembered them. He guessed that the two men who had been sent to pick him up would face consequences for hitting him harder than Frankie Falzon apparently intended. He knew that the blow could have killed him. It was a tiny crack in Falzon's armour and one that he knew the Maltese would undoubtedly punish. He had little doubt that Falzon would kill if it suited him, but he would see the murder of a serving police officer as several steps too far unless he regarded it as absolutely necessary.

'Sit up, Sergeant,' he said irritably. Barnard eased himself into a sitting position with difficulty, knowing that Falzon would be happy enough to have him at a disadvantage. 'And now tell me how I can help you, if that's what you want. I did hear that you and Ray Robertson are not as close as you once were.'

Barnard tried to mask the surprise which he was sure was obvious on his face, but his head was not yet able to cope with subtlety.

'We were schoolfriends,' he said. 'But those things don't last forever. We went in different directions.'

'And you helped convict his brother?'

'Yes,' Barnard said. 'One of the better things I've done over the years. Georgie was always a bit crazy.'

'So how can I help you now?'

'There's a growing concern over drugs,' Barnard said carefully. 'A young girl died after falling out of a window – you probably heard that. We haven't even been able to identify her yet, but we know she'd taken a cocktail of illegal substances. What's going on is growing more common and there are two people around who I can't place: a man calling himself Minelli and another who identifies himself almost exclusively as Bob. No surname.'

'And you want to know if I have any connection with them?'

Barnard nodded, which sent another spasm of pain through his skull. 'Is Minelli Maltese?' he asked.

'Not as far as I know,' Falzon said flatly. 'The name could be Italian. Many Italians came here to work after the war. But on the whole they prefer to run grocery shops than anything illegal. I have never regarded the Italians as a particular threat of competition here. Although they are well organized in Sicily and Calabria as you probably know. Perhaps they have ambitions in

London but I am not aware of that. Although there seem to be people in London now who seem to be as ruthless as the Sicilians are reputed to be.'

'So Minelli is not one of yours?'

'Definitely not,' Falzon said.

'And the other one?'

'Bob, you say? I have no idea. I am still working mainly with the girls, sticking to the agreement I have with your schoolfriend Robertson not to tread on anyone's toes. I have no desire to sell drugs. No desire at all. But I have not spoken to Ray Robertson for months.'

'No one has,' Barnard said. 'But I was told today that his mother has died.'

'Ah,' Falzon said, crossing himself. 'I too lost my mother recently.' For a moment, Falzon almost aged visibly before he gave himself a shake and seemed to return to the conversation, reluctantly. 'I do know that the rising trade in drugs is causing your colleagues at Scotland Yard some concern. I'm told they are planning to set up a special unit to clamp down on drugs, new ones as well as marijuana and heroin, the old staples. There is instability in Soho suddenly, as you know, threats and even murder. That is not good for my trade. It tends to keep the customers away.'

Barnard knew better than to ask how Falzon came to be privy to information from the Yard which few in the local police stations had access to, though in his experience this was not unusual. And he wondered whether the new unit being set up to tackle drugs would be quite as amenable to the sort of accommodations which had been current for years between Falzon and the Robertson brothers and some senior officers in the force. Now he had met DI Jamieson, an ambitious young man with his eyes firmly focused on his own career and the expanding drug trade, he doubted if relationships would be as cosy as they had previously been. The new drug squad would want to do well and be seen to be doing well and the effects would be felt by the rest of the force as well as the crooks moving into the area with their new products and customers evidently ready and willing to try them. Jamieson would have mixed feelings about the trade: the dealers' expanding market was a possibly lethal threat to users but a beckoning opportunity for him to shine.

Barnard looked at the man who sat so close to him that he could see the blood pulsing at his temple and realized that Falzon was very ill and that he knew himself that he was very ill. If he lost his grip on his empire with Ray Robertson's attention already apparently fading, the current uncertainty around Soho could only grow and violence increase as their successors fought for a legacy from their predecessors' power and profits. How many more deaths might follow, Barnard hardly dare imagine.

'Can I ask you a favour?' Barnard asked, suddenly feeling very tired.

'You can ask, Sergeant,' Falzon said, though without much sign of enthusiasm.

'Will you talk to Ray Robertson? You've rubbed along together for years without too much friction. Can't you discuss how you might get along together for a bit longer, just long enough to see if you can hold these newcomers off between you until we've got on top of the drug problem and the violence? It would be doing everyone a favour.'

Falzon did not reply for a moment, the chilly eyes inscrutable, and Barnard was about to dismiss his own suggestion as an ill-advised joke when the Maltese nodded almost imperceptibly and his face sagged again into a picture of old age.

'Find out when his mother's funeral is,' Falzon whispered, his voice faltering. 'Let me know and I will be there to pay my respects.'

'Are you sure?' Barnard asked.

'I'm sure,' Falzon said.

Barnard still hesitated for a moment as possible disastrous consequences swirled through his imagination like bad dreams.

'No violence?' Barnard asked.

'We are not savages,' Falzon said, getting to his feet with obvious difficulty and turning to the door. 'My men will take you home.'

He did not look back.

A convoy of large and comfortable limousines had travelled in close formation through south London from their gathering point close to the offices of the Rainbirds' agent in Charlotte Street without excessive speed or fuss. Kevin Dunne had told them where to wait when Kate rang him, although she hesitated before she

dialled, thinking for a moment that the number seemed familiar
although she could not remember why, and after the initial excitement on Dave Donovan's part at experiencing the sort of luxury
Bentleys and Jags offered, they both settled down to enjoy what
the driver had said would be a three-quarters-of-an-hour drive to a
village close to Godalming. It was there that Jason Destry had
bought his house and, according to the quickly shared gossip
exchanged with some of the other guests en route, was planning
some major building works after the celebration party was over. It
was, they were told by those who had been there before, a large,
rambling house, but long neglected with part of it fallen into
complete disrepair. He had, it seemed, made the restoration of the
swimming pool a top priority. The October evening was not especially warm but some people had apparently brought their swimming
gear. Kate kept quietly to her determination that there was no way
she would be persuaded to step out of her lime green silk to doggie
paddle around a chilly pool. That was not her idea of a party.

The cars, on time, eventually pulled up in a phalanx alongside
a series of flaming torches at the foot of a broad flight of stairs
leading to the front door which was flung invitingly open. Jason
Destry himself stood at the top of the stairs in his signature red
jacket and personally welcomed each guest leaving staff to take
coats and usher guests into spacious rooms where drinks were
being served. It could, Kate thought, look much like the many
parties and receptions which had been held here over the years if
you kept your eyes away from the cracked plaster and the flaking
paint, but even from the drive it was obvious this was different.
She doubted very much that previous owners had greeted their
guests with rock and roll played at a volume that could probably
be heard in Central London.

'I'm glad you could come,' Destry said to her as he welcomed
the twenty or so people who had been ferried out by car from
Charlotte Street, with an unexpected kiss to the cheek for Kate.

'I'll see you later, honey,' he said. And there was a more believ-
able and warmer greeting as they went inside from Kevin Dunne,
who looked slightly relieved to see some faces he recognized.

'How's it going, whack?' he said, clapping Dave Donovan on
the shoulder. 'It's nice to see a few familiar faces from north of
Watford. And you, Katie.'

'From the way Destry was going on about his housewarming, I thought he'd at least have the Beatles lined up and champagne on tap,' Donovan said.

Dunne pulled a face. 'You could say the place is a bit rundown,' he said. 'But you have to put that down to the previous owners, apparently. There was a major legal row when the old boy who owned it died and it stood empty for years after the war when a fire in the tower at the back made it unsafe. They were pretty happy to almost give the house away when Destry came to look at it.'

'But no Beatles,' Donovan said plaintively.

'You might find some champagne but I don't think Jase and John Lennon see eye to eye about much,' Kevin Dunne said in spite of the fact that the speakers were pumping out the Beatles latest hit 'Help', their eighth number one, while the Rainbirds' latest still languished in the middle of the charts, rising but only very slowly. 'Anyway, aren't they away on tour again?' Kevin said. 'Though I heard this is supposed to be their last trip to America. They reckon they work eight-day weeks on tour and are getting fed up with it, apparently. Though I don't think Brian Epstein will be keen on them giving up. He won't know what to do with himself if they stop.'

'Yeah, well, he's getting a bit above himself isn't he, Brian Epstein,' Dave Donovan put in sourly. 'He didn't need to put Marie off the way he did when she went to see him. He could have shown her a bit more respect.'

'Have you seen her at all while you've been down here?' Kate asked Dunne. 'I thought if she was put off by Jack Mansfield she might have gone looking for a few Scouse shoulders to cry on to make her feel better.'

'Not to my knowledge, though I've been pretty busy since I arrived. Sorry, Dave. Can't help you with Marie. Anyway, come in and enjoy yourself. There's booze that way and food that way and I guess if you want anything stronger you should ask Jase.'

'You sure?' Donovan asked. 'I thought there were new laws about that sort of thing.'

'I don't think Jason's noticed if there are,' Dunne said with a grin. 'Anyway, this place is pretty isolated. I don't suppose PC Plod will even notice we're here. Though there's going to be fireworks later on too, I'm told.'

'That might tell the police there's something going on up here,' Kate said, glad of the warning that there were things she'd do well to avoid if she and Harry Barnard were to remain on speaking terms.

'They won't bother, especially if they know that the Rainbirds are heading to number one themselves when the new record's released next week. That's partly what this party's about,' Dunne said. 'The Beatles had better look out once we really get going. Everyone's waiting for that bubble to burst, aren't they?'

Kate turned away, took a glass of what looked like red wine from the glasses already filled on a makeshift bar in the room to the left of the front door and went for an exploratory stroll around an extensive and visibly aged house which had a curiously unfinished appearance. If Destry was genuinely restoring it the process seemed only half begun and was likely to take a significant amount of time – years she thought, rather than just months. The rooms at the front of the house had been given a coat of paint, the smell still lingering, and some furniture had been moved in, but towards the back rooms were closed off. What must have been the kitchens facing an enclosed courtyard were not even half finished and some of the doors were locked. Glancing out of the tall window halfway up the stairs, Kate could see a couple of caterers' vans parked close to dilapidated outbuildings which said clearly that little or no preparation had been done here for the party. The place might be intended as Destry's new home but it looked unlikely that he was intending to live in it any time soon.

She pressed on slowly up the stairs but the sense of abandonment only increased and it did not seem that anyone could have slept here recently. Somewhere boards creaked and she took shelter in a corner where a narrower staircase led up to another level where some of the boards were charred, her breath coming too fast as she hovered on the edge of panic. Some of the space was taken up with piles of boxes sealed up with plastic tape. She wasn't sure how Destry would react to this intrusion but she guessed it might not be well. At the last moment at the flat she had tucked her camera into her bag and she had taken a few shots on the way up the narrow staircase and as she turned she took a shot of the sealed boxes too. She held her breath, realizing that away from the blare of the music below there was no sound at all above and that the creak of boards was coming closer. Someone else was coming up. To her relief, she recognized Dave Donovan's voice calling to her as the steps got closer and she moved out of her sheltering alcove.

'I'm here,' she said in a near whisper.

'What are you doing upstairs?' Donovan asked quietly. 'Does Jason know you're exploring?'

'I hope not,' Kate said. 'This house is not what I expected. It's pretty well falling down in places. This part seems just to be used for storage. And there's been a fire at some time.'

'So I see,' Donovan said.

'I wondered where these stairs go,' Kate asked, glancing up.

'I reckon exploring up there's an even worse idea than on this level,' Donovan said cautiously. 'You brought your camera,' he said, sounding surprised.

'Come on, just a quick peek,' Kate said. 'Two minutes.'

'Very quick,' Donovan conceded reluctantly, and switched on the light which illuminated little apart from cobwebs and dust on uncarpeted stairs which gave on to two half landings and a series of doors which were all locked.

'When we were at the front there seemed to be some sort of tower at the back of the house, black and white like those old places in Chester, you know?' he said. 'You must have gone on school trips to Chester? This must be the tower or we wouldn't be able to get up so high.' Kate peered out of one of the windows and took a couple of shots looking down at the partygoers below.

'I can see the swimming pool,' she said and took another shot. 'Yes, I remember Chester, but this isn't as old as all that, is it?' she asked.

'Come on,' Dave Donovan said urgently. 'I don't know why he's bought an old ruin but I'm sure he won't like us wandering around up here like this. Let's get back to the party.' They tiptoed back down the stairs to the landing and then hesitated at the top of the main landing where they met Kevin Dunne coming up.

'I wondered where you'd got to,' he said, stopping halfway. 'What are you doing up here?'

'I was looking for the lav,' Kate said quickly.

'Downstairs on the corridor to the kitchen,' Dunne said. 'Jason's planning a big building job on this place but nothing's been started upstairs yet, only a few architects coming round and contradicting each other. Some of us told him to leave the party till the place is a bit more ready but he wouldn't. He's an impatient beggar. And he's been told that parts of the tower are not safe.'

'Right, thanks,' Kate said. 'I'll go then. I'm busting.' She hurried past Dunne, closely followed by Donovan with Kevin Dunne watching them from above. He crossed the landing as soon as they were out of sight and went straight to the narrow staircase leading up to the next level. The landing was carpeted and offered no clues to Kate and Dave's movements, but the next stage told a clear tale. Two people had gone another floor up leaving footprints in the dust going up and then coming down again.

'Jason's not going to like that,' Dunne said under his breath.

SEVENTEEN

B y the time the fireworks were due to start in the garden around midnight, Dave Donovan was seriously worried about Kate O'Donnell's state of mind. He knew he was mildly drunk himself and guessed that she was much drunker than he understood: her eyes were becoming unfocused, her gait unsteady, and he had not exchanged a coherent sentence with her for at least an hour. He had watched her weaving between the guests taking photographs now and again as people milled around in crowds refilling glasses and eating the buffet food awkwardly as there were few places in the main rooms to sit comfortably. She seemed to be keeping the camera low and the flash turned off and he wondered if the pictures would come out at all but he assumed she knew what she was doing. As time went on they moved closer to the windows with the rest of the guests until the lawns and shrubberies were illuminated gold and red and blue and silver, the trees lit up by sparkling bands of light and the dark skies filled with soaring cascades of fire. He put an arm round her and to his surprise could feel her trembling.

'I think you need a little break, Katie,' he said. He took her glass out of her hand. 'Let's find somewhere to sit down for a while.'

'I like the pretty stars,' she said, suddenly speaking clearly but shrilly, pulling herself away from his arm and half standing leaning against the glass to gaze at the display outside again.

'Have you been mixing your drinks?' Donovan asked anxiously, guiding her with some resistance to a sofa where she slumped back against the cushions and closed her eyes and began to shiver.

'Kevin gave me a cocktail,' she said. 'That was nice.'

'Yeah, he offered me some of that but I didn't finish it. It tasted a bit odd,' Donovan said, wondering just what it was that had given the sweet drink such a weird flavour. But the amount of alcohol he had drunk seemed to make it too difficult to get back to his feet and ask Kevin the question.

Kate suddenly pulled away from him and then flinched.

'What is it?' Donovan asked, beginning to feel nauseous himself.

'I thought . . . something was coming through the window . . . flying . . . on fire . . .'

'It was just one of the fireworks, Katie. Nothing to worry about. The windows are all closed. It must have been a reflection in the glass. Where's your camera? Give it to me and I'll look after it for you. You don't want to lose it, do you?' She did not respond but handed him her camera and her bag. What had seemed like shivering was now more like shuddering and he noticed her arms, barely concealed by her flimsy silk dress, were covered in goose-bumps. He took her hands and felt how icy cold they were, took his jacket off and wrapped it round her shoulders.

'You're not very well, Katie. I'll ask Kevin if we can get a lift back to London. I think you should be going home. It's late.'

'It's not late,' Kate shouted so frantically that even the sound of the explosions outside did not mask her distress and many of the watchers at the windows turned to look at her for a second or two with uncomprehending eyes before the display took their attention again. 'It's not late,' Kate said again more quietly. 'We only just got here. It's not late.'

Donovan glanced at his watch but did not argue.

Kevin Dunne watched them from the far side of the room where he and Jason Destry were paying little attention to the pyrotechnics outside.

'I think you'd better move soon,' Destry said.

'The same as last time?' Dunne asked.

'I think so,' Destry said. 'It worked fine with our other little friend who took a trip. There's been no comeback?'

'Not a cheep,' Dunne said.

'Just make sure Donovan has had enough to keep him quiet. She's obviously well away with the fairies. Just a pity she won't remember much about it tomorrow. I'm not sure we've got the dose right yet. No one will want to buy this stuff in the clubs if it knocks people out completely.'

'Well, it certainly seems to have done that for Kate. Pity, I quite fancied her,' Dunne said regretfully.

'Keep your mind on the job,' Destry said sharply. 'This is important. We might get to the top of the hit parade or we might not, but there are other ways to make money in swinging London.

There's a new club or restaurant opening almost every week and people with money are flocking in. I saw Terence Stamp in Alvaro's last week and Marianne Faithfull the week before. It's not just rock musicians – its actors and film stars and dress designers. The whole of the West End is swinging. Do you know Alvaro's phone number is ex-directory? He runs the place just like another club. If your face fits you're in, if it doesn't you'll never get in.'

'Right,' Dunne said impatiently. 'I'll take these two out the back way before they're both completely out of it. I asked two of the cars to wait at the back in case we needed them. Looks like we do.'

Destry circulated among his guests again as the smoke from the display drifted away and the spectators at the windows headed back to the bar and the food which had now been laid out, and only the sharpest eyes noticed that the trees beyond the lawns harboured black-clad figures who did not seem to belong to the technicians who had supervised the fireworks. As soon as the display team moved off to their vans parked by the front gates the new arrivals moved smartly out of the shelter of the trees and round the sides and back of the house until a whistle was blown at the front and DI Brian Jamieson and DS Steve Pendleton hammered on the door, turned the handle and to their surprise found it opened easily.

'They felt pretty secure out here, didn't they?' he said. Closely followed by a dozen uniformed officers, Jamieson turned off the lights briefly to attract attention in the rooms where the party was still in full swing and a puzzled silence fell.

'Police,' he said, hardly needing to raise his voice. 'Stay where you are, please. We will need names and addresses to start with and then more details from some of you. Mr Destry, you are under arrest.'

In the melee of musicians and guests and police officers no one noticed Kevin Dunne slide out into the hall and quickly make his way to the stairs of the half-ruined tower at the back of the house with a bundle of what looked like kindling in his hand.

Dave Donovan was as oblivious as Kate seemed to be on the drive back to London and their unceremonious ejection from the car which had taken them there. As far as he knew, neither of the men in the front seats had said a word during the journey. But the shadowy darkness which was all he could see when he eventually and reluctantly opened his eyes told him nothing about where he had been dumped on an uncomfortably hard and dirty floor, or whether Kate was still with him or not. He felt incredibly cold, knew that he was shaking uncontrollably and felt an overwhelming fear that he had lost contact with Kate somewhere on the journey and that he would not be able to ever find her again. Somewhere he thought he heard a woman scream which panicked him enough to enable him to stagger to his feet, but when he tried to cry out to attract attention he could achieve no more than a faint moan. His mouth was as dry as sandpaper and he had little certainty in the dark void he had been consigned to of even remembering his own name. Struggling for breath, he dropped to the floor again and only then realized that he was not in fact alone. Someone else was lying face down on the floor beside him, and when he forced his hands to reach out he could feel a bare arm, the flesh even colder than his own, and the soft touch of silk and then, when he persuaded his fingers to reach out a bit further, a face and hair spread out among the scattered debris of a filthy floor.

'Katie?' he croaked, although he doubted that he had said it loudly enough to register. But when he put a hand on her chest he realized that although she was not moving and did not seem to aware that he was there, she was at least breathing, even if only faintly. He struggled out of his jacket, wrapped it over her and hugged her close in an attempt to keep her warm, but as his head very slowly cleared, the faint light of what he assumed must be dawn revealed that they were lying under stone arches open on one side to a narrow, high-walled street with only one dim street light some distance away. As the daylight increased he could just about read his watch, although the face seemed to be changing shape, and saw that it said six thirty and at the same moment he heard the unmistakeable sound of a train passing, fading away and then braking to a high-pitched standstill. If they were near a station, he thought, surely he would be able to attract someone's attention and get help even early on a Sunday morning.

He waited a while until he felt strong enough to scramble to his feet again, although he knew Kate needed help. He did not want to leave her and be unable to find his way back. He did not look at his watch again as a sort of helplessness engulfed him and the face of the watch seemed to grow and shrink again more or less at random, but he realized that the sound of the trains was becoming more regular. Somewhere out there a day was beginning and when Kate stirred and began to whimper and moan, he struggled to his feet, pulled her upright and staggered towards the street.

'Come on, Katie, we have to move. People will be looking for us.' But he realized that although she was upright she was making no attempt to walk. Half carrying her and half dragging her, still wrapped in his jacket which meant that he was shivering uncontrollably himself, he could see no obvious way through the neglected huddle of arches and narrow, littered streets which he could tell from the increasing sound of trains must conceal a station where he knew there would be help. Kate's agitation grew and she started a panicked and incoherent monologue, behind which lay the belief that she was surrounded by a raging fire which threatened them both.

'There's no fire,' Donovan said, struggling to hold her upright. 'You're safe, Katie. There's no fire. What you saw was the fireworks, just fireworks.'

'The tower was on fire. I saw it, blazing,' Kate said mulishly and kicked and struggled until in desperation Donovan picked her up and carried her over his shoulder, although he knew he could not keep that up for long. To his intense relief, Donovan eventually saw a red phone box on the corner of the next turning. He struggled on, pushed Kate inside the neglected and smelly box and dredged through his coat pockets for loose change. Tess answered her phone quickly and he could tell that she was unusually eager to talk to him.

'Can you get hold of Kate's boyfriend?' he asked. 'She's not well.'

'What's happened?' Tess asked. 'I fecking knew something was wrong when I got up and found you hadn't come back from the party.'

He glanced down at Kate, who had slid down the glass and was sitting on the floor with her head in her hands, shaking again. He opened the door and glanced across the road to the street sign on the corner.

'We're in a phone box on the corner of Partick Street. It's close to a station – we can hear the trains. King's Cross maybe. Or St Pancras. Can you get Harry Barnard down here? Katie needs help and he needs to know what's happened. Be quick, Tess. Katie's not looking good. She needs a doctor.'

'How does Harry find you?'

'I've no idea,' Donovan said, and there was a note of panic in his voice. 'He'll need a map. Partick Street.'

'Give me the number of the phone you're using and I'll get him to call you,' Tess said with all the authority of someone used to organizing thirty fifteen-year-olds who were not terribly moved by the Shakespeare play she had to persuade them to read. 'Hang up and wait there. And look after Kate or Harry Barnard is likely to kill you and post you back to Liverpool in bits.'

Donovan realized later that it cannot have been more than a few minutes before the phone rang, but at the time it seemed like hours.

'How's Kate?' Barnard asked, and Donovan could hear the suppressed fury as if the sergeant was already standing no more than a yard away on the deserted street outside the airless refuge the phone box provided.

'She was out of it when I woke up, but then she came round and now she's shaking and shivering and talking nonsense. I think some bastard spiked our drinks.'

'Have you called for an ambulance?'

'I only had change for one call—'

'Right, I'm on my way and I'll get an ambulance down there. Partick Street? The ambulance will probably be first to reach you.' There was a pause and Donovan could hear pages turning close to the receiver at the other end. 'You're at the back of King's Cross station. Favourite haunt of toms and alcoholics, and the odd maniac. Those streets have never been touched since the war. It wasn't so much that they got bombed as that they simply fell apart. Don't move. I'm on my way.'

Barnard's car pulled up with a squeal of brakes. Donovan had no idea how long he had taken, despite frequent glances at his watch, which still seemed to be liquidizing into unusual shapes and sizes, proving that his eyes were still not behaving as they should. He had sat down on the floor of the phone box beside

Kate and kept his arms round her. She was still shivering violently and seemed to have lapsed into unconsciousness again.

He knew that Barnard's reaction would be unpredictable and quite possibly violent. The sergeant was out of his car within seconds and pulled the door to the phone booth almost off its hinges as he squeezed into the narrow space and pushed Donovan out of the door. Kate, still sheltered slightly by Donovan's jacket, was trembling, but when he spoke to her she did not appear to hear him.

'Do you know what they spiked your drinks with?' he asked Donovan as he tried to lift Kate up.

'I've no idea,' Donovan said. 'She seemed to be seeing things that weren't there. I'm sure I got a dose too, but it doesn't seem to have affected me so much.'

'If it's this new drug which seems to be hitting the streets it seems to be affecting people in different ways. You're bigger and heavier. That probably makes a difference.' He laid Kate back down gently against the side of the phone box as an ambulance appeared from the direction of King's Cross. Barnard went to meet the two uniformed men who jumped out.

'We think a drug overdose,' he said, flashing his warrant card. 'Do you know what the effects of LSD look like?'

'I saw some pillock who'd taken it trying to wreck a casualty ward a couple of months ago. I reckon he ended up in a police cell until the tranquillizers kicked in. It's nasty stuff, LSD.'

'Someone was spiking drinks at a party these two were at,' Barnard said. 'Someone thought it was a joke apparently.'

'It won't kill you like a heroin overdose can, but some people react very badly, go a bit doolally,' the ambulance driver said. 'It looks like that's what's happened to this young lady. It's certainly no joke.'

'You'd better take them both to Casualty,' Barnard said. 'We'll need to talk to them later and find out exactly what happened.' While the ambulance men lifted Kate on to a stretcher, Donovan grabbed his jacket as Barnard pulled him out of earshot.

'Who do you reckon?' he asked.

'Jason Destry,' Donovan said flatly. 'I doubt anyone else would have taken it to his party, not without him knowing anyway.'

'OK,' Barnard said. 'Go and get checked out and I'll catch up with you later.' He watched the ambulance draw away from his car, fighting down the urge to drive down to wherever the party had been held and have it out with Destry, but he knew that would finish off his already threatened career in one easy move. Instead, he pulled away from the kerb slowly and followed the ambulance at a steady pace to Casualty, where he parked as close as he could to the ambulance bays and caught up with Kate's stretcher as they manoeuvred it through the doors. Dave Donovan was still following closely behind and as they approached the expectant medical team waiting for them, the ambulance attendants urged Barnard away and said to the doctor who seemed to be in charge that they had two patients to be seen.

'And you are?' the Casualty doctor asked Barnard. He got out his warrant card again, determined to stay within reach of Kate.

'Drugs,' he said. 'Mr Donovan here claims their drinks were interfered with at a party, possibly by LSD. I need to keep an eye.'

The doctor looked surprised. 'I knew there was supposed to be LSD around but I can't say I've seen a case before,' he said. 'I'll have a look at the young lady first, as she seems to be the worst affected, but I may have to consult a colleague who knows a bit more about these things than I do. If you take a seat over there in the waiting room I'll get back to you when we've examined her.'

Barnard bit back an angry retort and watched as Kate was wheeled into one of the cubicles at the side of the ward and the doctor and a nurse prepared to examine her while another nurse ushered Donovan into the next cubicle along. Barnard leaned back in one of the hard chairs set against the wall and took a deep breath. As far as he could tell, Kate's condition did not seem to have changed on the journey to hospital: her complexion was pale, her breathing barely noticeable and, apart from an occasional involuntary tremor, she did not move. He closed his eyes for moment and opened them again quickly when he realized that in the battle which raged in his head between fierce anger and utter despair, despair seemed set to win. And Kate deserved more than that.

After about half an hour, Donovan reappeared and took the seat next to Barnard.

'They can't see any damage,' he said. 'Go home and sleep it off is all they can recommend.'

'They've got some specialist in to have a look at Kate,' Barnard said, glancing at the cubicle where the curtains were still tightly drawn. 'Ingleby, he's called.'

'She's not come round then?'

'No.'

'I suppose you reckon it's all my fault,' Donovan came back quickly.

'Well, I thought she was more drunk than I'd seen her after she went with you to the Late Supper Club and came in late,' Barnard said quietly. 'I was a bit preoccupied with other things that day. And now this . . .'

'Destry could have had a go that night,' Donovan admitted. 'He was giving us champagne as if it was water, celebrating his new record, he said. I had a bad hangover the next morning, I remember. A bit like I feel now.'

'I'll talk to the doctor,' Barnard said suddenly. 'There's something I'd like to check out while it's still daylight.' The doctor pulled the curtain back quickly when Barnard called him, revealing Kate curled on her side on the bed breathing quietly but with no other sign of consciousness.

'No change?' he asked. The doctor looked at his colleague on the other side of the bed.

'It takes some people days to regain consciousness,' he said. 'They seem to be living in another world inside their heads and it's not always a very pleasant one.'

'I'll drop in later to see if she's come round,' Barnard said. 'We need to talk to her as soon as possible.' He turned away and sat down again beside Dave Donovan.

'You can do me and Kate one favour,' he said. 'I need to go down to Destry's house and get a good look at the place today before anyone has the chance to clean it up and move any evidence. Will you stay here until I come back so Kate has someone with her when she wakes up? Please.'

'Do you think you can pin something on Destry?' Donovan asked.

'I'll have a bloody good try,' Barnard said.

'All right,' Donovan said. 'But be quick. It's not me she'll be wanting to see, is it?'

EIGHTEEN

D S Barnard found Jason Destry's house hidden away down a narrow lane in the Surrey hills where houses were few and far between and he reckoned contact with the neighbours was rare. He parked discreetly close to the open gates and walked the last few hundred yards to the main door. There was no sign of anyone at home that he could see and no cars parked on the forecourt or near the garages at the back. The place was unexpectedly deserted given that it had allegedly been the site of a major party the previous evening. He walked right round the property, meeting no one at all, seeing only the remaining debris from a fireworks display on the lawns and through the downstairs windows the abandoned remnants of drinks and food left on tables and the floor which had not yet been cleared away. It was a substantial house, looking well kept at the front but much more dilapidated at the rear with the tower on the back corner suffering from what looked like significant and relatively recent fire damage for much of its height.

Barnard tried the doors at the back but they were all securely locked, and when he heard the sound of a car coming up the drive he turned back and approached the front door along the terrace and watched as a sports car parked on the forecourt. He had driven all the way from central London hoping to find Jason Destry himself, even if he was still sleeping off a hangover from the previous night, but the person who uncoiled himself from the green MG was unexpected and not necessarily a welcome sight. DI Brian Jamieson looked as startled as Barnard did himself.

'What the hell are you doing here?' the DI asked.

'I could ask you the same question, guv,' Barnard said.

'That was your parked car I passed down the lane then? The red one? I thought it might be a late visitor loaded down with illegal substances.'

'I came to talk to Jason Destry,' Barnard said.

'Did you now?' Jamieson asked. 'Well, you're a bit late. I

arrested him and some of his group last night, and he and the rest
are in cells at various police stations in London as we speak. It'll
be all over the morning papers tomorrow. This is a first outing for
the new drug squad and we got here a bit too late last night to
make the front pages this morning. We'll have to do better next
time.'

'Drugs?' Barnard asked.

'Of course drugs,' Jamieson said flatly. 'So your turn now. Why
the hell have you turned up on my crime scene completely out of
the blue and totally uninvited? What do you want with Destry?'

'A couple of friends of mine were at the party here last night . . .'

'Names? We took everyone's name though we only arrested the
major players and sent the rest home.'

'You won't have got these two names. They left early and
went back to London. But they were off their heads on something
and one of them's still unconscious in hospital. Or she was when
I left.'

'What was it? Heroin? Coke?'

'More likely LSD, the doctors think. They claim someone spiked
their drinks and I think it had happened before when Destry was
around at the same time they were at the Late Supper Club in
Soho together,' Barnard said, knowing there was no way out of
this conversation now and no way of knowing where it might lead
him. 'It might help the doctors if they knew exactly what they
were dealing with. That's what I wanted to ask Destry.'

'And you think he might have told you? A friend of yours,
is he?'

'I've never set eyes on him,' Barnard said quickly. 'It's a long
story involving musicians from Liverpool and a singer who seems
to have disappeared.'

'So who's this young woman friend of yours who came to the
party?'

'My girlfriend,' Barnard said quietly. 'She and an old friend
from Liverpool were invited to the party by Destry when they met
him at the new club in Soho.'

'And you weren't?'

'I told you. I was working late anyway. You know what's going
on in Soho at the moment.'

'Ah,' Jamieson said, comprehension dawning. 'So when she

turned up off her head it was worth the effort of coming all the way down here?'

'If it helps her, of course, guv. I want to know what she took,' Barnard said. 'Or was given.'

'Well, you won't get any help here now. We turfed everyone out at about two last night and told them not to come back until we'd searched the place thoroughly. If there's LSD in there – or anything else, for that matter – I'll let you know. Now if I were you I'd get back to the girlfriend while you can. Didn't I hear that you have a serious interview with your DCI on Monday morning? Is it twos or threes they say troubles come in?'

'Something like that,' Barnard agreed and turned away, not wanting to let the DI see the fury he felt.

'We've put her in a side room for now,' the ward sister explained when Barnard tracked Kate down when he got back to the hospital and found that she was no longer being treated in Casualty. 'Most of the time she seems to be sleeping. We check her regularly, of course. But every now and again she becomes very agitated and has been disturbing other patients.' She led him into a small room off a main ward where Kate lay unmoving and still unconscious.

'Is her life in danger?' Barnard asked the question whose answer most frightened him.

'The specialist, Mr Ingleby, doesn't seem to think so but of course we have no idea exactly what she's taken or how much.' The sister did not hide her distaste.

'I don't think Kate knew either,' Barnard snapped. 'The friend she was with said someone put something into their drinks.'

'Right,' the nurse said with a sceptical look. 'If you say so. She's reacted very badly to it whatever happened. We're seeing more and more of these drug-related cases and most of them are self-inflicted: heroin, amphetamines and now something called LSD.'

'And some of the victims do end up dead,' Barnard said. 'One way or another.' He sat down beside the bed. 'I'll stay,' he said and the nurse made as if to object but then thought better of it and bustled off into the main part of the ward to chivvy the junior nurses into action. He leaned back in his chair and closed his eyes for a moment. He had told Dave Donovan to go back to Tess's flat and get some sleep.

'Don't go back to Liverpool yet,' he had said. 'The drug squad will want to talk to you about what happened. They've arrested Destry and some of the others and will want you as a witness to what went on at that party.'

'I didn't notice anything at the party which worried me but drinks were being poured out without anyone really knowing what they were. There was one so-called punch I thought was a bit dodgy . . . had a funny taste.'

'Get some sleep and try to remember everything that happened,' Barnard said. 'We'll have more questions for you later.'

'That place they dumped us was dodgy, though,' Donovan had added. 'There were people there – voices, like someone hiding, someone screamed.'

'I'll tell the DI,' Barnard had said, turning back to Kate and taking her hand. For a moment he thought her fingers gripped his, but then they went limp again and he reckoned he had imagined it. In the end the overheated room defeated him and he fell asleep in the visitor's chair still holding Kate's hand, and only woke when he became aware that he was no longer alone with her. DI Jamieson was shaking his shoulder and the ward sister was close behind looking thunderous.

'This is completely out of order,' she said. 'It's only because it's Sunday that Mr Ingleby hasn't been in again to see the patient. He will throw you both out when he comes – you can rely on that.'

Both men looked appalled, but it was Barnard who hesitated and Jamieson who spoke.

'Sister, someone has put this young woman's life at risk, probably deliberately, which would make it a case of attempted murder. Your responsibility is to save a life – mine is to identify a possible killer. It would be a very good idea if we treated each other with some respect.'

The sister glanced at the watch pinned to her uniform apparently with no answer to Jamieson's argument.

'I will telephone Mr Ingleby,' she said. 'I'll warn him what to expect.' She quickly checked Kate's condition and then turned on her heel and closed the side ward's door behind her.

'Thanks, guv,' Barnard said.

'I only came in to see if Kate had come round. Obviously I need to talk to her as soon as she's able. In the meantime, I'll catch up with Dave Donovan if you tell me where he is.'

'He's gone back to Tess Farrell's flat. He looked almost as bad as Kate, to be honest.' He gave him the address. 'One thing he said before he went was that he thought there were other people under the arches where they were dumped,' Barnard said. 'They could hear voices and screams.'

'I'll get the local nick to take a look,' Jamieson said. 'And I'll see you and Kate later.'

Tess Farrell answered an imperious ring on her front doorbell just as she was making Dave Donovan a cup of tea. She had realized as soon as he had explained everything that had happened to him and Kate since they had left to go to Jason Destry's party in the country that Dave was not likely to be departing for Liverpool tonight. In fact, she guessed that he would not be very keen to go home at all until he was sure that Kate O'Donnell had recovered and left hospital. He and Kate had gone through a stormy relationship several years ago which had started at Liverpool College of Art and sunk after Dave had unsuccessfully tried to launch his band in London. But Tess knew he had never accepted that it was all over, however fervently he had claimed that Marie had taken Kate's place. When he had explained to Tess briefly what had happened at the house in Surrey he had more or less collapsed on the sofa and was still asleep.

When Tess opened the door she found herself faced with two men, neither of whom she recognized.

'Miss Farrell?' the older of the two asked. She nodded. The man reached into an inside pocket and flashed a card with an ID photograph in her direction. 'I'm Detective Inspector Brian Jamieson. I understand you have a David Donovan staying with you and I need to ask him some questions about what happened last night.'

'You'd better come in then,' Tess said, and led the two men up the stairs to the first-floor flat. 'He's been asleep for hours. I don't know what happened to him at Jason Destry's party but whatever it was it wasn't good. Do you know if Kate O'Donnell has woken up yet? He told me she was unconscious.'

'She hadn't when I left the hospital about half an hour ago,' Jamieson said. 'DS Barnard is with her.'

Tess nodded, wondering if Harry was there as her boyfriend or one of DI Jamieson's investigating team or, more cynically perhaps, both. Tess shook Donovan's shoulder. 'Wake up, Dave,' she said. 'There are two policemen here to talk to you.' Donovan groaned but succeeded in opening his eyes and slowly sitting up, eyeing the two officers in jeans and leather jackets with deep suspicion.

'DI Jamieson and DS Bentley from the drug squad,' Jamieson said, displaying his warrant card again. 'I understand you were at a party last night in Surrey, at Jason Destry's house. Is that right?'

Donovan grunted and nodded. 'That's right,' he said. 'But not for long. Kate O'Donnell didn't feel too good so we came back to London after the firework display. I asked the driver to bring us back here but they more or less chucked us out of the car somewhere else. It was pitch-black and Katie was rambling by then and eventually fell asleep, or passed out – I couldn't get her to wake up. All I knew was that she was still breathing. I was out of my mind. I thought she was going to die.'

'We know there were drugs available at the party. So what did she take?'

'She didn't take anything as far as I know,' Donovan said angrily. 'I know you bizzies think anyone in a band must be on drugs, but I'm not and Kate wouldn't touch anything willingly. You must know her boyfriend's a bizzy himself.'

'So you're saying someone spiked her drink?'

'And mine,' Donovan said. 'By the time we told Jason we wanted to go back to London because Kate wasn't feeling good and I was feeling pretty weird myself. I wasn't sure whether I was awake or dreaming in the back of that car. And Kate was hysterical before she passed out completely. Said the house was on fire. She seemed terrified. I begged the driver not to dump us but he wouldn't listen.'

'Well, as fairy stories go that's quite a good one,' Jamieson said. 'My problem is the doctors say some drugs don't leave any traces in the body so there may be no way we can check what it was. It's a pity that.'

'Or even if it was a drug at all,' Donovan said, sounding more confident by the minute.

'Given the way your friend Kate has reacted I don't think there's much doubt she was drugged and is probably lucky to be alive. And it's my job to investigate what happened at that party. DS Barnard told me you were planning to go back to Liverpool?'

'Tomorrow morning,' Donovan said. 'But only if Kate is OK. She's an old friend.'

'I'd rather you didn't,' Jamieson said.

Donovan opened his mouth to argue but Jamieson did not give him time. 'I need you here as a witness,' he said. 'I need statements from you and Miss O'Donnell. I could arrest you as you've admitted that you and Kate O'Donnell were under the influence of drugs when you left Destry's party. But if I did that you might end up in the dock alongside Destry and his mates. If you help me with the prosecution you should be OK.'

'That's not fair,' Tess said sharply from the other side of the room. But Jamieson shrugged.

'Drug convictions are going through the roof,' he said. 'New drugs like LSD are coming on stream and it sounds as if that's what you took – or were given. Scotland Yard want it stopped. Sorry, but that's where we are. What's it to be, Mr Donovan?'

Donovan looked helplessly at Tess. 'Looks as if I'll be staying if you put it like that, whack,' Donovan said, leaning back on the sofa and closing his eyes again, defeated.

'And there's one other thing I need from you, Miss Farrell,' Jamieson added. 'In the circumstances I'm within my rights to search your flat. We can do that two ways. You can give me and DS Bentley permission to search now and get it over with, or I can apply to a magistrate for a search warrant, in which case one of us will try to track down a magistrate, which might not be easy on a Sunday afternoon, and the other will stay here until the documents are ready and then do the search. Which would you prefer?'

'My God, you're a bastard,' Donovan muttered.

'I'm doing my job,' Jamieson said without a hint of an apology.

'You can search now,' Tess said. 'And if you're carrying anything you shouldn't, Dave, it's on your own head. It's absolutely nothing to do with me.'

*　　*　　*

Barnard sat beside Kate's bed as the afternoon wore on. He had drunk cups of tea after he had decided that what they called coffee in the canteen tasted of dishwater and had eaten nothing all day, and felt his eyes closing intermittently. Every so often he had shaken himself awake when he persuaded himself that Kate's eyes were flickering, but every time she had lapsed back into immobility almost at once. As the afternoon dragged on the only thing that really roused him was the regular visits of a nurse to check on Kate's condition as he sank closer and closer to total despair.

In the end it was Kate who took him by surprise; he guessed that he must have fallen asleep again only to find that Kate's eyes were finally wide open and she had half a smile on her face and was watching him sleep.

'You're awake,' he said. 'How are you feeling?'

'Not great,' she said. 'What happened?'

'I don't know. I wasn't there. What can you remember?' As soon as Barnard saw her face crumple in distress he knew that was the wrong question to ask, too soon almost certainly and quite possibly ever.

'Don't worry,' he said, taking her hand. 'Forget everything if that's what you want. You don't have to talk about it, especially not to me. Just concentrate on staying awake for now. You're going to be fine. And you have no idea how good that makes me feel. Let me get the nurse. She'll know what to do now you're awake.' He went to the door of the side ward and waved to the ward sister at the far end close to the nurses' station. She hurried towards him. If he had even half doubted how serious the medical staff felt Kate's condition to be, the look of relief on the nurse's face convinced him.

'Is she awake?' she said, taking his arm and preventing him going back to Kate's bedside. 'Is she talking normally? That's what the doctor said he needs to know.'

'She's talking but is very emotional – scared even. She doesn't want to talk about what happened. Not yet anyway.'

'I'll phone the doctor,' the sister said. 'He'll want to see her now, I'm sure.'

'There'll be a lot of people wanting to see her and ask her lots of questions, as DI Jamieson explained,' Barnard said.

'That will be up to Mr Ingleby,' the sister said sharply. 'He won't want anything done which might disturb her mental balance. Some of these drugs are very dangerous things.'

'I know,' Barnard said. 'Will Mr Ingleby talk to me, do you think? We're not married. I'm not her next of kin.'

'That will be up to the consultant,' the ward sister said. 'He'll make his own decisions. You'll have to explain the circumstances to him. Shall we have a look at Miss O'Donnell before I make the phone call? You can stay with her if you wish.'

'I think that's a good idea,' Barnard said, and he followed the nurse back into the side ward feeling the tension build as Kate submitted to the routine checks on her well-being.

When the ward sister finally left to make her phone call Barnard threw hospital rules aside, sat on Kate's bed and put his arms round her. 'Tell me about it,' he said. 'If you feel up to it. A lot of people are going to want to know what happened so you can try it out on me first.' She cried then, long, wracking sobs which told him nothing except she was adrift in a place he could not even imagine, confused and consumed apparently by images of fire.

'There were fireworks, Dave said. Just fireworks. Nothing dangerous,' Barnard tried to reassure her.

'No, no, there was a fire in the tower,' Kate insisted. 'It was on fire and I couldn't get out. Every time I opened the door someone – or something – pushed me back in. There were flames everywhere. Even now I can see it and smell it and think I'll choke on it. I was in the middle of it and I thought it would never stop. I was looking for you. I wanted you and I couldn't find you anywhere . . .'

'I wasn't there, sweetheart,' he said. 'Where was Dave while all this was going on?'

'I don't know,' she said.

'You're not hurt,' Barnard said, feeling completely helpless. 'You're not burnt. They said they gave you a thorough going over when you were brought in and found nothing to worry about, nothing physical anyway.'

'It was in the car, the fire. The car was burning.' She examined her hands and arms carefully.

'No,' Barnard said gently. 'The car wasn't burning. Can you remember being in the car?'

She looked puzzled for a moment. 'I thought I'd got drunk again, like after I went with Dave to the club. I felt woozy. The driver said they would take us back to London but I can't remember much after that.'

Barnard felt rather than heard someone behind him, and he turned his head to see the ward sister and the specialist enter the room.

'We were lucky,' the ward sister said. 'Mr Ingleby had already been called in to deal with another patient so it didn't take long to find him.'

The consultant did not look pleased to see Barnard, still sitting on the bed. 'And you are?' he said, frost in his voice and eyes.

Barnard shrugged slightly and stood up. 'I'm Kate's boyfriend,' he said. 'She's a long, long way from her family.'

'Right, then you can tell the sister here how to get in touch with them. Do you have any idea what this young lady took, or how much?'

'I wasn't with her when it happened,' Barnard said.

'Right,' Ingleby said, and there was a wealth of accusation in the single word. 'Then you can leave us to examine the patient.'

'Visiting hours are long over, Mr Ingleby, as you know, sir. I have told him that several times.' A note of outraged authority was very evident now in the nurse's tone.

'Can I take her home tonight?' Barnard asked without much hope.

The doctor shook his head angrily. 'I will want to keep her under observation at least until tomorrow, possibly longer. You can ring the ward sister after midday and she will tell you whether I think it's safe for her to leave and you – or her family – can come and fetch her. Some of these episodes are slow to clear up. The hallucinations come back unexpectedly . . .'

'I'd like to go home soon,' Kate said with just an echo of her usual determination, which Barnard rejoiced to hear.

'And I had a bag with me at the party,' she said. 'A bag and my camera. I wanted to take some pictures, and I think I did. But I'm not sure whether I brought it back with me.'

'I'll find it, sweetheart,' Barnard said, feeling a faint stirring of optimism at last. He leaned around the ward sister to give her a hug. 'I'll see you tomorrow.'

'And there's something else,' Kate said, avoiding the sister's annoyance and grabbing Barnard's hand tight. 'It's important. Kevin Dunne gave me his phone number so we could get picked up. I couldn't understand why it sounded familiar until much later when I realized that I'd heard it before. It was the same number that Marie Collins left with her agent.'

'You think that's where she was staying,' Barnard said. 'With Kevin Dunne?'

'We thought she'd go looking for the Scousers, didn't we?' Kate said, her voice breaking.

'So where is she now? You didn't see her at the party, did you?' Barnard asked.

'No, Kevin came in the cars with the rest of us but there was no sign of Marie. So where was she then?' For a moment they were left speechless until Barnard decided that the conversation was not going to offer an answer and that Kate was becoming very anxious.

'Don't worry, Katie,' he said. 'Kevin's safely tucked up with Destry on remand so he's not going anywhere. I'll feed what you've said into the system. Now get some rest. I'll see you soon.'

DI Brian Jamieson was sprawled in a chair close to the main doors when Barnard left Kate's ward and he stood up as the sergeant came down the stairs.

'You and me, we need to talk,' he said.

'Right, guv,' Barnard said. 'Have you interviewed Dave Donovan yet?'

'I caught up with him at the flat in Shepherd's Bush. That girl's a bloody teacher. You'd think she'd know better than to get within a mile of illegal substances.'

'I'm sure she does,' Barnard said. 'It was Kate who arranged for Donovan to stay there, just for a couple of nights it was supposed to be, while he looked for this girlfriend who's allegedly gone missing. None of us knew all this would happen. Kate's just given me a new take on the missing girlfriend as it happens.'

'Yeah, right. Anyway, I tend to believe the story of your girl and Donovan having their drinks spiked. It's just the sort of thing Jason Destry would think was funny. The drug problem is London-based, so unless someone's hoping Donovan will flog

LSD for them on Merseyside I think he's just collateral damage, like your girl.'

'"My girl", as you call her, is a photographer and she just told me she took her camera with her to Destry's party, but she doesn't know what happened to it.'

'You're kidding,' Jamieson said. 'No one's found a camera at Destry's house to my knowledge. So she could have left it in the car or dropped it where they were dumped under the arches. Do you fancy a quick trip to King's Cross? I asked the local lads to see what they could find down there but they might need geeing up. What do you think?'

'Let's do it,' Barnard said.

NINETEEN

Jamieson drove the MG fast through the quiet Sunday afternoon streets and made a sharp turn into a side street between King's Cross and St Pancras, the two mainline stations. The road was lined on one side by neglected-looking brick archways which, close to the Euston Road, had been taken over by depressed commercial enterprises until even those petered out and there was no sign of life left, just wind-blown litter and cavernous openings which gave on to nothing but darkness. Round a bend they came across a squad car parked to effectively block the road completely and Jamieson parked alongside.

'They've only sent one car,' he said angrily. 'It could take them a week to find anything in there. Come on. We'll have to have a look ourselves. I've got a flashlight.'

Full of foreboding, Barnard followed the DI into the gloomy interior of the arches, trying to avoid thinking about what Kate had gone through here and what they might still find. The DI kept the torch focused on the littered floor where the detritus made it all too obvious what normally went on here, at least where the arches were close enough to the outside world to enable the prostitutes and their clients to see each other in the twilight and the drinkers to recognize what they were drinking before they slid into oblivion. But there was no sign of anyone using the space now and Barnard guessed that if there were a couple of uniformed officers prowling these rambling corridors no one would come back until they were sure the police had returned to their cars and driven away.

'Dave Donovan didn't seem sure how far he walked to get out of here and to the phone box,' Barnard said. 'He said he carried Kate some of the way.'

'Sounds as if you owe him,' Jamieson said, flicking the beam of his light over the accumulated rubbish at the sides of the tunnel, causing an occasional rustle from a startled rodent.

'Maybe I do,' Barnard said, which was an admission he never

thought he would hear himself make about Dave Donovan. They plodded on in silence until Barnard stopped suddenly, almost tripping Jamieson up.

'There!' he said, pointing and then dodging along the DI's flashlight beam to something much cleaner than anything else in sight.

'Wait, don't touch,' Jamieson said, pulling gloves out of his pocket and putting them on. 'There'll be prints. Is it Kate's bag?'

'I think so, yes,' Barnard said, sounding strangled by conflicting emotions.

Jamieson picked the bag up carefully and opened it. 'Yes!' he said, lighting up the interior and showing Barnard the camera, which fitted neatly into one of the compartments. 'Hers?'

Barnard nodded. 'I think so.'

'So, we need to get any pictures she took at that party developed and printed fast. Destry and his mates will be in front of the magistrates tomorrow and if there's any incriminating evidence on here I want it in the hands of the prosecution. I'm supposed to be able to use the resources at the Yard. We'll see how good that promise is. With a bit of luck I can get them remanded in custody. That'll give the newspapers something to shout about and tell the public that the drug squad is up and running.'

As the two of them turned round to retrace their steps, Jamieson stopped and raised his hand.

'Did you hear something just then?' he asked. They stood for a moment in silence until they recognized the sound of heavy running footsteps behind them. Jamieson aimed the torch beam further into the dark and identified a uniformed officer running erratically towards them.

'Whoa,' Jamieson said. 'DI Jamieson, DS Barnard,' he said. 'We wondered where you'd got to.'

The constable bent over with his hands on his knees breathing heavily and almost unable to speak. 'Sir, we found . . . we need an ambulance . . . though it may be . . . too late . . .'

'Take your time,' Jamieson said.

'It's a young woman, says she's been here a long time . . .'

'She's alive, though?'

'Just about.'

'Right, you go and get help; we'll catch up with your partner . . .'

'I'll do that, guv,' Barnard said. 'You could go to the Yard and get the pictures done.'

Jamieson thought about that and then nodded his assent. He pushed his flashlight into Barnard's hand. 'What time's your interview with your DCI tomorrow?'

'Twelve o'clock.'

'Destry's in court at eleven. It won't take long. I'll see you after that.' And he turned on his heel and followed the uniformed officer back the way they had come.

Harry Barnard came out of Casualty for the second time that Sunday with Dave Donovan following close behind him. The musician looked as if he had been run over by a bus and Barnard did not look much better.

'I'm sorry, mate,' Barnard said. 'You said you knew there were other people in those passageways. We should have taken more notice of that. We should have searched them earlier.'

'The doctor said she was too far gone,' Donovan said. 'He couldn't save her. He said she had pneumonia. She dyed her hair red for nothing, didn't she, silly cow? Her parents are coming down to identify the body. What's left of her. She looks like she hasn't eaten for weeks. God only knows what they'd given her.'

Barnard glanced at his watch and put a hand on Donovan's arm. 'The pubs won't be open yet,' he said. 'We'll go back to my place and have a drink and then I'll get you back to Tess's flat. You need to sleep, if you can. Remember they spiked your drink as well as Kate's.' He put Donovan in the front passenger seat and set off fast towards Camden Town.

'I heard someone talking to the car driver,' Donovan said. 'They'd been there before. I guessed Kate and me were not the first to be dumped like that.'

'Are you sure of that?'

'I'm not sure whether Kate heard. She was pretty far gone by that time. But I'm sure Destry was picking up girls and giving them drugs to get them into bed. I knew he had his eye on Kate – that was obvious. He couldn't keep his hands off her. I found her hiding upstairs to keep out of his way. And it's quite likely he had picked Marie up too. He had other Scousers around the band. He must like the accent – the only person down here who does. Kevin Dunne's been with the Rainmen a while, and someone called Pete I heard mentioned was going to audition. Drummer, I think.'

'We found her bag and her camera too. The drug squad will get them developed. They'll want them for evidence.'

'I wondered where that had gone,' Donovan said. 'I was supposed to be looking after it.'

'Don't go anywhere or do anything until you hear from me or DI Jamieson tomorrow. I'm in an important meeting in the morning but whatever happens I'll find out who's the senior officer looking into Marie's case and we'll take it from there. It'll be handled initially by the local nick, but it looks as if the shiny new drug squad may get a look in.'

When Barnard woke to the grey light of morning he found himself still fully dressed lying on his bed and spent a good half hour piecing together his memories of the day before. And the more events he remembered, the more depressed he became. He glanced at his watch to discover it was only six thirty – more than enough time to get rid of the thumping headache but not nearly enough to stop him worrying instantly about Kate and to a lesser extent about the interview he was booked to have later that morning. Yesterday, he thought, had been bad for Kate and Dave Donovan; today could see him out of the Met for good, the inadvertent victim of Ray Robertson in spite of his own best efforts to avoid that fate.

After a shower and some breakfast Barnard felt marginally better and at half past eight he rang the hospital and was put through to Kate's ward. The nurse he spoke to was cagey but in the end admitted that Kate had slept well and that Mr Ingleby might possibly let her go home when he had seen her on his ward round later.

'What time will that be?' Barnard demanded and was told somewhat huffily that it was usually between ten and eleven.

'I'll ring again later,' he said, and hung up. He stood for a moment in front of the mirror in the hall before pulling on his coat and was shocked by the face which stared back at him. There were dark circles under his eyes; the bruising Ray Robertson had inflicted at his mother's house was still only too evident and he was so irritated by the dark, conservative tie he had chosen as a sop to senior officers who considered even a single identifiable flower or a colour more flamboyant than maroon to be an open confession of sexual deviancy that he pulled it off and went back to his wardrobe to choose one of his cheerful Liberty prints. 'May as well be hung for a sheep as a lamb,' he muttered as the phone rang.

'Jamieson,' the voice at the other end announced.

'Guv?' Barnard asked, irritated that the DI was bothering him this morning.

'Can you stall this interview of yours?' Jamieson asked.

'I shouldn't think so,' Barnard said. 'DCI Jackson's been waiting for this for a very long time. And DI Fred Watson's not one of my greatest fans either. They've both got a grievance now. Either I'm Ray Robertson's best mate and have been for years or I've been sleeping with a well-known tom and tried to get in on the inquiry into her murder by hiding the fact that I knew her. The first charge could see me out of the Met, the second will wreck my relationship with Kate as well.'

'Doesn't sound promising,' Jamieson conceded. 'Meet me in the Blue Lagoon and I'll show you the pictures. About eleven thirty? Too early for a pub. I have to be in court first to see Destry remanded and make sure nothing goes wrong. The press will be there in force. We're already getting calls about drugs and the music scene. I'll come straight over to your nick and talk to them afterwards. I've got your girl's photos developed and they're a goldmine. Did you know she took some pictures at the Late Supper Club as well? Everything's on one roll of film and gives us enough unanswered questions to keep us going for a month.'

'Right,' Barnard said. 'No, I didn't know that. She was staying with Tess Farrell for a few days so she could help Dave Donovan out. I was tied up with the Grenadier killing, working all the hours God sends so I didn't see her for a couple of days.'

'See you later,' Jamieson said and hung up.

Barnard made himself more coffee and then drove to the West End and parked close to the nick, giving himself time to cross over Regent Street and make his way into the narrow Soho streets. The police tape around the Grenadier pub had been taken down now and the whole area looked unusually calm. To his surprise he saw Vince Beaufort heading in his direction with a firmer tread than he had seen him use recently.

'Flash Harry,' Vince said, almost cheerily. 'I was going to catch up with you at the nick later. I was thinking about what you said about standing up to these bastards, and then I heard the details of what happened to Evie. And I saw the chap who's been chatting up your Kate. He's all over the place like a rash and I finally discovered his name from the manager at the Delilah. He's called Bob Cotton. Will that help?'

'It might do,' Barnard said. 'Keep in touch, Vince. I think we might be making some progress at last.'

'Good,' Vince said.

'But mind your back,' Barnard warned. He glanced at his watch, turned towards the familiar door to the Blue Lagoon and saw DI Brian Jamieson making his way inside.

'A quick coffee, guv?' Barnard asked, and Jamieson nodded. By the time Barnard brought the coffees back to the table the DI had spread a bundle of photographs across the Formica.

'My God, she was busy, wasn't she?' Barnard riffled through the prints that Jamieson had divided into those taken at the Late Supper Club and those showing the party at Jason Destry's house in the country.

'Do you know him?' he asked, pointing to an image of the man he had just been discussing with Vince Beaufort.

Jamieson gave him a sharp look. 'Why do you ask?' he said.

'There's a few people who wonder what he's up to, including Kate. He's been pestering her and asking questions about her boyfriend, in other words me.'

'You obviously never worked out he'd followed you to Ma Robertson's house. He's called Bob Cotton, he's a DS and he works for me. He told me he reckoned that you were still in touch with Robertson and told your DCI the same. But it didn't take much detective work on my part to find out what actually happened when you met Ray Robertson. I went down there and found someone who'd seen you go into the house, followed by Robertson, and come out distinctly the worse for wear.'

Barnard touched the bruises on his jaw with an exploratory finger and nodded. 'I didn't dodge fast enough,' he said. 'I should have told Mr Jackson the whole story. I was worried that if I

admitted to seeing Ray at all the DCI would put the worst inter-
pretation on it.'

'It would have avoided a lot of trouble,' Jamieson said as Barnard
picked his way through the prints. 'I've told Jackson what happened
to you and Kate over the weekend. I thought he needed to know
before your interview. It's relevant as Destry and some of his mates
were arrested and charged, which means it will be all over the papers
any minute as soon as the *Standard* and the *News* are on the streets.'

'I'm not sure he'll think there's anything there to help me,'
Barnard said. He turned back to Kate's pictures. 'Here's your man
Cotton at the Late Supper Club, and I saw him myself coming
out of the Delilah. Is he bent? What the hell's he up to?'

'I'm not sure yet,' DI Jamieson said with a shrug. 'But I intend
to find out. I've a suspicion he could have been bought, but no
reliable evidence.'

Barnard flicked over another print. 'So there was a fire in that
tower. Kate didn't invent it, though it obviously scared her rigid.'

'We'll have to talk to her about that eventually. We think Destry
may have been storing stuff in the tower and someone set it alight
deliberately. I've got the forensic team sifting through what's left.'
He looked at Barnard for a moment in silence.

'Would you consider joining the drug squad?' he asked quietly.

'You're joking,' Barnard said. 'Why the hell would you want
someone with my record?'

'Partly because of what I think Cotton's got up to so quickly
over the last couple of weeks. If he's been bought, and that's
always a risk with cops who are dealing with criminals who have
large amounts of money, I'll have him.'

'And you think I can't be bought?' Barnard asked slightly
incredulously.

'Given what's happened in Soho since these new thugs have
tried to move in, and how close to home it's come for you, I think
I can be pretty sure that you'll always know which side you're on.'

Barnard took a deep breath. 'Can I think about it?' he asked.
'And talk to Kate.'

'Sure,' Jamieson said. 'I need to tie up some lose ends around
the Destry case. I'll see you after your session with the brass.
Good luck.'

*   *   *

DS Harry Barnard stood for a moment outside the DCI's office door and gave himself a moment before he knocked. When the call to enter came he squared his shoulders and followed the secretary's wave to go into the inner office. As he expected, Jackson was not alone. DI Fred Watson was standing looking out of the window behind the DCI with his hands behind his back and, when he spun round as Barnard came in, he had a look of extreme dissatisfaction on his face. The two senior officers did not speak for a moment, leaving Barnard to take in the table where four seats were waiting with pads and pens and glasses of water ready for a formal meeting. DCI Jackson eventually stood up.

'DS Barnard, I have to tell you that this interview has been postponed for the time being. I have been informed by DI Jamieson what has happened over the weekend and how you became involved in an operation launched by the drug squad. I suggest you take the rest of the day off and we'll discuss your problems later in the week when your young lady has recovered from her unfortunate experience.'

'Thank you, sir,' Barnard said, feeling even more disoriented by relief than he would have been if they had suspended him on the spot. He turned and headed back to the door, aware that DI Watson was following very close behind him.

As he turned towards the CID squad room, Watson came up alongside him and leaned close. 'Don't think that's the end of it, Barnard,' the DI said. 'He said it was postponed not cancelled. Next time I should bring a union rep with you. You'll bloody well need one.' Watson accelerated towards the stairs and did not look back while Barnard headed to his desk and picked up the phone to ring the hospital, but before he had time to reach Kate's ward, DI Jamieson had appeared at his side.

'I gather it didn't happen quite as planned for you,' he said.

'That was down to you, was it?' Barnard asked. 'Fred Watson is not best pleased. Anyway, thanks.'

'It's a get out of jail free card for now, but we won't make it stick unless I can derail Cotton and prove he's lying. If he persuades them that you're still in cahoots with Ray Robertson they'll have you out, one way or another.'

'So what do you reckon?'

'This man Minelli is the key. Cotton is easy enough to read, I can deal with him. But we're no further forward with Minelli. Who the hell is he? Where does he come from? Who is he working for? And what exactly is he selling? We need much more. Tell me who to talk to. You see how your girl's doing and take her home. And get some sleep before you come in tomorrow. We'll talk then. I've told my boss that I'll be here working on this case. That will keep you out of trouble for a bit.'

Barnard collected Kate from the hospital at the end of the day, with the consultant's acquiescence if not blessing, and put her to bed.

'Sleep,' he said after he had made her a mug of hot chocolate and tucked her up with a kiss. She was, he thought, already looking more her normal self and he was slowly beginning to believe the doctor's verdict that no serious harm had been done.

'It wasn't your fault, Harry,' she said. 'Dave and I decided to go to the party.'

'That's one take on it,' Barnard said non-committally. 'We'll talk about it in the morning. In fact, there's quite a lot to talk about in the morning.' He dropped a plastic bag on to the bed.

'The nurse gave me that. It's your belongings they took off you in Casualty. I'm afraid your green silk dress looks pretty bedraggled. I don't think that will be going to many more parties. I liked that dress,' he mumbled before he realized that she was already asleep.

Barnard had reluctantly spent the night on his sofa and was wakened by a phone call soon after seven. He picked it up in the hall and hoped the sound had not wakened Kate. Jamieson was at the other end and sounded stressed already.

'I tried to find your mate Vince Beaufort last night without any luck. I know he's a poof and could have slept anywhere from Maidenhead to Margate, but do you know if he has a place of his own?'

'He's usually around Soho but recent events have probably made him much more cautious about where he's seen,' Barnard said. 'And it's very early for him to be out of bed.'

'What's your situation? How's the girlfriend?' Jamieson asked, almost as an afterthought.

'She's home and asleep.'

'Can you get into the nick today? I think you should if you can. Bob Cotton is a loose cannon and he won't give up if he thinks he can still get away with anything. I wanted to go to my boss and get him taken out of Soho but the guv'nor says we haven't got enough evidence. I think he'd prefer to get you suspended for the duration.'

'Give me an hour, guv,' Barnard said, not wanting to be bullied into anything Kate could not cope with. 'I'll call you at the nick by eight thirty.'

'Do that,' Jamieson said as Barnard realized that Kate was standing in her pyjamas by the living-room door listening to him.

'I'm sorry,' he said. 'I didn't realize you were awake. How are you feeling?'

'I feel fine,' she said with a smile which she no doubt thought was normal but was not quite there yet. 'Do you have to go to work?'

'I'm afraid so. I thought maybe you would be OK if I took you over to Tess's place so you're not on your own. And I'll ring the agency to tell Ken you won't be in for a few days.'

'Fine,' she said.

'And you won't let Dave – or anyone else – take you to any parties? The drug squad want Dave to stay in London while he makes a statement about everything that happened so he'll be around. Tess won't be too pleased with that.'

'I think I'm all partied out,' Kate said with a shudder.

'Your photographs were brilliant by the way. They'll make or break the case, DI Jamieson says.'

'That's good,' Kate said.

'Get dressed, sweetheart, and I'll take you over to Shepherd's Bush.' He put his arms around her, kissed her with a sense of profound relief and struggled to let her go again. 'I'm sorry I have to go to work but if I don't get these bastards off my back I'm finished.'

By eight thirty Barnard was at the nick and found DI Jamieson had taken over his desk and had Kate's photographs spread out in front of him. He looked up as Barnard hung up his coat and thrust a bundle of photographs into Barnard's hand.

'Look for anomalies,' he said. 'We need more than we've got

so far. People of interest are Destry, DS Cotton, Minelli and Mercer. Who are they talking to? Are they carrying anything that might contain drugs? Who is behaving as if they might have taken drugs? If drinks are being spiked have we got a picture of that going on? We weren't there but this is almost as good as.'

Barnard pulled up a spare chair and they worked slowly through every picture that had been developed from Kate's film. The pictures taken at the Late Supper Club came first and then those taken at the party with her venture into the tower first where there was plenty of evidence of the top floor being used as a store, to a series taken back in the main rooms where the partygoers could be seen beginning to enjoy themselves. He wondered how she had concealed her camera so effectively but realized she had taken most of the shots close to the windows where the light was better, and a lot of them were taken at oblique angles at which it was sometimes difficult to recognize faces.

Ten minutes in, Barnard whistled between his teeth. Among the pictures taken at the party, Kevin Dunne had been caught on camera carrying a heavy punchbowl into the room where the food was laid out. In the background it was obvious that the firework display was about to start outside and while most people had their backs to him at the windows, Jason Destry had been caught by the camera pouring something from a small bottle into several glasses and then topping them up with punch. He and Dunne were laughing in the next shot as they carried the glasses to willing drinkers in the crowd including, Barnard was gutted to see, Donovan and he guessed Kate as well, no doubt with her camera well hidden.

'That's when it happened,' he said. 'And she only took a couple more shots after that. It must have hit her almost straight away.'

By mid-morning DI Jamieson was a relatively happy man. 'So, we've got them on drug charges at the party, and supplying, with the picture Kate took of the boxes in the tower, before the fire started, and we know what we're looking for at the Late Supper Club. The fire brigade say not everything was completely destroyed in the Surrey fire so we'll start taking the place apart later today. We know that Mercer at the Late Supper Club was on good terms with Minelli and Cotton and Destry. What we don't know is who Minelli is and where he's getting his supplies from. Is that a fair summary?'

'I think so,' Barnard said. The phone rang on his desk and he picked it up thinking it would be Kate, but the line was poor and he only identified the voice with difficulty as the elderly Maltese boss, Frankie Falzon. He grabbed Jamieson's arm and indicated that he should listen.

'Mr Falzon?' he said. 'Can I help you?' Both of the detectives could hear Falzon laugh and his attempt to speak ended in a fit of coughing.

'You wanted to know about Minelli,' Falzon said. 'Not Maltese, I told you already. Not Italian either. He is from Corleone.' There was more coughing at the other end of the line before he was able to speak again. 'Corleone is in Sicily.' Barnard thought the line had gone dead but after a long pause Falzon spoke again. 'Evie Renton was one of my girls years ago,' he said. 'She told one of my people a few weeks ago that Minelli was threatening her.' And with that the line went dead.

When Barnard passed that message on to Jamieson the horror on the DI's face told Barnard all he needed to know about the implications of that. If he had begun to wonder if Soho was sliding imperceptibly into a war, it had now been openly declared.

EPILOGUE

Kate had pleaded with Harry Barnard not to go to Ma Robertson's funeral. He had come home from the nick the previous night grim-faced to tell Kate that the mystery of the girl who had plunged out of the Late Supper Club window had been resolved at last. DI Brian Jamieson had been with Barnard when a middle-aged couple from south London had called at the nick's front office. Their local police station where they had reported their fifteen-year-old daughter Jackie Greenwood missing had suggested they talk to the police in Soho where an unidentified girl still lay in the morgue. She had been at school with Jason Destry, who had been a few years older than her, the parents said, but they had no idea that she had been in touch with him again. The morning paper reports of Destry's arrest had made them wonder. Life had been difficult with Jackie for some time, her parents said, and when she had stormed out of the house the night before she died, she had said she was leaving for ever. It was not until they had identified her battered body that they realized that this time she had probably meant it.

'It looks as if she tried to renew her friendship with Destry,' Barnard told Kate. 'We think she maybe waited outside the club until she saw him go in. He seems to have been lying about her from the beginning. When I questioned him about her he insisted she was a stranger and that he had merely told her to go home. He claimed he had left the club before she fell out of the window, something the manager confirmed readily enough.'

'That's very sad,' Kate said. 'Destry seems to damage everyone he touches. Like Ray Robertson. You really don't need to go to his mother's funeral,' Kate said, putting a hand on his arm. 'Please, Harry. You know Mr Jackson will be furious. Forget Ray Robertson, for goodness' sake. He's over.'

'It'll be fine,' Barnard said as he tightened the knot on his black tie and pulled on his black jacket. 'She was around all the time I was a kid. You don't know how close those relationships were during the war. The place had been blown to bits. Ray Robertson's dad had died in Normandy. We were just beginning to believe we might be winning the war when Ray and Georgie and I finally got back to the East End after being evacuated. It didn't matter that Ma was probably keeping half-a-dozen of her husband's illegal enterprises going. I didn't know about all that. I was only a kid, but I did know that she was keeping that half-wrecked community going as well. I have to go to the funeral.

'There won't be any trouble,' he said to Kate as he left the flat. 'I checked whether they were letting Georgie out but the Home Secretary turned the request down apparently. It'll be a traditional East End funeral but with only one son there. Nobody there will care about me. They won't even remember who I am. And Falzon has said he will behave. There'll be no trouble.'

The streets had been lined with spectators as the black horses pulled the traditional hearse slowly through Bethnal Green to the church. But the crowds had largely dispersed by the time the coffin had been lowered into the grave and the ritual handfuls of earth dropped on top. Barnard had kept well back because he could clearly see Ray Robertson himself among the family group into which Ray had evidently incorporated Frankie Falzon, his former rival in Soho, accompanied by a phalanx of stocky, dark-haired minders. It was all, Barnard thought, out of time, a reminder of when men like this dominated East London, but this was the sixties and their time was over. They were reduced to burying an old woman and she would certainly be the last of the family to gain even this faded recognition.

But as the mourners moved away from the grave back towards the limousines which would carry them to the funeral meats, Barnard was horrified to hear a shot ring out. There was no doubting what it was and Ray Robertson seemed to stumble for a moment before recovering, taking Frankie Falzon's arm and leading him away quickly while his minders spread out looking for the gunman.

Further down the street, making it impossible for the cars to move away, Barnard could see a group of uniformed police in some sort of a tussle and moved quickly himself to join the departing mourners. He put his hand on Robertson's arm.

'Ray Robertson, I'm arresting you for perverting the course of justice. You don't have to say anything but anything you do say may be used in evidence . . .'

Falzon's minders surrounded him very quickly and hustled him away, and Barnard and Robertson were left alone for a moment until the police reinforcements moved closer, DI Jamieson among them.

'At least you waited till Ma was laid to rest,' Robertson said, not making any attempt to move away. But he looked, Barnard thought, defiant as they watched the approaching officers and he knew he was not going to be easy to convict.

'I think it was Minelli with the gun,' Jamieson said. 'I caught just a glimpse of him but he had a car waiting. Difficult to know if he was aiming at Robertson or Falzon or you, but no doubt we'll be seeing more of him.

'He's not holding back then?'

'Did you think he would? He's not playing games, he's trying to take over.'

'Falzon thinks he's to blame for Evie's death. Maybe he didn't kill her himself but he wanted her dead to keep the rest of the women in order.'

'Could be,' Jamieson agreed. 'Did DCI Jackson know what you were planning for Robertson?' Barnard shook his head.

'He's got questions to answer. I thought if I'm going to join you in the drug squad we'd better have a clean start. No baggage, guv.'

'Good,' Jamieson said. 'Let's make it work then. OK?'